The Springs

The Story of Othniel and Acsah

CYNTHIA LEAVELLE

Dear Chris,

May God bless you
as you read.

Love,
Cynthia

James 1:5-8

This book is dedicated to
my beloved friend, Rhoda Royce,
whose encouragement and help
have made all the difference.

Caleb said, "I will give my daughter Acsah in marriage to the man who attacks and captures Kiriath Sepher." Othniel son of Kenaz, Caleb's younger brother, took it; so Caleb gave his daughter Acsah to him in marriage. One day when she came to Othniel, she urged him to ask her father for a field. When she got off her donkey, Caleb asked her, "What can I do for you?" She replied, "Do me a special favor. Since you have given me land in the Negev, give me also springs of water." So Caleb gave her the upper and lower springs.

Judges 1:12-15

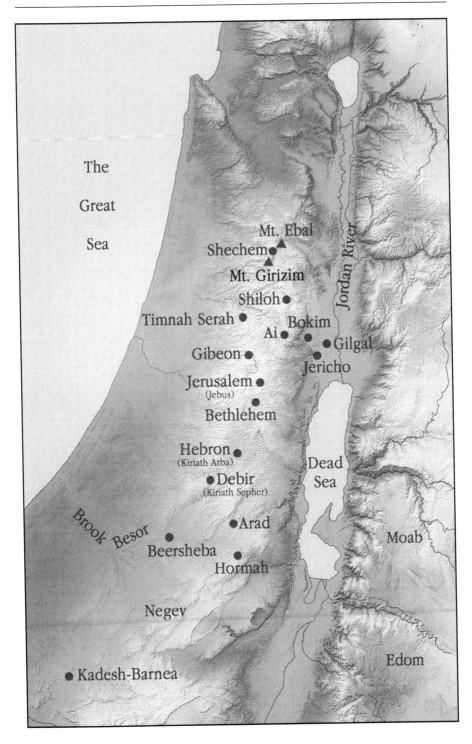

The
Great
Sea

Mt. Ebal
Shechem
Mt. Girizim
Shiloh
Timnah Serah
Bokim
Ai
Gilgal
Gibeon
Jericho
Jerusalem
(Jebus)
Bethlehem

Hebron
(Kiriath Arba)
Debir
(Kiriath Sepher)

Dead
Sea

Brook Besor
Arad
Beersheba
Hormah

Jordan River

Moab

Negev

Edom

Kadesh-Barnea

Contents

Chapter 1 3
Chapter 2 13
Chapter 3 21
Chapter 4 31
Chapter 5 41
Chapter 6 47
Chapter 7 59
Chapter 8 63
Chapter 9 69
Chapter 10...77
Chapter 11...83
Chapter 12...89
Chapter 13...93
Chapter 14...101
Chapter 15...107
Chapter 16...117
Chapter 17...123
Chapter 18...129
Chapter 19...141
Chapter 20...149
Chapter 21...153
Chapter 22...161
Chapter 23...169
Chapter 24...175
Chapter 25...183
Chapter 26...193
Chapter 27...199
Chapter 28...205
Chapter 29...213
Chapter 30...221
Chapter 31...227
Chapter 32...237
Epilogue...243

Part I

1

Othniel peered down at the Jordan Valley from a sharp promontory. The eastern sun blazed in his eyes, but still he could spot the small brown dots—the tents of Gilgal. His weariness from the long march through the mountains fell away at the sight. Today he would see her, after eight long months of constant maneuvers and bloody battles. He had waited for over six years for Acsah. Although he believed she loved him, an obstacle greater than this mountain stood between him and marriage—her father, Caleb.

His friend Salmon shouted up to him, "How close are we?"

"I'd say about three hours out."

"Let's get going then."

"I'm on my way." He leapt down with renewed energy. Catching up to Salmon, he teased, "I can't imagine what your hurry is."

Salmon looked at him with a twinkle in his eye. "As if you didn't know. The most beautiful woman in the camp is waiting for me."

"Not so. She's waiting for me."

"My wife likes you, Othniel, but not that much."

Othniel turned to his two Kenite captains. "Jethro. Heber. Let's get those troops up and on the move."

"Yes, Sir."

No one grumbled as men passed this command. All rose to their feet, each picking up his share of the battle plunder. Othniel knew they wanted to get to their loved ones as much as he did.

Othniel joined Salmon at the head of their column as they marched down the rocky road to Gilgal. "I know it was tough for you to lose your command, but I benefited from having you fight with me and my men after your nuptial year was up."

"It was hard seeing Hamul leading my men. I mean, I did understand that the fighting would go on after I married Rahab. I missed all the battles in the South. But these last eight months, I've appreciated being able to fight with you and your men."

"I've been blessed to have you with me." Othniel reached out and grasped his friend's hand. "Thanks for everything."

Salmon nodded at the men behind them. "You've done a wonderful job of uniting and training them. Not many men could have done that."

"Uniting Israelites, Kenizzites, and Kenites? I struggled for a while. But they work well together now, don't they? I wouldn't trade this group of men for any other in Israel."

"Speaking of marriage and Caleb, when will you ask for Acsah's hand?"

"I don't know. I'm waiting for the right moment."

"Does Acsah know how you feel?"

"She may now." Othniel didn't elaborate, but his thoughts turned to a kiss he had given Acsah before he left on the last campaign. The pleasure of her lips on his still lingered after all these months. He longed to hold her again. What had it meant to her, and how would she treat him after that kiss?

A shout made him look up. Gilgal waited ahead. His heart pleaded, *Lord, please make it possible for Acsah to become my wife.*

As they approached the camp, he turned and spoke to his troops, keeping his speech short. "Men, you have fought well. Go and be blessed with your families." Then he turned and walked toward Caleb's campsite in the alien section of camp, carrying his plunder. Soldiers from other units hurried by, going in all directions.

His brother Seraiah caught up with him. "Are you giving all your plunder to Caleb again?"

"Most of it. Why?"

"I'm keeping mine for Azubah and me. We're a separate family now. Don't you need to start saving for a bride?"

"I'm sure if I marry Caleb will give me what I need for a bride price."

"That depends on whom you marry."

Othniel watched his brother hurry away. Seraiah had a point. Caleb would have a strong opinion about that, too. But if he married Acsah, would he even need a bride price? Of course, Jacob's uncle Laban demanded 14 years labor from Jacob to marry Rachel and Leah. Surely Uncle Caleb would be fair. After all, everything he had belonged to Caleb, and he brought 25 sheep and 10 oxen back this time as well as the grain and gold he carried.

The family circle of tents came into view. Acsah's brothers, Iru, Elah, and Naam, were hugging their wives. Elah's son Kenaz dashed around among everyone's legs before being swept up into Elah's arms. Next to Naam's tent, Othniel saw Seraiah holding his wife Azubah with tears running down his face. Her advanced pregnancy was obvious even to his bachelor gaze. He was going to be an uncle.

Even that thought couldn't keep Othniel from looking around for the one person he longed for. But he didn't see Acsah. Where had she gone? Had something happened to her? His heart froze. She must not care, or she would have been here. He walked over to Caleb's tent and set the bags of gold, barley, and other food items down next to it, first removing a smaller bag containing all the items he had chosen with Acsah in mind. "Acsah, are you in there?" No answer came.

⚊•⚊

That morning, Acsah had sensed a change in the atmosphere, a stirring of anticipation in the voices she heard through the goat-hair tent walls. Perhaps today the army would return. Her maid, Dinah, appeared in the tent doorway. "Do you want some breakfast, Mistress? I have some dried figs and barley bread."

Acsah rose to wash her face and comb the tangles out of her long black hair. She took the food Dinah brought. "Is there any word about the men?"

"Yes, they've been sighted ten miles away, but they won't get here for several hours. Are you anxious?"

"You know I am." Ever since her father had acquired Dinah with the rest of her Gibeonite family, Acsah had found the girl capable with the spindle and loom, but Dinah could also be canny about her secret affection for Othniel. Would that cause trouble with her father later?

Acsah finished her breakfast. "I think I'll spend the morning with Rahab and her baby."

"All right, Mistress." Dinah began clearing the breakfast things.

As Acsah moved between the tents, she tried to remember. Had Salmon left Gilgal before Rahab realized she was pregnant? How surprised he would be! Acsah wanted to see his reaction. Then she could get back to her own tent before Othniel arrived there.

Othniel. The thought of him stirred an unnamed longing in her. She imagined him before her—a head taller than other men, with broad shoulders and sinewy muscles and eyes twinkling with kindness and wisdom. When he picked her up in his arms to swing her around, she felt no fear. The comfort and security made her want to hold on forever.

5

How could such a man have killed hundreds of people, as her brothers had told her? After all this time, would he have changed?

———◆———

Acsah approached the cluster of tents that housed Rahab and all the servants belonging to Salmon. Rahab's servant Shamar stirred porridge in a pot over the cooking fire. "How's your little daughter, Shamar?"

"She's well, but a handful right now. Babies are much easier at the age of that one," Shamar nodded at the baby in Rahab's arms.

Rahab stood at the opening of her tent and beckoned. "Come talk to me while we wait."

Acsah looked at the tiny boy. "He's changed in the last few days."

"Yes, his hair's beginning to thin some. I think it will grow back thicker than ever."

"He's so alert. He's going to be smart like his parents."

Rahab took a seat on a woven mat and indicated another for Acsah. "I hope he will be wise."

Acsah hid a chuckle. Rahab always managed to say thought-provoking things in the most everyday of conversations. "Is there a difference between being smart and being wise?"

"Oh, yes. I've known some very intelligent people who made one wrong choice after another and ruined their lives. Haven't you?"

Acsah nodded. "Yes. I have. What do you think makes someone wise?"

"In those cases, I would say choosing not to be so smart."

"That doesn't make sense to me."

"Doesn't it?" Rahab paused while she unwound the swaddling clothes and allowed her son to kick freely while she cleaned him. "I mean someone might think he or she is too smart to have to obey the Lord, but a wise person knows he or she isn't smarter than God and just obeys."

Acsah knew Rahab spoke the truth. But the word *obey* made her feel edgy. Changing the subject, she said, "When's your purification?"

"In one week."

"Are you glad Salmon will be here for it?"

"Yes. I'm sorry he missed the circumcision."

"I know you must be excited about showing him his son for the first time."

"I am. I don't think he knows."

The baby started fussing, so Rahab opened the slit in her loose shift and nursed him. The look of love she gave her baby moved Acsah deeply and stirred a longing in her. "He's precious, Rahab."

Rahab smiled and put a finger next to her son's hand. He reached up and grasped it in his tiny fist. "I love it when he does that."

"I worried when you didn't get pregnant right away after you married."

"Did you? That first year, we were so happy. I thought I shouldn't expect anything more from the Lord. But I admit I did hope for another baby." Sorrow shadowed her face for a moment. Acsah's heart broke a little, remembering that Rahab had been forced to sacrifice a baby alive in the fires of Molech in Jericho. "After Salmon left, I realized I had conceived. Planning for this baby has kept me busy and happy while he's away. The Lord has blessed me so much."

Acsah watched Rahab nurse. Rahab had experienced unbearable horrors in Jericho—the sacrifice of her baby, an abusive marriage, gang rape, and all the degradation of being a prostitute. Rahab's first baby had never even had a name. That reminded her to ask, "You haven't picked a name yet, have you?"

"No, I want Salmon to choose."

"Any ideas?"

"I want something that glorifies the Lord."

"No doubt Salmon will have one. Just think, soon all three of you will be together as a family."

"Yes." Rahab's eyes sparkled. She looked down at her now sleeping infant, then gently laid him in a nest of blankets in the corner. "Now that he's satisfied, how about we eat something? I'm ravenous all the time since I've been nursing."

Acsah took the bread and cheese Rahab offered her and began eating. "I hope you're close by when we get settled. You know so much about housekeeping and babies."

"Why? Are you planning to have babies and keep house?" Rahab's teasing made Acsah sigh.

"I'm beginning to doubt I will ever marry." Acsah looked around the comfortable tent, envying Rahab her marriage to a man she loved.

"If your father won't let you marry Othniel, won't you agree to marry whomever he chooses?"

"I don't want anyone but Othniel. I'd rather be single."

"Not marry or have children? You don't understand what a blessing you would miss and how lonely you would be. I do know. Your father loves you, and he's a godly man. Surely, he wouldn't choose someone unsuitable."

"My father cares only about getting me a husband from Judah, not about my happiness."

"Because he isn't really from Judah?"

"Right. We're Kenizzites, descendants of Esau."

7

"Jacob's older brother?"

"Yes, so although we're descended from Abraham, we're not part of the twelve tribes. My father has always felt rejected and wants at least some of his descendants from Judah."

"But you aren't willing to make that happen, right?"

"Not if it means I can't have Othniel. You don't understand how much I love him. You didn't love Salmon that way."

"I learned to love Salmon."

Acsah knew what Rahab was implying, but Rahab couldn't possibly understand this yearning she had for Othniel, her desire to become his wife.

In the silence between them, they heard sounds outside the tent.

"Do you think...?" Acsah's heart quickened in anticipation.

"Perhaps. Let's go out and see." Rahab picked up her sleeping son and rose, pulling aside the tent flap so they could see out. People hurried to the western side of camp. "We should stay here. They can find us more easily than we can find them."

Acsah agreed, trying to decide whether to go back to her own tent immediately or wait. All around them men entered the camp, many carrying sacks of grain and other plunder while women and sometimes children clung to them. The anxiety in Rahab's eyes made her think she should leave, but before she could, a familiar figure came striding toward them.

Salmon's eyes widened as he spotted Rahab. His pace increased until he reached them, flinging his arms around Rahab, baby and all.

Acsah said, "Be careful, you're going to smother the baby." But neither Salmon nor Rahab paid any attention to her. He held Rahab for a long time, dipping his head finally for a long, deep kiss. As Salmon pulled back a little, Acsah could see tears running down his cheeks into his beard as he looked for the first time into the face of his little son. Then he and Rahab smiled at each other.

Only then did he acknowledge Acsah, "Hello, Acsah. It's wonderful to see you. You're more beautiful than ever." He turned back to Rahab, "As are you, my wife."

Acsah realized she was intruding on a private moment. "I'd better go to my tent now."

"You have a father and cousin anxious to see you," said Salmon, smiling at her.

"I'll let you know about the purification ceremony next week," said Rahab.

"Next week!"

Acsah laughed at Salmon's expression. "You two have a lot to talk about. See you later."

Now that she knew Othniel had arrived in the camp, she regretted her decision. Why hadn't she stayed with the family? How would she act when she got there? What would he say? Moving swiftly between tent groups, she saw more families reunited. Her pulse beat faster as she neared her own circle of tents.

She could see Othniel turning this way and that as though looking for someone. The disappointment on his face transformed into a bright smile as their eyes met.

She had rehearsed this scene so many times in her imagination. The reality felt dreamlike. How she wished she could have an embrace such as Salmon had given Rahab. She joined Caleb where he stood with her sister-in-law and her nephew Kenaz.

Caleb enfolded her in his arms. "Acsah, my daughter," he crooned.

The rough wool of his cloak against her cheek gave her a sense of well-being. That she had missed her father as well as Othniel hadn't occurred to her until this moment. She basked in the glow of having him home and safe.

Now each of her three brothers gave her a hug before she reached Othniel and could naturally embrace him without raising suspicions. He lifted her up as he had since her childhood. Into his ear, she whispered, "I'm so glad to see you home, Othniel."

His arms tightened around her. She pulled her head back to look into his dear face and saw moisture in his eyes. The sight brought a clutch to her throat and a deep desire to do more than just hug him.

Zebidah, her old nursemaid, had organized the servants without her. Some brought water to wash the returning soldiers' dusty feet, and others served bowls of stew made from a goat slaughtered for the occasion. She hoped her father didn't know how little she had done to help, but clearly the meat stew, bread, and fresh fruit were adequate to feed the thirty or so family members and servants in their area. As people sat in groups around the shared fire, Acsah rejoiced when Othniel joined the group near her tent door where she could listen to the conversation.

"I understand Salmon has a fine son," Caleb looked at Othniel.

"I hadn't heard. Praise the Lord. I know he wanted to have a child."

"Anytime you want, I'll arrange a marriage for you. If the Lord wills, you can have a son of your own. Your younger brother's wife is expecting, I see."

Acsah watched Othniel's face in the firelight. She understood him well enough to know he was struggling with strong emotions, and if he

9

tried to speak, he would start stuttering. Her father often had that effect on him.

Othniel didn't respond, so Caleb turned to one of his sons, Elah, who joined them. "Tell Othniel how many times I'm approached every week by men wanting to arrange a marriage with their daughters."

Elah laughed. "You could have your pick of any woman, Othniel, not just Kenizzites but anyone in Judah."

How would Othniel answer? Acsah bit her lip in the shadows.

"I....I'm s...sorry, Uncle Caleb," said Othniel. "I...I'm n...not ready for marriage yet. I w...want to wait until I have a permanent home for my bride."

"Commendable thinking, nephew. You want to provide, but you don't want to wait too long to settle this sort of thing."

Othniel changed the subject abruptly. "I...I haven't h...heard about the last battle from your perspective. What happened where you were?"

As Caleb warmed to this subject, she observed that Othniel could relax and respond easily. Othniel lost his composure and faltered only when her father started talking about marriage. What went through Othniel's mind when he spoke of marriage?

Others around the campfire asked questions about the battles, and Caleb told of a huge battle near the Waters of Merom where the enemy assembled. Nine kings marshalled an army of tens of thousands, with chariots and horses. "They were an insurmountable obstacle, but Joshua told us we could defeat the enemy in one day if we attacked first and early."

"Is that what happened, Grandfather?" asked little Kenaz, who slipped into the circle next to his father.

Caleb paused to smile at his only grandchild. "Yes, that's what we did. We attacked them before dawn when they weren't looking. Salmon and Othniel did a thorough spy job, so we knew their chariots would be useless in the hills. We attacked them in their camp, before they could descend into the plains where the chariots would have given them the advantage."

"What happened, then, Grandfather?"

"Our men defeated them. They scattered in a panic. We pursued them all the way to Sidon, way up on the coast. Others ran into the valley of Mizpah, but our men followed them there as well. None of them survived."

"Did you bring back a lot?"

"As a matter of fact, we did. We burned Hazor because the king of Hazor led the alliance against us, but we conquered all the other cities without fire and claimed all the plunder."

"Which towns?"

Elah stopped his son. "Kenaz, you ask too many questions."

"That's all right. I have missed the child's voice." Caleb listed the ten cities for little Kenaz.

"How many does that make so far?"

"Thirty-one kings. But we haven't completely driven all the people out yet. That's our next task—to move into the cities themselves and take the surrounding countryside from the people that still survive."

"Which cities?"

"Well, Jebus, Kiriath Arba, and Kiriath Sepher still need conquering. Jebusites and Anakites fled to those cities."

"Does that make a difference?"

"It shouldn't make any difference to God's people. But Anakites are huge people, as big as giants, and some of our men fear them, just as the people did during that time over forty years ago. I said it then, and I say it now, 'The Lord will be with us and defeat our enemies for us.' We must not make the same mistake as before. For fear of the Anakites, we spent forty years wandering in the desert instead of coming on into Canaan and conquering it then. I have an idea..." He paused and appeared thoughtful. Then, as though waking from his reverie, he said, "I think it's time for a young boy to find his sleeping mat. Tell everyone good night."

Taking Caleb's remark as an order, the group broke up for bed. Soon, Caleb came into the tent, where Acsah sat listening.

"It sounds like you succeeded."

"Yes. The Lord was with us. He promised he would be."

"So, how long do you think before we settle somewhere?" Acsah quietly finished smoothing out her father's sleeping mat for him.

"Several issues are still unsettled. I'm going to talk with Joshua soon to plan the next move."

Acsah had many more questions, but she could sense his weariness, so she simply moved to the inner room and rolled out her pallet. She called through the dividing curtain, "Good night, Father."

"Good night, Acsah."

In the quiet, they could hear crickets chirping and the low voices of people in nearby tents.

"Father?"

"Yes, Acsah?"

"It's good to have you back."

"I'm glad to be back."

She snuggled down under her blanket, anticipating the next day. Surely Othniel would declare himself soon to her father.

2

T he next day Othniel woke to the sound of his uncle's voice outside his tent. "Othniel, I have a task for you."

Groggy from the first sound sleep he had allowed himself in months, Othniel struggled to rise and get to the tent opening.

"You're slow today. We have things to do, and we must get started."

Othniel rubbed the sleep from his eyes and tried to look more alert. "Yes, Sir, what do you want me to do?"

"Gather the leaders of ten thousand in Judah and bring them here. We're going to have a conference with Joshua."

"What about, Sir?"

"I'll tell you all at the same time. Oh, and bring your friend Salmon, too. I may need him."

Othniel's mind now worked, and a dozen more questions sprang into it, such as when they would get a break. "Yes, Uncle Caleb. When would you like them to come?"

"Immediately. We need to settle this before someone else tries."

Breakfast would have to wait. Taking only enough time to fasten on his belt and dash some water into his face, Othniel set off to seek out the leaders, knowing they would not want to come out so soon.

Seven other men led the 76,000 soldiers of Judah. He delivered his message to the bleary-eyed and disgruntled leaders before he turned toward Salmon's tent. He especially hated waking Salmon from his first night in so long with his wife, Rahab. Finding Salmon awake and outside his tent surprised him.

"Salmon, you're up already."

"Well, the newest member of my family decided to wake up early."

"I heard last night you had a new son. Congratulations! What do you think of him?"

"A fine boy. He'll be a great man some day. But right now, he isn't interested in much except sleeping, being held, and drinking milk."

Othniel laughed at this typical father observation. "I remember feeling that way about Acsah's nephew Kenaz, but he's become more interesting lately."

"So why are you up and about when you could have slept in?"

"Caleb. He wants you to meet with him and the leaders of ten thousand immediately."

Salmon's eyebrows lifted in surprise. "We got back just yesterday. You don't think he's planning to go to battle immediately, do you?"

"I don't know; so we'd better go right away."

Salmon went over to his tent and murmured to Rahab before joining Othniel for the walk to the outskirts of camp.

"How's Rahab?"

"Beautiful as ever and unfortunately still unclean for another week. I had to take a bath last night because I hugged her before I knew, and I haven't touched her since." Salmon's expression was disgruntled, but Othniel could see he felt supremely happy with his beloved wife and new son.

"At least you can touch her after a week."

"I know. You've waited so long for Acsah. After all you've done for Judah, Caleb should want you for his son-in-law."

"Last night he talked about marrying me to someone from the tribe of Judah. I need to let him know my intentions, but every time I try to talk to him about it, I start stuttering. I rarely stutter with anyone else."

"Why do you have problems with Caleb?"

Othniel thought of all the times he had cowered in the presence of his dynamic uncle. "I don't know. I've done everything he wants— obeyed his commands, turned over all my plunder to the family group. Nothing makes a stronger impression on him than my sounding like a simpleton when I talk to him. And really, it only happens when we talk about marriage. Perhaps I lose control because I don't want to ruin my chances."

"I don't understand why he cannot see what a great person you are."

Ahead they could see the tops of Caleb's tents, and a few strides put them by the fire where the other leaders and Caleb sat, looking impatient.

Caleb thought about the next campaign. He knew the country around Kiriath Arba and Kiriath Sepher. He had seen it 45 years before, and he never forgot the juicy, plump grapes they had picked there. With the largest tribe in Israel, he had an obligation to get that land. Hadn't God promised it to him? He needed to get his request to Joshua as soon as possible, today.

The nine men sat on the ground in a circle around him. Caleb tamped down his feelings of inadequacy and summoned his strength. "I intend to ask Joshua today to make his decision regarding the allotment of land. I want you to accompany me to show you agree with my desire to lead out. Are all of you willing to demonstrate to the rest of Israel our faith that the Lord has given us this land?"

Hamul said, "We will follow you whenever and wherever you lead."

Caleb looked around and saw that the others were nodding.

"Good. I am planning to ask for the lands to the south, including Kiriath Arba and Kiriath Sepher."

Caleb felt rather than heard the intake of breath in the men standing around him. He knew he was asking for the hardest conquering—the most fortified cities where they would fight the giant men, the Anakites.

Hamul, still smiling and nodding, spoke again. "We admire your willingness to take on this challenge, but we are the largest tribe. We could have any land we choose. Wouldn't the lands to the north we've just conquered be settled more quickly?" Others nodded, with relieved looks on their faces.

"Did you not agree to follow wherever I lead?"

"Well, yes."

"Do you not believe the Lord has been faithful to give us the land when we go in his strength?"

"Of course, but..."

Now Othniel spoke up. "The Lord will deliver those cities and the Anakites into our hands. We will follow you."

Caleb looked around at the group of men, who, at least on the surface, seemed in accord. "Let's go see Joshua." He led them toward the tribe of Ephraim. Thank God Othniel spoke up. Always he feared people would turn on him and challenge him because of his lineage as a Kenizzite, as they had at Kadesh Barnea so many years ago. He could never let them perceive weakness in any situation.

Backed up by the nine men, Caleb approached Joshua by his campfire. "My friend, I request an audience with you about an important matter."

Joshua looked up with a pleasant expression, but Caleb thought he looked tired. Surely leading two campaigns would be hard on a man over one hundred years old. "Of course, you can have an audience. How are you, my old friend? I see you've brought the leaders of Judah with you. This must be important."

"Yes, I've been thinking about our next move."

"Always ready for action, aren't you, Caleb?"

"Well, I assume we're ready to divide the land."

"Of course, I'm sure the Lord wants us to do that soon. We've already made the allotments for the tribes of Reuben and Gad."

Caleb bowed his head, "Before you make any more allotments, I want to make a special request."

"Ask whatever you will."

"You remember when we were young men, and the Lord sent us as spies from Kadesh Barnea into the Promised Land along with the 10 others?"

"Of course, but speak for yourself about being a young man."

"Only you and I believed the Lord would give us the land. The other ten opposed us and said we couldn't conquer the land because of the Anakites."

"Yes, I remember."

"Well, at that time, Moses promised me the land on which I had walked. It's been 45 years. The Lord has kept all his promises to us. I'm 85 years old, but I can still fight like a young man."

"I believe you. So what do you request?"

"Let me have the hill country. I believe the Lord will be with me as he has all these years, and I will be able to drive the Anakites out."

Joshua nodded his head. "My friend, you shame me. I've been thinking I have no more energy to finish up this work, but you're ready to take on the hardest challenge. You're an example to the younger men of faith. May God bless you and make you successful."

"Thank you, Joshua."

"As a reward, your personal inheritance will include Kiriath Arba and all its surrounding villages and towns, if you succeed."

"We will defeat the Anakites there and in Kiriath Sepher."

"I need to make a general announcement about the allotment of land. But let's continue on together until we've assembled at Shiloh."

"When will that be?"

"Soon, my friend, but not immediately. I think the army needs time to rest before we move again. It's up to the Lord."

"Of course."

"Now why don't we let these young men go back to their sleeping mats while you and I have a visit?"

Caleb dismissed his leaders. "You may have the rest of today off."

Othniel and Salmon moved away, leaving Caleb with his friend.

"Come see my little son."

"I'd like that."

Together they threaded their way east past the tents of Ephraim, the tabernacle, and the tent of Salmon's cousin Eleazar the high priest before reaching Judah's section. As they passed the tabernacle, Othniel observed, "The cloud hangs low right now."

"Yes, I think the Lord knows we need a rest."

"Unlike Uncle Caleb. Yet I have to admit that his faith inspires me. He believes we can defeat the giant Anakites."

"He has seen the Lord work so much in the last few years."

"So have we, but he believed even before that, back before Israel had a trained army. I want to have that kind of faith."

"If I've learned anything from being married to Rahab, it's that wanting to have faith is the first step in having it," said Salmon.

"You missed her a lot, didn't you?"

"You know I did. She fulfills me."

Othniel sighed. "I suppose if I marry Acsah, I'll have to give up my command, too."

"That would be harder for you than for me. You have so many good friends among your troops. And they follow you so well. I can't imagine how anyone else could do what you have done with them."

Othniel shrugged off the praise. "There's your tent. Let's have a look at this little one."

Salmon slipped into the tent and emerged a few seconds later holding a quiet bundle. "What did I tell you? Eating, sleeping, and being held."

Othniel grinned as he looked at the tiny face below him in Salmon's arms. The little nose wrinkled up and the baby suddenly sneezed, then looked up with shiny, dark brown eyes at Othniel. Warm feelings stirred inside of him. "Have you decided on a name for him?"

"I think we'll call him Boaz—the Lord is our strength."

"A good name for a man of God. He has work ahead to grow into that name."

"I trust he will."

"I guess I'll go find that sleeping mat. Let's see if I really can take advantage of this day off. Who knows how long that will last with Caleb around? Thanks for showing me your son. You should be proud of him."

Othniel walked out to the alien section on the eastern edge of Judah. At the campsite, he saw no one around, so he slipped into his tent and settled on his sleeping mat in the inner room for a much-needed rest.

Acsah noticed first the standard of Judah in its place in the tent. Pleasure coursed through her veins as she remembered it meant Othniel had returned. But outside the tent, she didn't see him. In fact, very few people lingered in the area around the campfire. She ate a lonely meal wondering where everyone had gone. Wasn't Othniel as anxious to see her as she was to see him? The mornings offered a good time for them to be together without causing her father alarm. With a sigh, she opened the tent sides to make the outer room into a kind of porch, and she settled down to some spinning. It wasn't fair to expect Dinah to do all the cloth-making, and from this vantage point, she could watch everyone who came and went in the area.

Finally, she saw Azubah emerge from her tent, clumsy with the fullness of her pregnancy. "How are you, Azubah?"

"I'm all right. But my back's been hurting a lot lately. I wonder if that means something?"

"I've heard that could be a sign of labor." Acsah's many conversations with Rahab about her years as a midwife to Jericho's other prostitutes made her feel like an expert. "Can I make you some food?"

"Would you? I'd love that."

Acsah called to Dinah and began making some porridge with the water left from that morning. Dinah appeared, and Acsah commanded, "You fix the fire; I'll grind some more barley."

Dinah added fuel to the fire under the pot of water, then spoke to Azubah. "You're probably due any day. Do you have an Ashteroth figurine to ease your labor pains?"

Azubah gasped, and Acsah reacted to hearing that name. "Dinah, you shouldn't say such things. You know we can't worship idols."

"I wasn't asking you to worship it, just have it to help you. You might wish you had it when the pains start."

Azubah shook her head. "I'll trust in the Lord. He's the only God."

"But your god is male. How can he know what a woman feels?"

Acsah made a warning sound in her throat. Pouring the barley meal into the pot of boiling water, she thought about what Dinah asked. Such questions bothered her more than she wanted to admit. She knew God had condemned women to pain in childbirth because Eve had listened to the serpent. Did he care about them during the pain?

After a period of silence, Azubah said, "Acsah, could I have some of your porridge, or are you going to stir it all day?"

Acsah woke from her reverie and served her a bowl. "Dinah, would you go get another jar of water from the river?"

Dinah bowed her head in assent and, taking the jar, walked away.

Acsah turned to Azubah. "What do you think about what she said?"

"Don't let her suggestions bother you. You must remember she doesn't understand about our laws and our God."

"I know, but sometimes I do wonder. She seems so sincere in her beliefs."

"Yes, but a person can be sincerely wrong. All over the camp, Gibeonite servants are having these kinds of conversations with Israelite masters and mistresses. I wonder what effect having them among us will have."

"If we had destroyed Gibeon the way we did Ai and Jericho, we wouldn't have this problem."

"Did you ever hear exactly what happened?"

"Do you mean with the Gibeonites? They dressed up like travelers on a long journey. They even put old, moldy bread in their saddlebags. They told Joshua and the other leaders they came from a distant country. Othniel told me they were very convincing."

"But shouldn't we have known? I mean, Joshua can usually see through people." Azubah started cleaning out the empty porridge bowl.

"Othniel said the leaders just took the Gibeonites' word for it. They made a covenant. So when they came to Gibeon, out came those very same men. We couldn't destroy them, because of our covenant." Acsah shook her head in exasperation as she told this.

"So instead, we took them as slaves. I still think the Israelite leaders made a mistake."

"Azubah, perhaps we can convince them to worship the Lord."

"The leaders?"

"No, the Gibeonites."

"Do you think we could?"

"I don't know." Could she convert Dinah to worshiping only one god? Othniel would know the answers. She could talk with him. But for the rest of that long day, she saw no sign of him or her father.

3

The next morning, Acsah planned a good breakfast for her father. She knew cooking would put her out in the center of things and increase her chances of seeing Othniel. Where had he spent the day before?

Outside the tent, she met Dinah returning from milking the family goats. "I'm thinking about cooking some more porridge this morning. This goat's milk will complement that."

"What can I do to help you?"

"I'll need the large cooking pot again. Do we have plenty of water?"

"No. We used up all we had last night. I'll go to the river to get some."

Acsah spied Othniel emerging from his tent. "No, you just got back from carrying the milk. I'll go to the river. You can begin grinding the grain."

"All right." Then with a twinkle in her eye, "Perhaps Othniel will carry the water for you."

Acsah felt her face flush at being caught, but that didn't stop her from saying, "Good morning, Othniel."

"What are you doing up and about so early?"

"You needn't look so surprised. I'm fixing breakfast. I often do. But first I'm going for water."

"Would you like some company on the way?"

"Yes. I would." She tried to appear casual, but the grin Dinah gave her made it hard.

She lifted the large water jar to her shoulder, but hardly cleared the outskirts of camp before Othniel took it from her. "Carrying water is women's work," she teased him.

"I've been carrying my own water for several months now."

"Yes, but in a goatskin bag. What will people think?"

"Do you want it back?" He held the jar out to her.

21

"No, not really."

"Well, then." He paused and gazed at her with a look in his brown eyes that made her catch her breath.

"I looked for you yesterday, but I never saw you."

"To tell you the truth, I spent yesterday sleeping."

"Oh, I didn't think of that." She blushed at having been so personal.

"Would you have awakened me?" His teasing tone made her a little less embarrassed.

"No. I'm glad you got to sleep. You were exhausted."

"I was. I'm feeling much better now. Tell me what you've been doing."

"Cooking and spinning and weaving. I made some more wool blankets. I even used different colors in one."

"That's good. Do you enjoy weaving?"

"Not as much as Rahab and Dinah do. They're really skilled. Rahab can make a blanket in half the time it takes me."

"But you made them, nevertheless." His affirming words made her want to work even harder to please him.

"Yes, I want to have plenty of household goods in case I ever have the opportunity to have my own house." She glanced up at Othniel, but he was looking at a distant point.

"I'm sure you will have an opportunity as soon as all this fighting's over. What else have you done?"

Acsah launched into details of camp life—who had given birth, been ill, or died. She didn't realize how fast the time was passing until suddenly Othniel handed her the jar.

"You'd better take it. I can hear plenty of women up ahead, and I wouldn't want to make us the source of camp gossip."

Acsah flushed, realizing she had been gossiping herself, but a look in Othniel's face assured her he meant nothing by it.

They reached the path running down through the trees next to the Jordan River. She went toward the sound of women's voices. A long line of women waited to dip into the deep clear pool at the river's edge. They greeted her as she joined them. She fidgeted lest Othniel grow weary of waiting and leave her.

Finally, her turn came. Acsah lifted the dripping pot from the pool and placed it on her head. The cold drops of water soaked through her head covering and into her scalp. She balanced the heavy pot with one hand, then picked her way up the path between the trees growing near the riverbank. In the distance, Othniel stood with his muscular arms crossed on his chest, waiting for her. Her pulse increased, and her lips curved into a smile. He hadn't left. She would get to enjoy his company on the return trip. As soon as the women around them moved away in different directions, he took the dripping jar from her and carried it in one huge hand as if he held only a cup.

"How can you do that?"

"Do what?"

"Carry something so heavy with such ease." He wasn't straining at all.

"Perhaps carrying water shouldn't be women's work."

"The water jar isn't too heavy for me, but I can't carry it like that."

"But if I happen to be handy, you'll let me do it."

"You offered." Acsah looked up at his amused expression. He liked this banter. "I've been doing all the talking. Tell me about your experiences. Are you glad to be back?"

"Very much so. I missed having someone else cook for me."

"Is that all you missed?" She glanced his way again. Would he say he missed her?

His eyes softened as he gazed back, making her heart beat faster. "I missed female companionship."

"I thought you and all your soldier friends liked war."

Othniel grimaced. "War isn't fun, Acsah. I take no pleasure in killing. We do it because we must, because the Lord ordered us to."

Acsah's high spirits fell at his tone. "I'm sorry. I didn't mean to imply you liked killing people."

"No. It's my fault. You were talking about companionship. I do appreciate my men when I'm facing the enemy. And it's true we share some intense experiences. But lying on the cold ground night after night with little sleep and not much to eat—a man starts to wish for peace and the comforts only a woman can give him."

Did he mean comforts she could give him? Acsah longed to provide those. She started to say it, but as a woman, she couldn't speak so, at least not first. Perhaps she should change the subject. "We women miss men when they're gone, too."

"In what way?"

"Protection for one thing. With so many men gone, the camp didn't feel as safe."

"I can see that. Anything else?"

How could she tell him she missed being with him, seeing him every day, talking to him as they were now? "I just missed you—all of you."

Othniel smiled. Did he understand she meant him in particular? As they approached the alien section, he handed the jar back to Acsah. "I'm really glad to be home again. Eight months is a long time."

She looked around at the tents and laughed. "Do you call a tent encampment home?"

He smiled. "No, I guess not exactly. But…" he paused, "… a tent does provide shelter from sun and rain and wind."

Acsah shook her head. "I won't feel I'm at home until I have a real roof over my head and sturdy walls around me."

"How do you know that those things will make a place home? You've never lived in a real house."

"Well, then, what do you think? What makes a real home?"

"The presence of people we love." His look made her a little dizzy.

"Welcome home, Othniel," she murmured as he walked out of earshot. With a sigh, she turned back to her work, feeling a little flat. When they were together, she wanted to skip with joy, but a tension of unspoken desires and unanswered questions came between them. When, if ever, would Othniel declare his intentions?

———◆———

Othniel smiled as he walked away from Acsah. Clearly she enjoyed his company as much as he did hers. He longed to find the right time to talk to Caleb, ask permission to marry her, and discuss the bride price and dowry. In most cases, his father or closest male relative would do this, but his parents had died in the wilderness. Caleb was his closest relative. How could he handle this? And would Caleb even consider him? Perhaps waiting would make his uncle see their affection and let them marry. But probably not. Caleb had made it clear time after time that he wanted Acsah to marry into Judah.

Othniel sighed in resignation. The day was passing, and he hadn't checked on Caleb's flocks, though his cousins Iru, Elah, and Naam took primary responsibility for them. Still, with the new Gibeonite servants, he should pay more attention.

He arrived at the fields to find that Asa and Oren, Dinah's brothers, were the only ones watching the sheep. "Where's everyone else?"

Asa kicked at his shepherd's crook. "Someone came to take Seraiah back to the camp, something about his wife. I haven't seen anyone else all morning. But we're used to shepherding alone. You've all been gone."

"I'll stay out here with you, today." Othniel realized he didn't know Asa and Oren very well for the reason Asa had mentioned—the Israelite men had been gone to war since the Gibeonites had been acquired. "How do you like life in the Israelite camp?"

Asa averted his eyes. "You're very good masters, I'm sure."

"What did you do in Gibeon?"

"Farm. I had just inherited my own land when the Israelites came, but I'd worked the soil for years."

"What kinds of crops did you grow?"

"Grapes, figs, wheat, barley."

"I saw the land at Gibeon; it's mostly hills."

Oren separated two goats, fighting for the same grass. "Yes. But we did terrace farming. I wager you know nothing about farming."

"You're right; I don't. I helped harvest some wheat one time, but other than that I'm inexperienced."

"Then what do you want with our land?"

"We can learn to farm. Perhaps you can teach us."

Asa shook his head. "Honestly, I don't think you people have much of a chance with your one god. He couldn't be an agricultural god if you met him in the wilderness."

"He's the only God. Since he created everything, I think he can help us out with crops. He promised to."

Both brothers looked unconvinced, but Othniel didn't argue. What were they thinking, and would they ever understand about the Lord?

———

Acsah sat disconsolate by the cooking fire, listlessly stirring the pot of porridge when Dinah joined her. "He left, did he?"

Acsah nodded her head. "I can't read him, Dinah. Do you think he likes me as more than a relative?"

"Of course, Mistress. Anyone can see from the way he brightens up when you're around. You're very special to him."

"Then why doesn't he ask my father for my hand?"

"Why do you think?"

Acsah sighed. She really shouldn't talk about her father's concerns with her maid.

Dinah's mother, Mehetabel, came hurrying over to them. "Azubah's definitely in labor now. But her pains are quite far apart. Zebidah and I are going to stay with her for now, but we may need the two of you later. I'll get my supplies." Then she hurried away.

Acsah said, "I would like to get my friend Rahab to help, but she has her newborn to care for."

"Mother can handle this. She's delivered a lot of babies." Something about the way Dinah said this made Acsah aware again of the tension in camp among her servants, especially between Zebidah and Mehetabel.

"Dinah, how's your mother adapting to life here?"

Dinah shrugged. "She had her own household before and isn't used to following other people's orders—carrying water and wood all the time."

Acsah didn't respond. Zebidah had been the head woman servant for as long as she could remember. The old woman didn't tolerate laziness or insubordination. What would bring peace among the servants?

The atmosphere around the campsite changed dramatically. Seraiah hung around outside his tent, looking worried and clenching his fists every time a moan came from inside. Mehetabel would put her head out occasionally and ask for something, but mostly, they waited. Acsah knew delivering babies took time, but the delay weighed on her. She wanted to do something.

Caleb and the other men came to the campsite in the evening. When her father started looking for something to eat, she hurried to serve them the cheese and warm bread she and Dinah had prepared between errands. Would her father settle for so little attention? But she didn't have time to think about that because Mehetabel called for both girls to come into the tent to assist.

Zebidah positioned Dinah behind Azubah to give her support for pushing and told Acsah to have warm cloths ready to wipe and wrap up the baby after the birth.

Acsah didn't anticipate the look of agony on Azubah's face when the pains came. Although she'd heard many stories of births, she'd never assisted before. For the first time, she realized the seriousness of birth and the reality that birth and death exist close together. Would Azubah and the baby survive this?

As the pains increased and Azubah moaned in distress, Mehetabel began to make strange sounds, a chant of some kind. At first Acsah couldn't understand, but gradually, she realized Mehetabel was invoking the goddess Ashteroth. "Stop, Mehetabel."

Mehetabel did stop, but not without giving Acsah a troubled look. They had no time for a discussion. Azubah was pushing now, and the baby's head crowned. In less time than Acsah could have believed after such long suspense, the baby's head emerged with a rush of blood, soon followed by his little body.

All four stayed busy cleaning up the baby and delivering the afterbirth.

Azubah spoke through dry lips. "The baby?"

"You have a beautiful boy." Zebidah put the swaddled baby in his mother's arms.

Azubah soon had him at her breast and smiled with such radiance that Acsah had trouble believing she had been in such agony only minutes before. "The four of us will have to take a bath and wait until sunset to be clean. We've touched her blood."

Dinah sighed. "Your laws are so complicated. I don't know how you remember them all. But I don't mind taking a bath; I need one." She looked down at her bloody hands and clothes.

Zebidah was arranging the bedding around Azubah when Acsah saw her lift something out of the blankets. "What's this?"

Mehetabel took the clay figurine from Zebidah. "She needed something for the pain. I brought my own Ashteroth."

Acsah made a moaning sound in her throat. How could she fight against such persistent idol worship among her servants? "Take this away and bury it. I never want to see such a thing in the camp again. You must do this."

"But Mistress, I..."

"Do not question your mistress. Do what she says." Zebidah's voice held ice.

Mehetabel hesitated, but she left the tent, muttering something about slavery.

Dinah offered to stay with Azubah, and Acsah went to her tent, where she wept as she bathed. She didn't know if her tears came from joy and relief or from frustration. She wanted so much to talk to someone.

After sunset, she saw the men gathered around the campfire, congratulating the new father. She joined them, slipping in beside Othniel where he sat a little behind the others.

"You look pensive. Was assisting in the delivery too much for you?" The concern in his voice warmed her and made her open up.

"Oh, Othniel. I'm so confused about these Canaanite gods."

"What happened?"

She explained to him about the conversation with Dinah the day before and about Mehetabel's figurine and chant. "I can forbid them to speak of Ashteroth and order them to get rid of their idols, but I can't change what they believe."

"No. Only God can change their minds. But I think something more is bothering you."

"Well, I get the feeling Canaanite women take a lot of comfort from having a female god. They think she can understand what they go through better than a male god."

"I'm male, too. My answer may not fully satisfy you."

"I want to hear what you think."

Othniel looked at the campfire for a few minutes. "We all want someone who will meet all our needs without demanding much of us, don't you think?"

"I agree."

27

"If you are making up your own god, you can give him or her whatever characteristics you want."

"You're saying women make up gods to ease them in childbirth because that's the kind of god or goddess they want, not because God is really that way."

Othniel stared at the fire for a moment. "Do you worry about childbirth, Acsah?"

"All women do, I think."

"I wonder if Azubah thought much about it."

"I know she did; we talked about it. But she's firm in her faith in the Lord. She even said the Lord would help her. I wish I had her level of faith."

"I would die if anything happened to you in childbirth."

This statement so surprised her, Acsah didn't know how to respond. She waited for him to elaborate. When he didn't, she said, "I'm sure Azubah's glad Seraiah got back in time for the birth."

"Yes. He was as surprised as Salmon with his new son."

"Azubah wasn't sure for a long time. But nine months have passed since her last period, so I've been expecting it."

"Seraiah really wanted a son." Othniel nodded toward his beaming brother.

"Don't all men want sons?"

"Yes, of course. But daughters are nice, too. I'll never forget Uncle Caleb's pleasure when you were born."

"He already had three sons."

"True, but the celebration for your birth was as grand as for a son. You were such a beautiful baby."

"Were? I take it that has changed."

"Well, yes, of course. You're certainly no longer a baby." His expression told her the "beautiful" part hadn't changed.

She met his gaze, hoping he would say more. Then she noticed her father looking their way and studying them, so she looked away and changed the subject. "You remember my mother, don't you?"

"Yes, a wonderful woman. Don't you remember her?"

"I have vague recollections of a face full of love and a voice singing songs. Sometimes when I'm walking around camp, I hear a mother singing to her baby, and feelings of loss and longing come over me."

Othniel took her hand in a comforting squeeze, but suddenly, Caleb called, "Acsah, I want you to go in now."

Acsah said goodnight and moved swiftly off to the tent, her heart full. All that had happened this evening made her aware of Othniel's love. She lay on her palette under the wool blanket and stared into the

28

darkness, rehearsing every word, every look, every touch, until sleep overcame her.

4

Early on the day of Rahab's purification ceremony, Acsah sat thinking about the last few days. Helping take care of Azubah's new baby boy had taken up a lot of her time, so she hadn't spent as much time with Othniel as she had wanted. Yet every day, he had said or done something that intensified her deepening love. He accompanied her every morning on her trek for water. Two days before, she had found a string of shiny metal beads in her hand after he handed back the water jar. And yesterday, he had entrusted Dinah with a jeweled comb for her. But the looks he gave her as they walked toward the river for water or sat by the fire in the evening gave her the most hope. Why couldn't they have a normal relationship, open and accepted by all?

She rose and started after the water, one chore she never wanted to miss now. Othniel didn't disappoint her. He joined her as soon as she picked up the jar.

As they walked, Acsah inhaled deeply, her senses delighting in the fresh morning air and the virile man striding beside her. She wanted to talk about Azubah's baby, but what would he like to talk about? "Tell me more about the battles."

"You heard about the biggest the night we came back, the battle of Merom."

"Yes. I heard Father's version. Now I want to hear yours."

"Prepare yourself. War stories can be boring for those not there. The most fearful part came before the battle when their chariots and horses spread all over the valley. Defeating them seemed impossible. Yet the Lord helped us. We attacked them in their camp in the hills, and they had to fight us there, where their horses and chariots couldn't go. And some of our men got at the horses and hamstrung them. Then we burned all the chariots."

31

"I'm surprised you did that. Those might have been useful in future battles."

"Joshua ordered us to. He said the Lord didn't want us to put our faith in our weapons or armor, but in Him alone."

"The weapons weren't much use to your enemies in the end, were they?"

"No. When I think back to all the miracles the Lord has performed, I'm amazed. Think about the battle we fought against the kings who attacked Gibeon. Do you remember the giant hailstones?"

"They hit the enemy but not you."

"Right. And during that same battle, Joshua prayed, and the sun stood still."

"I remember we kept waiting for the sun to get lower in the sky to begin fixing the evening meal, but it didn't move. Finally we ate anyway. I think we fixed five meals that day."

Othniel shifted the water jar to his other hand. "It's interesting that we can't see what God is doing sometimes. You found it inconvenient to cook five times, but the longer day made it possible for us to win. Our limited view doesn't compare with His."

Acsah stepped along, pondering. "So you're saying we should trust God even when what's happening doesn't make sense because he may be working out a bigger plan we can't see?"

"Yes."

"I've heard my father say such things all my life, but sometimes I don't see the plan. Do you believe God is working even when your own life seems all mixed up?"

"Why? Does your life seem confusing?" He studied her as if to read her mind. Right now she'd prefer he didn't.

"Sometimes. I have a lot of questions I would ask God if I could."

"You can ask me anything. I won't always have good answers for you. But I'll try."

This sounded like a promise of a future together. But she couldn't ask Othniel her questions about why he hadn't asked her to marry him yet, or why her father could follow God so closely except regarding her future husband.

They reached the river where she got the jar of water and joined him for the return trip. They had walked for several minutes without speaking. Othniel turned to her. "Do you want to go with me to the purification ceremony this evening? Salmon has a grand feast planned."

"Yes, I'd like that." She looked down at her woolen shift. "I wish I had something more attractive to wear. This scratchy wool is shapeless."

"Well, I've got something I planned to give you later, but perhaps you need it more now."

"What is it?"

"Don't start begging me to tell. I'll send it to you by Dinah later."

"Oh, I want to know, please."

"You'll know soon enough, Little One." She recognized that stubborn set to his jaw. She'd have to give up teasing him. When they arrived back at the campsite, she reached for the water jar.

He grinned. "Are you afraid the other women will think you're shirking?"

She wanted to continue the banter, but her father came out, looking around. Doubtless he was searching for her and wouldn't like seeing her with Othniel. She walked quickly away from Othniel to the fire pit where Dinah waited for the water to soak some beans.

———

Othniel smiled at her retreat. What joy this small woman gave him. Her slender figure enticed him to follow her. That she thought the shift shapeless amazed him. Then he chided himself for the direction his thoughts tended and went inside his tent to dig through the small amount of plunder he reserved. He had to kick Elidad's sleeping mat aside. He needed to remind the servants to roll their mats up. They had gotten sloppy while he'd been away. He wasn't surprised to find Dinah waiting for him when he emerged from the tent, carrying what he had found. "Take these to your mistress."

"Of course." She turned away, but not before he caught a puzzled expression on her face. Didn't she recognize a linen dress when she saw it? He didn't have time to decode Acsah's enigmatic maid. He had promised Salmon he would help him get together the animals for the purification sacrifice and feast that evening. He made his way toward the herds.

Salmon already had a goat and a lamb when he found him. Othniel took the goat under his arm while Salmon got a firmer grasp on the lamb. "Are you going to slaughter the goat here?"

"We probably should. That will make it pleasanter for the women at the campsite. Women can be squeamish about these things." Salmon let the lamb go. "Are you ready?"

Othniel gripped the bawling goat for Salmon to slit its throat, then helped him drain the blood out as the law required. "Are you making goat stew for the feast?"

"I think that's Rahab's plan. The servants will take care of things while we're at the ceremony. I found a perfect lamb for the purification burnt offering, but I'm having trouble getting a pigeon. Do you have a good skinning knife with you?"

"Never without it." Othniel began skinning the carcasses. "I think I saw some pigeons down by the river this morning. Do you want me to go down there later and see if I can catch one?"

"Would you? Thanks."

When he finished the messy job of skinning the goat, Othniel picked up the meat and skin and carried them while Salmon got the live lamb again. Single file they made their way to Salmon's campsite.

"Here we are." Salmon gave his lamb to one servant, while Othniel handed the goat's carcass and skin to another and then washed in some water a third servant brought him. He wondered how he would feel being the patriarch of a family like Salmon, with servants jumping to serve. In his own campsite, his uncle treated him like a servant. But he wouldn't think about his uncle that way. He dried his hands and turned to Salmon. "I'll go look for that pigeon. Do you want me to bring it here?"

"You can bring it to the ceremony. I know you'll get one. See you this evening."

—◆—

Acsah looked up as Dinah entered the tent. "Here's what Othniel gave me for you." As she spoke, she shook out the bundle to reveal a dress of finest linen, dyed a rich blue color.

Acsah squealed. "How perfect! I can't wait to try it on." She pulled it over her head. It fit and felt cool and attractive. "Isn't it lovely, Dinah?"

Dinah refused to meet her gaze. "Yes, it is. But are you sure you want to wear it?"

"Why wouldn't I? Is something wrong in the back?" Acsah turned to show Dinah.

"No. If you like it, you should wear it. I'm sure Othniel will think you're very attractive."

Acsah thought Dinah's tone sounded suggestive, but she shrugged it off. She really shouldn't let Dinah takes such liberties with her, but right now, she was too happy to care.

That evening Acsah finished dressing for the purification ceremony. She combed out her long thick hair and chose earrings to go with a gold necklace.

She watched as Dinah put away her wooden box. "You have some lovely jewelry. Was it your mother's?"

"Some of it, but most of it came from my father's and brothers' plunder. Now my brothers give theirs to their wives. This set came from Othniel after the last campaign."

"And that has no effect on its value to you, does it?"

"Dinah." Her tone shut Dinah up.

Acsah emerged from the tent and watched for the reaction. All her relatives complimented her as she expected, but Dinah's brothers, Oren and Asa, stared and then looked away from her with embarrassed expressions. What was going on with the Gibeonites today?

Before she could question anyone, seeing Othniel approach distracted her. The admiration in his eyes gave her delight. All he said was, "Do you like it?"

"Very much. Thank you, Othniel."

"Are you ready to go to the purification ceremony?"

"Yes. Where's Father?"

"He's already gone."

Acsah looked at the bird in his hand. "Why are you carrying a pigeon?"

"I told Salmon I'd get one for the purification ceremony. They have to have one for the unintentional sin offering."

"Oh. Where did you find it?"

"Near the river where you get water. I learn things in those trips with you." His teasing made her giddy with pleasure.

As they reached the tabernacle, Acsah saw Salmon and Rahab coming toward them. Rahab carried their baby son, and Salmon led a lamb. Othniel walked past the crowd and handed the bird to Salmon. Acsah saw that Salmon's cousin, the high priest Eleazar, planned to perform the ceremony himself. He took the lamb and pigeon before going inside the tabernacle walls, followed by the men. The women waited outside.

Acsah watched Rahab standing outside the tabernacle, her lips moving in prayer. Why couldn't the woman cleansed by the ceremony participate in it directly? Acsah admired Rahab for worshiping the Lord, even outside. Rahab had such faith.

After a while, the men emerged from the tabernacle. Eleazar came out last. He raised his hands for silence and then announced. "The child has been given a name by his father. He will be called Boaz."

A murmur of approval rose before the crowd moved forward to congratulate the young couple. What a relief for Rahab to finish with her uncleanness after a whole month. Keeping up with the mats and rags irritated Acsah every cycle. And Salmon wouldn't have to wait any longer to sleep with his wife. Acsah sighed. Could she ever be with Othniel?

Othniel came to her then and said, "There's such a crowd around Rahab and Salmon that I think I'll wait to congratulate them until after the feast starts. Shall we move toward their tent?

"Yes."

"You really do look beautiful in that dress."

"Thank you. It's special to me because it's from you."

"Really, Acsah?"

"Of course. Where did you get the dress?"

"I believe at Madon, though I can't remember now, after so many different battles. At the time, it seemed that I could never forget each battle, but later the events started to run together."

"I think I understand. Some women have talked about their children that way. They didn't think they would forget which one said or did different things, but later they couldn't remember."

"You're comparing battles to children?"

She laughed. "They may be more alike than you can imagine now."

"Do you want to have children, Acsah?"

Acsah looked up at him, trying to judge the intent behind the question. "I'll need sons to take care of me in my old age."

"Yes. But do you think you will enjoy having children?"

Acsah could no longer make light of his question. "I love children. I want as many as the Lord sends."

"I envy Salmon so much right now. He has a wife and a child to come back to. I have only a bachelor tent."

"You have me, Othniel."

"Do I?"

"Always." She put as much feeling into the word as she could, hoping he understood all the depth of emotion behind those two syllables.

Othniel hesitated, started to say something, and then, sighing, turned back to the path.

———

Caleb watched Othniel and Acsah leave together from the purification ceremony. For several days now, they had been exchanging looks typical of lovers, not relatives. He couldn't let their affection for each other develop into something serious. He had his plans for Acsah.

He hurried to the feast and looked around. Several guests gathered around the fire in the center of Salmon's campsite. He had many servants, all hurrying about, offering food and drink. He could see Othniel talking to Salmon and Acsah to Rahab. Relieved for the moment, he took a bowl of the goat stew from a servant girl and started to eat the delicious meat. Several minutes passed before he realized Othniel had joined Rahab and Acsah. He needed to get over there to hear their conversation.

———

Hundreds of people stood or sat, eating the generous portions of meat stew, cheese, and fruit that Salmon had supplied. Othniel joined the men to congratulate Salmon. Acsah selected some figs and a piece of cheese from one servant and turned to look for Rahab.

When she spotted her, Rahab was looking at her with such distress she made her way over to her. "What's wrong?"

"It's your dress."

"Don't you like it? Othniel gave it to me."

"I hate to spoil your pleasure, Acsah, but I think you should know this belonged to a temple prostitute, from Madon by the look of it."

Acsah looked down at the colorful linen with its distinctive sash and elegant lines. "Well, no matter. Now it's mine. I think it's beautiful."

"Acsah, that's not the point. Tell me, how did your father's Gibeonite men react to your wearing this dress?"

How did she know? Acsah didn't want to answer this question.

"I thought so. Don't you understand what they will think about you if you keep wearing it?"

Acsah saw Othniel approaching them. But then he looked at their faces and backed away. "I'm interrupting a serious conversation. I'll come back later."

"No, Othniel. You need to explain to Acsah the reason she cannot wear this dress."

"Why shouldn't she wear it? I must have missed something."

Rahab lifted little Boaz to her shoulder. "I know you couldn't have known this, not having lived in Canaan as I have, but temple prostitutes wore this dress. For any man from Canaan who knows that, she might as well walk around naked as wear it. You can see why she must not, but she doesn't understand."

Acsah's cheeks flushed at this image. "Rahab, I don't understand why you're upset by this. This dress makes me feel attractive."

Othniel broke in. "You're so naive, Acsah. You don't know what men say when women aren't around." His voice held such vehemence she looked at him in surprise. "I don't want you to wear the dress any more, no matter how attractive it makes you feel. You're beautiful to me without this dress."

"Are you saying this as my kinsman, Othniel?" She tried to read his expression.

"I'm saying it as the man who loves you and wants to make you his wife."

Acsah's heart beat faster. The moment had come at last. Othniel was declaring himself.

Her father's sudden appearance beside her changed her elation to fear. "Acsah, come with me back to our tent." Caleb turned to Rahab where she stood holding the baby. "I thank you for your hospitality. Please extend my thanks to Salmon as well."

Acsah hesitated for only an instant. The stern tone of her father's voice meant she dared not disobey. She stole one look at Othniel's face and beheld such anguish there her heart sank. Did her father know about the dress? Or did he hear what Othniel said?

She turned and walked away, aware of her father's stiff posture. Neither said anything until they entered the tent.

Her father began. "How long has he been courting you?" His voice reflected inner fury, cowing Acsah despite her resolve.

"It's the first time he's ever spoken of marriage. Until now, he's treated me as a relative." Acsah thought about the exchanged looks, the treasured kiss when he left for battle in the North, but those didn't count, did they?

Caleb snorted. "Treachery in my own family—he knows what I plan for you, and yet he has the audacity to declare this intention. I won't stand for it."

"Oh, Father, I..."

"You what? You aren't going to tell me you want to marry this Kenizzite, not when you could have any man in Judah?"

Acsah took a deep breath to steady her voice. She would not get what she wanted by trying to coax her father in this mood, but desperation drove her. "He's been like a son to you, Father."

"No longer. He's an unwanted suitor. You may not see him until I have you married to someone from Judah." He stormed from the tent.

She changed her clothing, taking the offending blue dress outside and putting it on the fire. If only she had never seen it. What had started as a blessed day now had ended as the worst of her life.

———— ❧ ————

Othniel watched Caleb and Acsah walk away. He could hardly inhale, as if the breath had been knocked out of his body.

Rahab stood by him, looking sympathetic. "Are you okay, Othniel?"

"I... I... I.... Excuse me."

He fled on foot, away from the scene of his mortification. "That went about as badly as it could," he said to himself as he paced back and forth along the bank of the Jordan River. "Why did I blurt it out in public? Caleb knows now, and he isn't happy about it. Acsah knows, and I have no idea what she thinks. What do I do?"

Gradually he realized he had to go back and face the situation. A man couldn't declare himself to a woman and then leave her without making some attempt to fulfill his intentions. He felt like a whipped puppy as he crept back to the campsite. He planned to confront his uncle, but he had no confidence he could convince Caleb of his worthiness.

He didn't have to wait long for the meeting. Caleb saw him and came to him. To his surprise, Caleb said nothing about the scene with Acsah. Instead, he talked about the land allotment for Judah. "I want you to go south and begin the survey work, so that we can give out portions of land equitably. In your spying, you've worked at this before. Get details about the land—its suitability for farming and proximity to defensible cities. I expect all this will take you some time. Joshua plans to move the whole camp to Shiloh soon. You can rejoin us there, or, if we have moved, somewhere south of there, after you have finished the work. Keep careful records and try to include water on every man's section of land if you can."

Othniel felt stunned. Assigning portions of land for 76,000 men overwhelmed his comprehension. As if reading his mind, Caleb said, "Start with the southmost sections first near Kadesh Barnea and work your way north. We will take care of the northern parts as far south as Hebron.

Othniel's mind reeled, but he spoke up, "Uncle Caleb, b...before I go, there's so..o.mething I nee...ee...d to say...."

Caleb interrupted his stuttering speech. "Whatever it is, we can discuss it after you have finished this work. Now go to bed; I want you started first thing in the morning."

Othniel took this as a military command. How could he ask for Acsah's hand in marriage when he couldn't get out a whole sentence? Night had fallen, and Acsah slept in her tent. He realized Uncle Caleb wanted him to leave without telling anyone goodbye. Uncle Caleb might change his mind over time, but Othniel doubted it.

5

The next morning before dawn, Othniel gathered the supplies and disguises he needed for traveling as a spy in enemy territory. Though many major armies had been subdued throughout the territory, plenty of people there still would delight in assassinating an Israelite.

He slipped out of his tent and looked in the direction of Caleb's. Caleb stood waiting "and guarding the entrance," Othniel mumbled to himself.

Caleb stepped over to him and handed him a sack. "Here. This contains some Canaanite gold you'll need in your travels, although you may find food from farms along the way."

Othniel said, "Th...thank you," and put the bag inside his tunic.

"Do you have your hunting equipment and a water skin? Good, you should manage fine. Take some materials for recording your information."

Othniel nodded numbly. "Is th...there anything else I should know, Sir?"

Caleb looked at him in the gloom with an expression Othniel might have called pity from anyone else. "Acsah will be married before you return. You should use this time to reorient your thinking."

Othniel now saw the whole plan. Uncle Caleb wanted him out of the way in order to marry her to someone else. Othniel turned away and made his way south. His legs took him along the Jordan River, but his mind kept reviewing the last 24 hours. Acsah looked so beautiful in the blue dress. Why had he declared himself at the feast? Now Caleb would pick someone else for Acsah, and he had this long journey ahead with nothing to look forward to.

He walked 10 miles before his emotions caught up with him. In all his 44 years, he had never faced a pain like this one. Losing his parents, especially his father, had been difficult, but Caleb and Acsah had comforted him. Now he had no one. He cried out in agony, "Acsah is lost to me forever! How can I go on living?"

He stumbled. The wrench to his ankle stopped him. Below, the green Jordan Valley gave way to the barren cliffs of the Salt Sea. This symbolized his life from now on. All his hope for happiness and fertility was tied up in Acsah. Now the future stretched barren, desolate. A sob caught in his throat.

He resumed his journey, forcing himself to keep moving up one hillside and down another. The area became dryer and less vegetated, until all he could see were the bare hills and the beautiful but deadly waters below with their salt-encrusted shores, like the salty streams drying on his cheeks. It would be so easy to go down there and take a drink of those waters and then continue his journey until he dropped dead.

Oh, God of Abraham and Isaac, he moaned in his anguish, *I may not be a descendant of Jacob, but my loyalty has always been to you and to your chosen people. Is there no hope for me to have this one desire?* His heart continued to cry out as his legs moved along in the discipline of a soldier.

———

Acsah couldn't find Othniel or her father anywhere the next morning. Surely her father wouldn't do anything rash. Dinah told her what happened as she came back into the tent.

"Othniel's gone?" Her heart beat in her throat. "Gone where?"

"My brother said he overheard your father sending him south. It sounded like he left for several months."

"But he just got back!" Acsah's frustration erupted. "What's my father trying to do to me?"

The answer came a bit later. Caleb called for her to come walking with him out toward the Jordan River where they could stay in the shade and converse without being overheard.

"Father?" Acsah inquired after they reached the river's edge.

"I have two suitors I am considering for you, and I want to know if you have a preference in this matter."

Acsah's heart started beating faster, as she hoped he would name Othniel. "Yes, Father. Who are they?"

"One is Hamul, the oldest son of the Hamulite clan and a leader of ten thousand men. He has a good record in battle and has acquired much plunder and managed it well."

"And the other?" Acsah held her breath.

"Nadab, the son of Shammai of the Hezronite clan. He has an impeccable lineage and plenty of wealth. Do you know either?"

"No, Father." Acsah could not keep the disappointment out of her voice. He didn't mention Othniel.

"Then I will begin allowing them to make overtures so you can help me decide whom you should marry."

"But Father, what if I do know someone, someone I prefer already who wants to marry me?"

"Has this person asked me for your hand?"

Acsah realized that Othniel had not, at least before last night. "I don't know, Sir."

Caleb's voice betrayed his impatience. "What person dares to court my daughter without my permission?"

"Othniel wasn't trying to court me, Father. He only loved me, and I have learned to love him in return."

Caleb said with finality, "That situation has been remedied. I have sent your cousin to survey Judah's possessions. By the time he returns, I want you married to either Hamul or Nadab."

Acsah could not help objecting, though she knew it would anger her father. "Why don't you like Othniel? What about him isn't good enough for you?"

Her father's rage cowed her. "I have nothing against him personally. But I think we can do better for you. Being a Kenizzite has limitations for a man that you don't understand. I don't want to pass that on to your children. You have an opportunity to choose better for them. Do not disobey me in this matter."

Acsah knew the interview had ended.

She returned to her tent and, going into the back room, cried with great, wrenching sobs for a long time. She had been so young when her mother died, but she could still remember feeling abandoned, that no one loved her. This grief overwhelmed her, and her father had caused it. As a godly man, did he represent God? She knew Othniel did love and understand her, but her father had sent him away. What kind of God inflicted pain like this? Would Othniel say this belonged to the Lord's plans?

Much later, Acsah awoke, aware gradually that she had fallen asleep and that Dinah was calling to her. "Can I do anything for you, Mistress?"

Disoriented by her unusual daytime nap, Acsah struggled to speak. "Let me splash some water in my face. I'm going to visit my friend Rahab."

She held her emotions in check while she hurried to Rahab's tent, but as soon as she sat down, she burst into tears again. "Oh, Rahab, I'm so confused." A few minutes passed before she could compose herself. "I'm sorry; I don't know what's wrong with me. You see my problem, don't you? I want to marry Othniel, but my father won't let me."

Rahab reached over and held her in a motherly embrace. "I'm so sorry, my friend."

Acsah clung to her until her tears subsided once more. "You saw what happened. Father sent Othniel away."

"I've never seen a man in as much pain as Othniel last night. At least now you know he wants to marry you."

"Father plans to force me to marry someone from Judah. How could he do this to me?" She wanted to say, "How could God do this," but instead she asked, "Rahab, when you look back on all you endured in Jericho, do you blame God for making you go through so much pain?"

"No. Why do you ask?"

"Something Othniel said yesterday about trusting God's plan when we can't see what he's doing."

"You don't feel much like trusting God right now, do you?"

"I don't."

Rahab picked at the wool floss she had been spinning. "I didn't believe in the Lord when all the bad things were happening to me. Those resulted from my people's sin—lust, pride, and idolatry. When I put my faith in the Lord, everything changed for me."

"But I've been in Israel with law-abiding people around me, and I haven't rebelled against the Lord. Why should I have to suffer?" Her frustration must distress Rahab, but she didn't know anyone else to ask.

"I don't know, Acsah. You just have to trust."

Acsah didn't like this pat-sounding answer. How could her future husband be part of a bigger plan of God's?

❧

Caleb kept walking by the river long after Acsah left him. Why did she resist him about marrying into Judah? He hadn't argued with his own parents when they chose Abigail for him. She gave him three fine sons, who carried Judah's blood in their veins, though they couldn't claim Judah as their tribe. Abigail and he had a good marriage until she died of plague during the Dothan rebellion. He didn't want to admit even to himself that he'd never loved Abigail the way he loved Milcah, Acsah's mother. They had been so happy in their short marriage, and Milcah's daughter gave him a way to have grandsons born into Judah. They would never have to hear the taunts he had as a boy and even a young man—*alien, Edomite, foreigner.* How those words still rankled in his soul! Nothing he had accomplished in his life, no quantity of respect or position in Israel had ever erased those memories.

Why had Acsah taken to Othniel? Everyone talked about how well he led his troops. How could he lead when he stuttered so much? His friend Salmon likely did most of the leading. Oh, Othniel was a nice boy, handy to run errands and such, but the husband of his beloved Acsah? No. He would contact Nadab's father to discuss bride prices and dowry, but first he would make Nadab leader of ten thousand in place of Othniel. That should excite some gratitude and willingness to make Acsah his wife.

———◆———

Othniel had been walking so mechanically that late afternoon came before he realized how far he had come without a real break. He turned into a wadi, which spread red and rocky until it reached the edge of the distant hills where gray slopes rose. He could see what looked like a bit of green growing in a narrow side valley to the south. He trudged across the arid red plain before entering the valley. As his eyes adjusted to the dimmer light, what he saw comforted him—a fresh spring feeding into a large pool of water. The vegetation grew lush and green, and more water fell into the pool, perhaps from another spring further up. A fig tree had a few ripe figs hanging from the branches, though early in their season.

He spied a quail under the tree, and soon he had the quail captured, killed, prepared, and roasting over a small fire he skillfully set. The meal of roasted bird, fresh figs, and water refreshed him more than he hoped for in the Negev, the desert of Canaan. He thanked God for showing him kindness in his time of hurt and sorrow.

He lay down wrapped in his cloak. If only he could relive the day before, take out his unguarded speech, withhold the blue dress—anything to restore the hope he had before this day. He didn't cry anymore, but the ache in his chest made it hard to breathe. As tired as his body felt from the hours of marching south, he tossed on the hard ground for hours.

Then in a chill early dawn, in that surreal state between waking and sleeping, thoughts came to him from a voice or a dream. *Everything seems hard, but I have a purpose for it all, for you, for Acsah, for Caleb, and for all of Israel. Trust that all will be well, and do not despair.*

Where did the thoughts originate? Such an idea would not have occurred to him alone. Was the Lord speaking?

He rose and washed his face. Yesterday's anguish had dissipated, leaving him renewed and ready to face a new day and the challenges before him.

Taking time to record the land features he had seen, he made a special note. Though this land would not grow crops, the spring would be a delightful place to live.

Then filling his goatskin water bag from the spring, he left, swinging along in his strong stride toward Ziph and Kadesh Barnea, the furthest point south in the Promised Land.

6

---❦---

Caleb approached Shammai's tent. He had known him since Shammai was only a boy. Why should this visit make him so nervous—because normally the groom approached the bride's father? He had received offers from a number of men for Acsah, many from Judah, but he wanted the best and most respected line for Acsah. If Nahshon's son Salmon weren't already married, he had the best lineage, but Shammai's ranked second in his mind. Ahead, he could see Shammai sitting in the shade of his tent. "Shammai, may I speak with you?"

"Caleb, son of Jephunneh. Please do sit down." Shammai called his maidservant. "Miriam, get us some grape juice."

Caleb made the obligatory small talk about the weather and their health before finally coming to the point. "I've come to discuss the possibility of uniting our two houses."

"Do you mean my son Nadab to your daughter Acsah? I would consider it possible if all conditions were right. What do you propose?" Shammai took the cups of juice from the girl and handed one to Caleb.

"I'm willing to offer a dowry of 100 sheep."

Shammai's eyes narrowed. "A generous offer. But for my son Nadab? I must consider it for a while. As head of Judah, you'll have power to decide about land allotment. You would, of course, settle generously on your daughter and her new family."

Caleb didn't like the direction this was taking. He planned to cast lots for the Lord's help in assigning land. "I will pray the Lord gives me wisdom about those things, Shammai."

"The Lord. Of course. As I said, I need more time to consider your proposal. You can proceed with negotiations."

Caleb set the cup down and rose to his feet. "Thank you for your time, Shammai. I will talk to your son today with your permission."

"Certainly. He's inspecting our flocks today. "

Caleb bowed and walked toward the fields outside of camp. What did he expect? That Shammai would want to have his son marry an alien girl? Clearly the dowry would have to increase. Of course, he could also start negotiations with Hamul, whose parents died in the wilderness. He might convince Hamul without the interference of parents. Caleb sighed. He wanted this business over and Acsah married into Judah.

Caleb found Nadab amid Shammai's multitude of sheep and goats where they were grazing. He overheard Nadab berating a servant as he walked up.

"That's the second stillbirth this season. How can you be so careless? I should make you pay for the loss from your personal wealth."

The servant bowed his head. "I'm sorry, Master. These things happen, even to the best of shepherds."

"He's right, you know." Caleb walked into their line of sight.

"Caleb. I didn't know you were standing there." Nadab didn't appear as much startled as irritated by his interruption. "Can I help you with something?"

"Yes. I've come to discuss an important matter with you. Come aside if you will."

They moved a little away from the flocks, while the shepherd went back to his work with a grin on his face. Caleb got straight to his point. "I want to promote you from captain to a leader of 10,000 men."

If Nadab felt surprise or gratitude, he hid it well. "Whose unit will I take over?"

"Othniel's."

"Your nephew's? Why? Has something happened to him?"

"No. He's doing some survey work for me south of here. We'll fight some before he finishes."

Nadab turned from him to look at the flocks again. "So this is a temporary position."

"Not necessarily. I'm sure you'll prove yourself soon as an able leader." Marrying Acsah would make it temporary, but Caleb didn't mention that.

"Isn't Othniel's unit the one with 6000 Israelites and 4000 aliens of various sorts?"

Caleb winced at the word *alien*. "Do you have a problem with that?"

"Hmmm. No. I accept anyway. I'll make what I can of it."

Why did he feel as though Nadab had done him a favor by accepting?

———— ◆ ◆ ————

"I've always cooked porridge this way. No one has ever complained."

"You Israelites don't know the first thing about cooking. You should wait for the water to boil before adding the meal."

Acsah woke to this exchange outside her tent. She groaned. Zebidah and Mehetabel were arguing again. She pulled on her shift and hurried out to break up the fight. "Stop it, you two."

Zebidah straightened up. "I'm sorry to disturb your rest, Mistress, but this Gibeonite won't do what I tell her, and now she's telling me what to do."

"I wouldn't interfere if she did things the right way, but this porridge will taste like paste." Mehetabel waved her hand at the bubbling pot.

In this case, Acsah realized Mehetabel knew more than Zebidah, who refused to change her way of cooking, even when Acsah tried to reason with her. But Acsah couldn't undermine Zebidah's position as head female servant. "Mehetabel, I believe Zebidah asked you to supply the campsite with water and wood. Have you done that this morning?"

"No, I was starting to when I saw her ruining the porridge again. I refuse to eat her cooking anymore."

Acsah sighed. "You have my permission to cook food for yourself and your family separate from the rest of us as long as you adhere to the laws about food and it doesn't keep you from your assigned tasks. However, you may not criticize Zebidah's cooking or give her advice unless she asks you. Do you understand?"

Mehetabel shrugged and picked up a water jar, then headed to the river.

When she moved out of earshot, Acsah turned to Zebidah. "Well, what do you have to say for yourself?"

"I'm sorry I woke you. She makes me so angry sometimes."

"Yes, and you make her angry, too. What could you do to keep peace in the campsite?"

"She's only an alien. Why should I have to make peace with her?"

"I'm only an alien myself, Zebidah. Should I worry?"

Zebidah moved her hands in agitation. "No. You're my baby girl. I love you."

"If you love me, please make every effort to get along with Mehetabel. She may teach you some new things about cooking." Acsah wanted to laugh at Zebidah's expression at this last statement. She was the closest thing to a mother Acsah remembered having.

———

Caleb met with his leaders again about surveying the land and conquering it as soon as Joshua gave permission. He dismissed them to go about their business, but called out to Nadab. "Nadab, stay for a minute and let me speak to you."

Nadab came back. "Yes, Sir?"

"Are you still interested in my daughter's hand?

"I've discussed it with my father, and we're willing to continue negotiations. What were you offering as a dowry?"

Caleb hesitated. "One hundred sheep?"

"I understand you have a new bull calf."

"Yes. I could put that in as well."

"Then we can proceed."

"Did I miss it, or have you already told me what the bride price will be?" Caleb hated bringing this up.

"Five she-goats and ten sheep," said Nadab.

Such a paltry amount. Of course the real bride price was Nadab's family name and lineage. "That should be acceptable."

"So when will we wed?"

"I want Acsah to have a chance to meet you and learn to like you. Could you perhaps come by my tent day after tomorrow?"

"If you think that's necessary. I hope your daughter is in the habit of obeying the men in her life."

This comment disturbed Caleb at some level. Acsah had a bright, bubbly personality, the kind that made everyone around love her, but he couldn't say she obeyed him without question. He nodded his head to Nadab then started toward his own campsite.

————

Acsah heard her father calling her from outside the tent. As she emerged, she saw beside Caleb a tall, thin young man. Caleb gestured toward her. "This is Acsah, Nadab."

Acsah observed that Nadab held himself with dignity. The smile stretching his thin mouth did not project warmth. As a woman, she waited for him to speak first to her, but he turned and addressed Caleb instead. "She looks pleasant enough. Did you say the dowry included the bull calf as well as the sheep?"

Even Caleb seemed taken aback at Nadab's unloverlike attitude. "I want to give Acsah an opportunity to know you before we make final arrangements. You have my permission to converse with her, either here in the tent or walking about the camp."

Nadab nodded assent, "If you so wish. We can sit here as far as I'm concerned."

Acsah's discomfort with this man grew as she sat down on the mat a few feet from him. Nothing about him invited conversation.

At last he said, "I suppose I should give you information about myself. I'm sure your father has told you I am the son of Shammai. I stand to inherit a fair amount of wealth when my father dies, and I am assuming your father will grant us prime land in the allotments he will make for Judah."

Acsah's indignation at this speech kept her silent, so he continued, "We will, of course, have numerous servants, but I expect you to take an active part in providing for the household. I assume you have learned to weave."

"Actually, I rather dislike weaving." She delighted in speaking truthfully about this, not bothering to mention her reputation as a wonderful cook.

"Hmm. That's a drawback, but I might overlook that if you can bring a good weaver from among your servants as part of the dowry."

Acsah smiled as sweetly as she knew how, all the while thinking of the pleasure of telling her father what a mistake he made choosing Nadab. His next speech only hardened her resolve more.

"My father and I discussed at length whether or not to make your father an offer. Both of us decided your father's position as leader of Judah more than made up for his lack of pedigree. I considered several girls with direct descent from Judah, but you're my choice. Our children will still be considered direct descendants of Judah and thus Israel."

Acsah couldn't stop the girlish laughter that burst out at this speech. Her sense of the ridiculous overcame her fury at her father for putting her in this position. "What a relief. You don't know how much sleep I've lost over that very issue."

Nadab appeared unfazed by her reaction. She saw that his self-importance made it impossible for him to suspect she might be laughing at him. He almost managed a smile. "Good. I'll tell your father we can finalize negotiations."

"Thank you, but I would prefer to discuss the matter with him myself. I'm sure he will want to hear what I have to say about the subject. He can seek you out when he's ready."

"You're not at all what I expected in a wife." His tone held surprise. "But I find you quite acceptable. I look forward to wedding you."

Acsah managed only a faint smile at this. Would her father really insist she marry such a man? The idea brought steel into her heart. When would Othniel come and set things right?

On returning to their tent, she wasted no time before talking to Caleb. "Father, I've made my decision about Nadab. I do not want to marry him."

"Why not, my daughter?"

Acsah took a deep breath and tried to sound reasonable, but her voice shook. "Because he's a pompous, insensitive fool, who wants me only for the land you could give him."

"Those words are a bit harsh for a man from so prominent a family. I agree he talks too much about the dowry and bride price."

"How much for the bride price?"

"Five she-goats and ten sheep."

"So little. That's an insult to me and to you."

"Acsah, I know he doesn't seem so generous now, but in time, he will learn to love you as he knows you better."

"He's not a man I could ever care about, Father. Surely you see the disdain in which he holds all of us." Acsah gestured to the family campsite. "Why would you want me to suffer from condescension all of my married days, not only from him, but from his whole family? I would rather marry an orphan than go to such a family."

Caleb sighed. "I will bring Hamul to meet you soon. He isn't as wealthy or prominent, but if you're concerned about personalities, you'll like him better."

Acsah shook her head, but knew she couldn't mention Othniel's name at this time without enraging her father. "You asked me to give you my opinion."

"And you have. Please give Hamul a fair trial."

"I will try, Father."

But the very next day, the cloud rose into the air above the tabernacle, and the whole camp flew into frantic activity preparing for the first move in over a year. Acsah knew she had become lax in her readiness and assumed everyone else had, too. How did she pack the crockery? She wanted it compact and unbreakable. At last she emerged from the tent. "Elidad, Oren, this tent can go now. Here are the bundles."

She saw Azubah's tent still standing. Inside she found Azubah in tears. "I can't manage it all, Acsah."

"You sit and hold the baby. I can get this done." She wrapped blankets around the pots and rolled up the mats from the floor. "This move comes at a really bad time for you, doesn't it?"

"Probably every move is bad for some women in the camp. My turn has come. Thank you for caring, Acsah."

The last tent still standing belonged to the Gibeonites. "Dinah, Mehetabel, we have to leave soon. Do you need help?"

Mehetabel fussed. "When you said to be ready to leave at a moment's notice, I didn't think you meant it literally."

"Let me show you the best way to pack." Acsah hurried as fast as she could, but still the tent wasn't struck before the men came with the pack animals. What would her father say to her? A few minutes more and she, Dinah, and Mehetabel had all their goods tied up in blankets and the tents rolled into tight bundles.

Actually, she had done well. Israel delayed moving until much later in the day than usual. Acsah got the standard of Judah and took it to her father. He led the whole procession—all the more reason she needed to be ready. She could tell he chafed under the delay, but he looked excited. Moving made him happy. She hadn't realized that before. He liked going and doing. She saw the servants lead the loaded donkeys to the outside edge of the campsite and the people line up behind the banner, ready to move.

As they wound their way across the plain and up a steep mountainside, Acsah remembered this road, the same one Israel took two years before to Shechem where Joshua read the law to them between Mt. Ebal and Mt. Gerizim. She slipped up near Caleb. "Father, are we going back to Shechem?"

"From what Joshua told me, we're headed to Shiloh."

"Where's that?"

"You'll be glad to know it's much closer than Shechem, a day's journey, though with our late start, we won't get there until tomorrow."

The path wound steeply up out of the Jordan Valley. Acsah considered herself an active person, but it had been many months since she walked like this. After several hours, her legs ached. How could the older people and children manage? She dropped back to where Azubah rode on a donkey, her baby cuddled in a pack in front of her. "Are you all right?"

Azubah nodded. "Yes."

"This must be dreadful for you."

"Seraiah's so kind to arrange a donkey for me."

After making sure Azubah was not distressed, she found Rahab and walked beside her. Rahab also had her baby in a pack, but she wasn't on a donkey. "Didn't you want to ride?"

"I've had so little exercise lately I wanted to try walking. It's hard, but I'm all right."

"Let me carry him for a while."

Rahab surrendered little Boaz, who at five weeks had gained weight and looked adorable.

Acsah kissed his little head. "His hair is so soft. Like baby bird feathers."

"Caring for a baby takes a lot of time and energy, but the compensations are great. What could be sweeter than nuzzling a baby's neck?" Rahab's smile said that for her, the benefits of motherhood more than repaid any trouble. Then she asked, "So how goes your father's search for a husband?"

Acsah shifted the baby around in her arms. "If the first candidate represents his choices, I have a problem."

"You have to obey your father."

"I know. That's the law. At least he's giving me a choice in the matter, between Nadab and Hamul. I've met Nadab. He wants only to get richer and more prominent by marrying the daughter of Judah's leader. Isn't it ironic that at the same time some Israelites disdain my father for his lineage, they covet his position?"

"I don't know Nadab, but I think Hamul has something to do with Salmon's old unit. I'll ask him. You haven't met him yet?"

"No. I'll let you know when I do meet him."

Their talk moved on to Azubah's baby. Acsah told Rahab about Mehetabel and Ashteroth.

Rahab shook her head. "I once did all those things, too. You're right when you say you cannot change their beliefs."

"You changed yours."

"Because I had an encounter with the Lord, and he saved me from destruction. I don't think you can persuade Dinah or her family by commands or argument. They'll come to the Lord when they see that the Israelite God is superior, the only real God."

An uneasiness settled on Acsah at Rahab's words. Did she even believe that herself? No, she wouldn't ask that question. "I've got to go forward to check on Azubah." She handed Boaz back to Rahab. "Thank you for visiting with me along the way. It made the time go faster and gave me much to think about."

"Thank you for giving me a break. Come visit me often, my friend."

Acsah reached Azubah's donkey and noticed that Azubah's voice cracked with dryness, and her face looked pale. Kenizzite women had strength, but travelling only a few days after giving birth would challenge anyone. Perhaps they would halt early since they couldn't make it in one day anyway. Then she remembered. The Lord decided when they stopped, so she sent up a prayer on behalf of Azubah, Rahab, and all the others struggling on this journey. *Please, Lord. Please let us stop early tonight for the sake of these little ones and their mothers.*

No sooner did she voice the prayer than she saw the pillar of cloud descend. They were stopping. He had answered her prayer, just like that. For the first time, Acsah believed the God of Abraham, Isaac, and Jacob might care for her enough to listen to her personal prayers.

Acsah wanted to ponder that thought, but right now, she had a dozen things to do at once. She needed to get Azubah and the baby into shelter as soon as possible and get a meal ready. With the energy that comes from unselfish purpose, she went to her tasks, holding the baby while Azubah dismounted, getting her a drink of water and a soft blanket to sit on, and untangling the tricky knots of the donkey loads containing Seraiah's tent and food for supper. And all the time she heard singing in the back of her mind, "The Lord answers the prayers of those who call on him." She would love to tell Othniel about this experience, but sadly, she couldn't.

In the late afternoon, in the stillness after the activity of settling their tents, Acsah took a walk to inspect the area. Mountains surrounded them on many sides, but trees grew in the immediate area. She climbed one higher hill and could look down over where they had been. The plains of the Jordan looked very far away.

Then a movement caught her eye. She could see a figure walking up the road, walking very fast indeed. Curious, she fixed her gaze on him. Who was this person who never tired? A tall figure in a garment made of some material she couldn't identify entered the camp, and as he walked past, his eyes bore into hers with a look that saw into her soul. She followed him as he headed straight for Ephraim and the tent of Joshua.

She saw Joshua rise when the stranger approached and offer the traditional hospitality of food and drink, but the stranger said, "Joshua, beloved of the Lord. I have not come from Gilgal today to fellowship with you, but to rebuke you and warn you."

Joshua fell on his face and said, "My Lord, have mercy. What would you have me do?"

"Assemble the people. I will speak to them all."

Joshua sent a servant to call for the men who played the silver trumpets. Seeing her standing nearby, he said, "Daughter of Caleb, go to the high priest Eleazar and tell him to expect everyone."

At the command in his voice, Acsah flew to do his bidding. She found Eleazar in his tent. She panted, "Joshua says to prepare. Something terrible or wonderful is about to happen."

Before she finished speaking, the silver trumpets sounded. Eleazar looked around him. "The tent of meeting isn't set up, but everyone will come here. I must prepare." He went into his tent.

Acsah waited outside as more and more people arrived. Many were questioning. "What's going on?" "Why are we here?"

Then Joshua and the stranger walked up to the place where the tent of meeting would normally stand. Some younger men brought some heavy flat rocks to make a kind of platform for them to mount. Eleazar came out of his tent, dressed in his high priest's garments and looking a little flustered.

Again the trumpets played, this time to bring the huge crowd of people to silence. Joshua spoke first. "This man comes from the Lord. He wants to speak to all of us."

Acsah had a good position in the crowd, behind the leaders, who had been pushed forward by the people to stand between them and whatever danger this messenger represented. Everyone there had either seen or heard about the judgments of the Lord in the past. She could see her father near the front, looking at the man with expectation.

The messenger spoke as though he himself were the Lord; indeed, Acsah could never be sure he wasn't. "I brought you up out of Egypt and led you into the land that I swore to give to your forefathers. I said, 'I will never break my covenant with you, and you shall not make a covenant with the people of this land, but you shall break down their altars.' Yet you have disobeyed me."

At this point, he looked at Joshua, Caleb, and the other leaders in front. "Why have you done this? Now therefore I tell you that I will not drive them out before you; they will be thorns in your sides and their gods will be a snare to you."

Caleb stood mesmerized by the man's words. He remembered the day the Gibeonites came. Something hadn't seemed right at the time, but he hadn't said anything. Now the Lord was telling them they had broken covenant by making that agreement with the Gibeonites. The thought that the Lord wouldn't continue on with them hurt him terribly. He fell on his face, vaguely aware of Joshua and others around him moaning in grief. "Please don't abandon us."

Suddenly, Caleb heard a rustling sound, and a voice spoke into his ear. "I will be with you, Caleb, if you continue to believe in what I will do for you and for Judah." Caleb lifted his head to see who spoke and saw the messenger's retreating back. Caleb pondered the message's meaning. Why had the Lord singled him out in this way? Around him he could hear people weeping. But elation over his message kept him from identifying with their feelings. The Lord would be with Judah.

Then he realized Joshua had risen and begun speaking. "We must make sacrifices. Bring your burnt offerings. Perhaps the Lord will relent if we show our repentance. From now on, this place will be known as Bokim, the place of weeping."

Caleb rose at once. He would get his bull calf to make a burnt offering. What else could he do but dedicate his whole being to the God who had done so much for him and promised him success in battle?

As he hurried out to the herds to get the calf, Acsah caught up with him. "Oh, Father, what does this mean?"

Caleb looked at her and saw her look of surprise.

"Father? Are you all right? Your face is radiant."

"He spoke to me. The Lord spoke to me." The wonder of it still amazed him.

"What did he say?"

"He said not to fear; He would be with me." Then turning from her, he hurried to get the calf and bring it back to the center of camp.

The sacrifices took several hours, and almost everyone stayed to watch, many still weeping. Because the tabernacle hadn't been set up, the priests did the ceremonies out in the open on an altar made from uncut flat stones. Caleb led the bull calf forward and slit its throat, helping Eleazar and his son Phinehas catch the blood to sprinkle beside the altar before lifting the calf in his arms with a grunt to place on the altar to burn. He stood near the altar as the calf burned, praying. Would God accept his offering? He really did want to fully commit to the Lord, as the burnt offering signified. Was anyone capable of fully understanding the Lord's will? Could a man think he loved God and still be holding back?

Unbidden, his desire to be aligned with Judah crossed his mind as something he wouldn't surrender. No, as long as he trusted God for conquering Canaan, only that mattered. He ignored his restlessness about Acsah and marriage and watched the other sacrifices. Evening turned into dark night as several Levites helped the priests keep the sacrificial fires burning. Finally, very late, the Israelites went to their beds.

7

The second day of traveling started very much like the first, except the whole process of packing took place in relative silence. Only the animals were not affected by last evening's events. Perhaps the sacrificial fires had hidden its leaving, but today Acsah could see that the pillar of cloud no longer hovered near Eleazar's tent where the ark was stored. The cloud of the Lord's presence was gone. Did that mean the Lord would not travel with them?

Acsah knew everyone around her worried about the visit from the messenger, but although she had a lot to think about, the peace she gained from the message to her father stayed with her. His faith set him apart every time. She knew the story of the 12 spies sent out from Kadesh Barnea 45 years before, but realized she had never heard her father tell that story.

The people started out, and Acsah moved to the front where Caleb marched, bearing the standard of Judah. "Father, tell me about Kadesh Barnea."

"Oh, Daughter, that happened a long time ago. My first wife Abigail was living then, the boys' mother." He stopped as his mind wandered.

Acsah waited, trying to imagine her father as a young husband. Did he love his first wife? He had often told her he loved her mother.

At last, Caleb shook himself and continued. "Already I'd proven myself as a leader. You know that Salmon's father Nahshon led Judah before me?"

Acsah nodded her head, not wanting to interrupt him.

"Well, Nahshon chose me as a judge, but only among the Kenizzites. One day, Moses called an assembly of the leaders. He told them the Lord wanted us to send twelve spies into Canaan and asked for recommendations from each tribal leader. When Nahshon suggested my name for Judah, many objected. Eliab, the leader of Zebulun, declared I could not because I didn't descend from Judah. Many others agreed, but Nahshon pointed out the obvious advantage I had—I could speak fluent Canaanite. Finally, they gave in. Only Hoshea treated me kindly."

"Hoshea?"

"Joshua. Moses changed his name right after that."

"Oh. I forgot his name changed."

"Yes, he was older than the others and wise beyond his years even then."

"So were you." Acsah looked at him to see if he would react to this compliment, but he only shifted the standard to his other hand.

"I still remember the speech Moses made before he sent us out. He told us where to go and what to look for. I felt the huge responsibility we had."

"Where did you go?"

"We entered from the south, the opposite of the way we're going now." He waved his hand to indicate the lush scene before them of olive groves and vineyards. "We came up through the Negev. I wasn't particularly impressed with that area. It's dry, dusty desert. We sometimes found a spring of water, but rarely."

"Is that land part of Judah's allotment?"

"Yes, but I doubt if anyone will want that land. My spy is looking it over, but I doubt he'll find any land worth allotting."

"Do you mean Othniel?"

She saw her father's back stiffen as he ignored her question. They walked in silence for a few minutes before she attempted to resume the conversation. "I suppose no one lived in the Negev then."

"Not many did, but we saw a few Amalekites."

"Perhaps they survive the way we did in the wilderness all those years."

"The Lord provided manna and helped us find water. The Amalekites wouldn't have had that. Life in the desert taxes body and soul. Here, the Lord clearly wants us to make it on our own."

"So land allotment matters very much."

"Yes, it does. But we will have plenty of land like this. The Negev extends only so far north, then stops. When we went north, we topped a ridge and everything looked different: green fields, vineyards, olive and fig trees, fertile valleys surrounded by rocky hills."

Acsah looked around at the scene before her. Would Othniel have the same kind of experience in a few days? How long would he stay away? "Did seeing the good land make you excited about conquering it?"

"Yes. But then we also came to the cities. I'll never forget my first view inside Kiriath Arba. Egypt had large buildings and impressive agriculture, but the sight of those cities up on those hills, fortified with walls the width of houses and filled with men taller than trees, overwhelmed me. In some ways, I don't blame the other spies for being afraid. At times, I thought the situation looked impossible, too."

"But when the time came, you stood up against everyone and trusted the Lord."

"You already know this story. I don't know why I'm telling it to you."

Acsah laughed at his teasing. "Because I want to hear your perspective."

"Not much exciting happened after that. We took stock of the land, counting cities and evaluating crops. I've never forgotten the grapes we found in that valley north of Kiriath Arba. I'm looking forward to having those again."

"What happened when you came back to Moses and the other Israelites?"

"That's the odd thing. When the spies consulted together, we all listened to Joshua and agreed we could give a good report. We walked into camp carrying that huge cluster of grapes on a pole, and at first, we did talk about all the good parts, the fertile land and streams of water. But after that, well, the others gave in to fear. They started telling about the Anakites we saw in Kiriath Arba and Kiriath Sepher, how thick the walls were, and how well armed the men.

"Well, I couldn't stand it. I spoke up and interrupted them. I said, 'We should go up and take possession of the land, for we can certainly do it.'

"You would think I'd suggested we commit suicide. All the doubt they had about me and my worthiness came out in their statements. 'What does he know?' they said. 'He's just a Kenizzite.'

"Before long, I thought a riot would break out. The people's reaction so grieved me I tore my clothes in anguish. Only Joshua stood with me. He spoke up and said, 'The land we passed through and explored is exceedingly good. If the Lord is pleased with us, he will lead us into that land, a land flowing with milk and honey, and will give it to us.'

"Then I added, 'Only do not rebel against the Lord. And do not be afraid of the people of the land, because we will swallow them up. Their protection is gone, but the Lord is with us. Do not be afraid of them.'"

"Did your speech do any good?" Acsah asked.

"No, they started talking about stoning us. I think they would have, but suddenly an intense light appeared at the Tent of Meeting. Moses and Aaron fell face down on the ground in front of the Tent. We knew something was happening, but we could hear only a roaring sound.

61

"I should have been afraid, but somehow I wasn't, because I'd done the right thing. But the ten spies besides Joshua and me had reason to fear. While we were still standing there, waiting to find out what Moses and Aaron heard, the other ten suddenly clutched at their throats and dropped dead of plague."

"Oh, Father. If you hadn't had such faith..."

"Nothing has changed. It still takes faith, the faith to act according to what God has commanded. That's what I'm doing now."

"Those other men came from prominent families, but that didn't make any difference to God, did it?"

"No. The Lord cared more about their faith than their lineage."

"I think the Lord has the right idea about that. Faith matters more than lineage." She hoped her father would see the irony in his own words, but nothing changed about his demeanor. Acsah sighed. "I'd better go help Azubah with the baby."

"Thank you for walking with me today. Sometimes it's lonely being a leader."

Acsah smiled before turning to set up camp at Shiloh. She loved and admired her father. How could he be so blind to the truth about himself and faith?

8

Only two days later at Shiloh, Caleb announced at breakfast, "Acsah, today at noon, I'm bringing a guest. I want you to prepare the meal and to meet this man."

"Is he the other suitor, Father?"

"As a matter of fact, he is. But don't decide in advance. He's very different from Nadab, and I want you to try to like him."

Acsah's meek assent belied the rebellion in her heart. Must she keep up this mockery when her heart belonged to Othniel? And what could she cook on such short notice that would please her father? Beans or lentils wouldn't work, but she could bake fresh wheat bread and make a leek and barley soup.

She went to work, putting her barley on to soak in a pot near the fire and beginning the arduous work of grinding the dried wheat kernels. She had some sourdough left from the last baking and plenty of leeks and salt. Still the meal needed something else.

Then she had an idea. After her barley and leeks started boiling, and the wheat dough finished its first rising, she set aside a little dough. To this she added honey and raisins and shaped these into small loaves, sprinkling some precious cinnamon on top.

The fragrant baking attracted her father, who nodded his approval. "I think your cooking will impress Hamul."

"Thank you, Father. Rahab taught me a lot."

"You've helped her as well. You befriended her when no one else would."

Acsah smiled at her father, hoping to keep the lines of communication open between them, even as she wondered how she could change his mind about Othniel.

At noon, a stocky fellow appeared at their fireside, beaming and rubbing his hands in anticipation. "I could smell the food from far away and hoped it was yours."

Acsah looked up into good-humored eyes appraising her with delight.

"So you're the lovely Acsah. I've heard of your beauty, my dear." His tone caressed her, almost possessively. "And your father said you would prepare today's meal. So much to delight in."

Acsah's heart fluttered at his admiration. Othniel never said such romantic things to her.

The meal progressed pleasantly, with Hamul praising every dish as delicious and the cook as extraordinary. "These sweet loaves are beyond description."

"I'm glad you like them. Do have another."

Caleb took one, too. "Acsah keeps us well fed. I miss her cooking when we're away fighting."

Acsah sat back, well satisfied with their reaction. Othniel took her ability to cook for granted. She removed the dishes as her father and Hamul discussed battles. Hamul led ten thousand now. Whose place had he taken? She could ask her father later.

Hamul finally rose to take his leave. "I hope to talk with you again soon." His eyes were communicating something that made her heart race a little. Was she falling in love with him? If so, why did this feel like fear?

Several days later, she walked over to Rahab's tent. The week had gone well. Hamul had come to see her several times. Each time he had expressed appreciation for her beauty and talents. The flattery made her wonder if she could learn to love someone besides Othniel. She observed nothing objectionable in Hamul, though she didn't know much yet. A part of her wanted to give in, to make her father happy, and to marry this man. After all, she would obey the law by doing that. In her confused state, she almost walked right past Rahab's tent.

Rahab must have seen her. "Come in, Acsah."

She sat down on the floor matting across from where Rahab was spinning linen thread. Rahab spun with such skill. Acsah sat mesmerized for a long time without speaking.

"How has your week gone?" Rahab woke her from her reverie.

"Fine. I met Hamul a few days ago."

"And..."

"He seems like a nice enough man. At least he didn't treat me like an alien."

"So does this mean you are going to marry him?"

"Do you think I should give in and marry Hamul? Did you find out anything about him?"

"Well, I found out he's the one given Salmon's command."

"Oh, I'm sorry. I didn't know. Did that make Salmon happy or sorry?"

"Salmon knew he would have to give up his command when he married me. As a soldier, he respected the decision of his leader."

"My father, you mean."

"Yes." Rahab sat quiet then, without meeting her eyes.

Her silence made Acsah nervous. What did Rahab know that she wasn't telling? "Do you think my father made a mistake?"

Rahab stopped spinning to work with her wool floss, still not looking at her. "I think your father's choice surprised Salmon."

"Why?"

Rahab sighed. "I really don't want to interfere, but you did give me permission to find out what I could."

"Yes, I did."

"Well, Salmon has heard things around army campfires."

"What kinds of things?" Acsah wanted Rahab to look at her.

"Salmon said Hamul brags about all the conquests he has made among his slave girls and even among some Israelite women."

"Adultery?"

"Well, I don't know that he ever deliberately seduced a married woman. But Salmon says Hamul impregnated one Amorite servant girl, and when he refused to acknowledge his paternity, she did away with herself, and, of course, the baby."

"How horrible!" Somehow she wasn't surprised. Hamul's manner fit the profile of a womanizer. "He acts very charming in person."

"What Salmon has told me reminds me of my first husband. Ambaal could also be very charming if he wanted something."

"But had no concern for the consequences of his choices."

"Right."

Silence fell between them for several minutes while Acsah tried to process what she had heard. Finally, she asked, "Why would my father choose a man like that for my husband?"

"Your father comes from another generation. He doesn't know how much things have changed. He assumes everyone believes as he does and has the same values. For him the only issue is lineage."

"And he will provide the wealth and land to get that. I wish he weren't blind to the truth."

"Perhaps he's blinded by insecurity."

"What do you mean?"

"He believes Israelites are better than he is, not because of their character or accomplishments, but because of their prestige. If I learned anything from being a prostitute, it's that men do not become good because they are descended from prominent people, but because they individually choose to do noble and good things. Some of my most brutal and slimy customers were the king's sons, and the king of Jericho wasn't much better."

"How can we raise our sons rightly then, if lineage has nothing to do with character?"

"We can raise them to love God and obey his law. That's the only heritage that matters. God blessed me by giving me a man raised by a godly man, and he has chosen godliness himself. I pray we can send that on to little Boaz." Rahab looked with tenderness at her sleeping son.

"I know only one eligible man whom I consider godly."

"Othniel?"

"Yes. Rahab, do you believe God answers our prayers?"

"I know he does. Why do you ask?"

Acsah told Rahab about the cloud descending when she asked and how that made her feel. "I prayed unselfishly then. Having Othniel as my husband is a selfish request. And I don't want to estrange my father. Do you think the Lord would listen to such prayers?"

"I believe he would. I'll pray, too."

"Thank you." They sat in companionable silence, but Acsah finally shook herself. "Well, I'd better go."

Acsah left Rahab's tent mulling over what Rahab said. What kind of heritage did she want for her own children? She had a godly father—no one could dispute it—but why wasn't that the criterion he used to choose her a husband?

"Hello, Beautiful." She looked up to find Hamul walking beside her. Until today, she would have accepted his company gladly, but all she heard from Rahab about him made her greeting rather cold.

"What's the matter with you?" A slur in his speech warned Acsah he had been in the wineskins.

"I'm on my way home now. I need to hurry. Excuse me." As she started to pick up her pace, a hammy hand closed on her arm.

"Not so fast. You aren't warming up to me as you should. I know a way to change that." He pulled her into a place where two tents backed up to each other with no one to see. His arms went around her waist, and his thick lips sought hers.

Acsah wasn't strong enough to pull away from him, but thinking quickly, she brought her sandal down hard on the top of his foot.

"Ow, you little..."

Without waiting to hear what he called her, she sped away. Like a hunted animal, she dodged through the corridors between tents, hoping she had shaken off the lecherous beast.

Breathless and teary, she arrived at her tent site and saw no one. She hurried into her own tent, into the inner room, and wrapped herself in a blanket. To whom could she turn for comfort? She dared not go back to Rahab with Hamul out there. Her father would choose Hamul's side. Oh, how she longed for the protection and comfort of Othniel! *Please, dear God, help my father to see that Othniel is the right man for me.*

———◆———

Othniel walked through the streets of Hormah. He wasn't wearing his beggar's clothing, since he planned to stay only long enough to buy some supplies and survey the land and water situations. The marketplace reminded him of other Canaanite markets. Children dashed between the legs of haggling customers and merchants, snatching things from carts and running away laughing. One merchant caught a child with some of his figs and was beating him with a stick, all the while shouting curses.

Othniel stopped in front of a well-stocked booth. Mounds of bread such as Acsah baked for him made his mouth water and his heart ache. "How much for the bread?"

The merchant eyed his clothes. "Three pieces of copper."

He knew he should barter for a lower price, but gave in without comment. "Give me four loaves of bread and two pomegranates."

The merchant handed him the food and took his money. "Much thanks. Come again."

Othniel held up his limp goatskin bag. "Tell me. Where could I refill my water bag around here?"

The merchant pointed to the city gate. "Just outside you'll find a deep cistern. Likely a young maiden getting water would assist you." He winked.

Othniel ignored the hint. "You have no wells inside the city walls?"

"Not that anyone's told me."

"Thank you for your help." Othniel walked down the street, stepping carefully to avoid the filth and rotting food and to keep from being tripped. The merchant no doubt enjoyed their exchange. Well, let him. He needed to survey the lands around the city. Perhaps he could get a better view from the raised center of town.

He turned down one narrow street. A voice spoke from the shadows. "You look lonely. Do you need a friend?"

The words resonated so with his feelings that he paused to look for the source. A statuesque woman with uncovered hair flowing in black ringlets around her emerged from a doorway. She smiled and beckoned to him. "Come and eat at my table, for I have meat and drink enough to share, and my beds are softer than the hard ground."

Othniel moved one step in her direction. What she offered sounded so good. Why would a strange woman offer food and friendship now? Was she from the Lord?

She opened her door wide and took him by the hand. "My husband has gone away. Perhaps you would like to take his place?"

Othniel recoiled—an adulteress, probably a prostitute. He pulled free and fled down the street. After many turns, he stopped and rested while his breathing returned to normal and he composed his thoughts. How could he have let down his guard? Because he pitied himself instead of concentrating on his task? With a groan, he sat against the wall, trying to make sense of his behavior.

A sentence from the law came to him. "They shall have no inheritance among their brothers; the Lord is their inheritance." This verse applied to the Levites, but in some ways it applied to him. What if as a Kenizzite he never had Acsah as his wife, or good land, or respect in Israel? The Lord would still be his inheritance. He was enough. *Oh, Lord, if you will consent to be my inheritance, that will content me, even if I never have anything more.*

He sat for a few minutes, then gathered himself and continued his work of surveying and traveling south, his heart calmer than it had been in a long time.

9

They had resided at Shiloh now for many days. Acsah hungered for Othniel to return before her father pressed her about Hamul and Nadab. The thought of Othniel brought bittersweet pain. Unlike Hamul's selfish pawing, Othniel's embraces gave her comfort and delight. The one kiss they had shared right before the last big campaign still thrilled her. She had stood with her sisters-in-law watching the men put on their armor and gather their supplies. The other women had wept, but she had not cried. Instead she had waited for a sign, anything from Othniel to indicate he hurt as much as she did. He had avoided her gaze, but she hadn't let that discourage her. Surely, she had thought, before he left he would say something. But the men had finished preparing, said their goodbyes, and started away. Othniel hadn't shown her any special attention.

The other women had turned back to their tents and left Acsah standing alone. She had started to move to her own tent to hide and cry, when she had heard a sound. Suddenly, Othniel had stood beside her. Without giving her a chance to react, he had bent and given her a tender kiss before turning and disappearing again.

Today, she held the memory of that kiss next to her heart. When would she see him again? Would he have changed toward her? If they moved again, would he find them?

Caleb strode to the tent of meeting, but his enthusiasm dragged. For many days, he and the other leaders had sat with Joshua and Eleazer as the high priest threw the Urim and Thummin over and over. Joshua would ask a question, and the Lord would answer by lots.

"Is Kiriath Sepher in Judah?"

"Yes."

"Is Jebus in Judah?"

"No."

"Is Jebus in Benjamin?"

"Yes."

Caleb knew the method should keep tribes from fighting over border towns, but yesterday, Hanniel and Kemuel had complained that Mannasseh and Ephraim weren't getting their share of land. No doubt they were jealous because Judah received so much. Joshua could have given in to their demands; after all, he was from Ephraim himself. He hadn't. How could he, if they believed the cast lots? The whole business made him tired. Perhaps today they would finish.

He sat in his position of honor next to Joshua. "Hello, Shemuel." He greeted the head of the tribe of Simeon.

"Caleb. It appears we'll be close neighbors."

"Yes, we will." Something about his manner made Caleb realize Shemuel regarded the fight ahead with less confidence than he. Perhaps he could offer to fight together.

Joshua rose. "The Lord has spoken to me. We must start today's business by casting lots for the cities of refuge, as we are commanded."

Caleb always felt awed when Joshua said the Lord spoke to him. Joshua talked about God as a personal friend who communicated with him. Would he ever have that experience?

The casting began. Six tribes were chosen, Judah among those. From Judah, Kiriath Arba was chosen. That meant his inheritance would serve as a refuge for those who committed manslaughter and needed protection from enemies. So be it.

With that done, Joshua rose again. "We have guests today. The heads of families from the Levite tribe have a request to make."

Eleazar rose to speak for the group of men who stood behind him. "As you know, the Levites do not receive an allotment of land. We accept that the Lord is our portion and inheritance, but the Lord commanded through Moses that you give us towns to live in, with pasturelands for our livestock."

The leaders nodded their agreement, and Caleb watched as Eleazar cast lots again.

"Which family group should go first? The Gershonites?"

"No."

"The Kohathites?"

"Yes."

"Which tribe should give them cities? Judah?"

"Yes."

"How many cities? One?"

"No."

Caleb listened as the number rose until it reached thirteen. Thirteen of Judah's cities would go to the priests. They called all the cities of Judah until the lots fell positive for thirteen, including his own inheritance, Kiriath Arba. Should he object? How could he, when the Lord had spoken through the Urim and Thummin?

Joshua looked at him. "My friend, I know I promised you Kiriath Arba, but the Lord has chosen otherwise. Do you want a different city, or would having fields and villages in the area satisfy you?"

Caleb couldn't think of a single walled city not selected for the Levites. "I'll take the villages and fields."

"Does everyone agree that Caleb will have these around the city as his possession?"

Shemuel answered for the group. "Of course. That's only fair."

The casting of lots continued until every family group of the Levites had cities among the tribes. Caleb's head ached from listening and trying to accept the change to his expectations. He would be a farmer, not a city dweller.

After every tribe received its inheritance, Levite cities, and cities of refuge, Joshua held up his hands. "I believe that concludes our business."

"Wait, Joshua." Caleb found himself on his feet. "Where will you live?"

Joshua looked at the leaders. Caleb knew that as an Ephraimite, Joshua should live in Ephraim. But after their complaints, he probably didn't want to antagonize them by claiming a city for himself. A sigh of relief went up when Kemuel spoke. "He will live among us, of course. What city do you want, Joshua?"

"I don't need a city, Kemuel. I would settle for the town of Timnath Serah."

Kemuel turned to the others. "I say, so be it. Do you all agree?"

"Yes." The rousing chorus of voices settled the manner.

Caleb started to leave the meeting, but Joshua stopped him and said simply, "Thank you."

On his way to the campsite, Caleb felt his spirits rise. At least the tedious business had ended, and the action could begin. And if Joshua, who had done so much for Israel, could live in a town, he could live in a village. First, he must conquer the city.

The next day, he called the leaders of Judah to meet with him again. He overheard Hamul grumbling to Nadab about so many meetings, so when he started, he made a point at once. "I've been in meetings every day this week to see the allotments of land. I thought you might want to know something about that, but to save time, I will get to the point. Simeon's lands and our lands abut. Shouldn't we ask Shemuel to fight with us and promise to fight with them?"

An older soldier spoke up. "I think we can use their help."

"We must help them in their turn." Caleb looked around the group, missing the sight of Othniel and Salmon, who always supported him.

"Of course," said the soldier.

"Then we are agreed?"

"Yes." All eight responded.

"Let's go then."

They approached Shemuel where he sat in the opened area of his tent on a mat. Caleb stood before him. "Shemuel, may I sit with you?"

"You are my honored guest. And why does Caleb, the son of Jephunneh, visit me in all this state?"

Caleb cringed at the mention of his father's name, reminded again that no one ever could forget they were Kenizzites. "As you know, the lands for Judah and Simeon lie in the same area."

Shemuel nodded without speaking.

"Come with us and fight beside us against the Canaanites, and we in turn will fight beside you for your lands."

"I see the wisdom of going together. I haven't talked to my military leaders, as I see you have with yours. I'm sure they'll agree, though. Frankly, I didn't look forward to capturing those cities with our few men."

"We will appreciate your help as well."

———◆—◆———

Her father went to meetings every day with Joshua, and Acsah wanted to know what they decided. That evening after Caleb came in looking tired, she asked him about the plan.

"Joshua has received the reports from the spies he sent out to survey the parts of Israel not assigned already. He and Eleazar have cast lots to decide the boundaries."

"With the Urim and Thummim?"

"Yes. They finished that yesterday. Today, they chose the cities of refuge."

"What took you so long?"

The Levites came and reminded Joshua that they needed cities as well. They gave the Levites 48 cities."

"Which ones in Judah?"

"Kiriath Arba, Libnah, Jattir, Eshtemoa, Holon, Kiriath Sepher, ..."

"But Father, I thought Joshua gave you Kiriath Arba as your personal possession. How could it also be a Levite city?"

"No one can argue with the Urim and Thummim. Besides, Kiriath Arba will be a city of refuge, too, assigned to the descendants of Aaron. We'll have priests near us."

"It doesn't seem fair."

"I still retain the ownership of the fields and villages surrounding the city, but not the city itself. Oh, Little One, I know how you feel. But I'm concerned about something else."

"What's that?"

"I have to motivate the army to conquer the Levite cities even though I cannot assign them as a reward to the conquering leader. That's going to be a problem, because Anakites have moved back in them."

"I don't understand. I thought Joshua and the army conquered those cities when you won Southern Canaan before." Acsah couldn't keep the frustration out of her voice.

Caleb nodded, "Yes, we did conquer some kings in the battle of Gibeon, but not all. And we're going south toward Jebus this time, a different direction than before. We left some cities we conquered unoccupied, and that's how some Anakites reestablished themselves. We have to return now, rout those men, and actually move in."

"How long do you think that will take?"

"It depends on how quickly we mobilize our men and how much we can surprise our enemies."

This unsatisfactory answer made Acsah restless. How would Othniel find them if they started moving all over the countryside? Still, she knew nothing would be settled until they fully conquered Canaan.

She was still thinking about this the next morning when she had an unwelcome visitor.

"Acsah, someone's here to see you." Caleb's voice held command.

She peered out and grimaced when she saw Nadab standing in the shade of the tent. Sighing deeply, she emerged.

A change had come over Nadab since the first time they met. He smiled and spoke directly to her. "Hello, Acsah. Would you like to take a walk with me?"

She looked to her father, who nodded his head. Quaking inside, she said, "If you like."

They moved with swift steps to the edge of camp, past the Kenite tents. One of Othniel's captains, Heber, was standing near his tent and spoke. "Nadab, I'm surprised to see you in this part of camp."

Nadab only nodded his head at Heber without speaking. Acsah could see the surprise on Heber's face at seeing her in the company of a man alone. She squirmed. Heber might tell Othniel. She wished her father would stop placing her in such awkward situations.

Out of Heber's hearing, Nadab complained. "I really wish I were in a different unit."

"Why do you say that?"

"Our unit contains aliens, the only one that does. Heber's in my unit, another captain. But I don't think he should speak to me so familiarly. He wouldn't be a captain if..." He stopped abruptly.

"You mean if Othniel weren't the leader of your unit."

"I wasn't criticizing your relative."

Acsah kept quiet, but she seethed inside at this additional sign of his prejudice.

"I don't mind Kenizzites so much; after all, you're descendants of Abraham. But we don't even know where the Kenites come from."

"They're devout followers of the Lord."

"Yes, so they say. Anyway, I didn't bring you out here to discuss other people. I want to talk about our marriage."

"You speak as though my father agreed."

"I know he will. How could he not? I know his desire to have a son-in-law from Judah."

"What exactly did you want to discuss with me?"

"Joshua has given your father control over allotting the land to the family groups in Judah. You have some influence with your father. When he's planning the allotments, ask him for land near Bethlehem. I think that's the most fertile country we have seen. And another thing, remind him he promised his new bull calf as part of the dowry."

"My father sacrificed his calf as a burnt offering at Bokim."

"He promised that calf to me. He had no right to waste it."

"I don't think sacrificing to the Lord could be called wasting. Besides, I had the impression you and my father had not finalized negotiations. Perhaps that indicates his decision regarding you."

"You will have to make sure about the land allotment anyway, and try to get him to give me additional stock to make up for the calf."

"I don't believe it's my place to influence my father's decisions." Acsah knew she didn't really believe it, but she didn't want to tell Nadab.

His brow furrowed. "When you're my wife, I will decide what you believe or not. I hope you understand that."

"Then I will make every attempt to make sure I am not your wife. Please excuse me. I am tired." She turned and walked toward camp without a backward glance.

The next day Acsah worked hard all morning preparing the feast for Azubah's purification ceremony, with help from Dinah and Zebidah. Her brothers' wives also contributed food. They expected a fairly large crowd. Azubah left for the tabernacle before Acsah could get ready. She hurried to finish up and get to the ceremony. At the tabernacle, she couldn't go inside, but she heard the baby's name when the priest announced it. "They have chosen the name Joab, son of the Lord."

Acsah wanted to cry. The last time she had gone to a purification ceremony, Othniel had been with her. He should have been allowed to see his own nephew named. She missed him.

Many people came to the feast, including Salmon and Rahab. Their baby Boaz looked around alertly. He had bright brown eyes that saw everyone and everything. She took him from Rahab, and he grabbed her beads and held on. She laughed as she extricated them.

Rahab smiled. "It's good to hear you laugh again. You haven't had much to smile about lately."

"You're right. But celebrating the new life and naming of a baby makes me happy."

"Is there anything I can do for you, Acsah?"

"Pray for me, Rahab."

⁻⸺•⸺⁻

Silver trumpets blew the next morning after Acsah finished bringing water from the spring and fixing some breakfast. Everyone in Israel had to assemble.

Joshua stood tall in front of the tabernacle, flanked by Eleazar and Phinehas. He spoke loudly enough that all could hear. "Let the Reubenites, Gadites, and the half-tribe of Manassah come forward."

For a few minutes, people shifted about, some trying to get to the front, others trying to back out of the way. Finally Joshua raised his hands and spoke again. Acsah had to strain to hear what he said. "You have done all that Moses the servant of the Lord commanded, and you have obeyed me in everything I commanded."

He went on to praise them for their loyalty and remind them of the arrangement Moses made that they could settle on lands east of the Jordan. "But be careful to keep the commandment and the law that Moses the servant of the Lord gave you, to love the Lord your God, to walk in all his ways, to obey his commands, to hold fast to him and to serve him 'with all your heart and all your soul.'" Then he blessed them and reminded them to share their plunder with their brothers.

As soon as he dismissed them, the two and a half tribes dispersed. Their leaders planned to break camp immediately. As they struck tents and packed their animals, Acsah shed tears. They had to move apart eventually, but something in Israel would never be the same again as when they all had lived together and acted with one purpose under God's leadership through first Moses and then Joshua.

Before Joshua dismissed the entire group, he announced that Judah and Simeon would also leave, but not until the next morning. Acsah's mind turned to all the chores she needed to do that evening if they wanted to have a smooth departure in the morning.

10

"You look like a stranger."

Othniel spoke his dialect of Canaanite. "I am. Could you tell me something about this place?"

"Kadesh Barnea? We're as far south as you can get and still be somewhere."

"You have a lot of goods for sale."

"We get a lot more travelers going north than you would imagine, and going south like yourself, too. They need supplies for the deserts west and north of here, so we supply them. What can I get you today?"

"I'll take some of those figs and some of that roasted grain."

"Three shekels."

Othniel handed him a piece of gold from Hazor.

"Oh, I see you're from way north. That area's been overrun by some Semites from Egypt."

"What have you heard about them?"

"I actually got to see them as a boy. What a huge group! We thought they would pass right through and head north, but something happened."

"Really, what?"

"Some kind of disagreement. Anyway, they just went back out into the desert. Disappeared. Then suddenly, after forty years, they're up by Jericho and wreaking havoc on town after town. Canaan will never be the same."

"What towns have you heard about?"

"Oh, too many to name. I've heard rumors they may be breaking up now, heading out in smaller groups. I hope none head south."

"Do you have a pretty good supply of water?"

"Couldn't be here if we didn't. We've got a couple of good wells, but not enough to grow crops. We keep a few sheep and goats. But mostly we import. That's why everything costs so much."

"So I observed. Thank you for your help. I'll enjoy the figs and grain."

"Come see me again sometime." Othniel walked around the area of Kadesh Barnea for quite a while, making notes about the land features and the limited water supply while he took a break to eat some roasted grain and drink water. Surveying like this taxed him more than being an army commander or spying. The loneliness made it hard. He missed his buddies in the army. Heber and Jethro always joked with him, but when he had a tough command, they never hesitated to obey. He knew they trusted him not to put them in impossible situations—dangerous maybe, but not impossible. Salmon, as a fellow spy, also provided him with companionship. God blessed him by letting him work so much with real friends.

But mostly, he missed Acsah. That one little woman had such a pull on his heart. The ache of realizing she might marry before he got back threatened to fill him once again with despair. *Lord, God, you've made no promises to me, but you know my desires, and I trust your bigger plan, whatever it may be.* Picking up his bag of essentials, he started walking northwest toward Beersheba.

The day after the tribes of Reuben, Gad, and Manassah left Israel, the leaders of Judah and Simeon roused their people and began their separation from the larger camp. Acsah realized with a start that now her own father would be the leader. He would listen for the Lord's guidance for all their lives. A rebellious thought came to her: "How can my father lead the tribe of Judah to do the Lord's will when he can't even choose me a good husband?"

She moved to the front of Judah where her father walked as they made the long march south. If only today she could say something to influence him to think better of his choices. But her father looked at her so affectionately, she hesitated.

"Do you know why I named you 'Acsah'?"

"No, Father."

"You know Judah's son Perez had two sons: Hezron and Hamul?"

"Yes, and Hezron had three sons: Jerahmeel, Ram, and Caleb. Your parents named you after that Caleb, didn't they?"

"Yes. All those sons made a large contribution to the tribe of Judah, which the Lord has blessed above all other tribes."

Acsah waited for her father to come back to the subject. His mind wandered more often now. After a bit, she prompted him. "So you named me Acsah…"

"Because that Caleb had only one daughter, and he named her Acsah."

"It's very important to you to identify with the tribe of Judah, isn't it?"

"Ever since Kenaz went into Egypt with Judah, we've identified with them."

"Your mother came from Judah, I think."

"Yes, but lineage descends through the man, not the woman."

"That's true, but it didn't keep Moses from choosing you as the spy for Judah, or Joshua from choosing you as the head of Judah."

"Nevertheless, having a father descended directly from Jacob is important."

Acsah chose her words carefully. "You can never make that true for yourself or your sons, Father, and it may not matter to my sons."

"You don't understand." His voice became edgy. "I want you married to a descendant of Judah, and I want that soon—so that I have some chance of holding my grandsons on my knee."

When her father started talking like this, Acsah became nervous. Did he think his life would end soon? Compared to Joshua, he was young. She had experienced so much loss in her life. Would God take her father from her, too?

———

A few hours later, they stopped to camp for the night. Caleb looked up to see the two spies he had sent on ahead running toward him.

"Ten thousand men are lying in wait for us on the other side of that ridge of mountains," said one.

The other gasped, "Had we kept moving today, they would have attacked us as we started up the hill; but since we stopped, they plan to wait until morning." Caleb could hardly understand them because they were so breathless.

"You are sure of this?"

"We saw the men with our own eyes and overheard the orders from their officers."

"Then we have no choice but to attack them now. Get Shemuel and the leaders of ten thousand to meet me here as soon as possible." He had to think. How could he best surprise the enemy? Could he get the army up the hill without alerting them?

Acsah approached him, "Would you like some cheese or fruit to eat?"

Caleb's mind churned with battle plans. But the food reminded him of his hunger. "What's that? Eat? I suppose I should."

He gobbled the food without talking at all. As he was finishing, the seven leaders gathered in their cooking area. He noticed Acsah slipping into the tent when Nadab and Hamul came into the campsite.

"Men, contact your leaders of a thousand and get the troops ready for battle immediately."

"Tonight, Sir?" Hamul's questioning of his authority rattled Caleb for only a second.

"Ten thousand men are lying in wait for us now. We must attack tonight, as far away from the camp as we can. We must operate by absolute stealth until you see my signal. Any more questions?"

"No, Sir."

The soldiers clearly understood the urgency of the situation. In only a few minutes, the units of soldiers were forming up, armed and ready to go. Caleb spoke to the men. "God will give us this land. He goes before us. Put your trust in him."

Then silently, the soldiers began to move. The climb up the hill in the growing dusk after a day of travelling challenged Caleb's strength. How good of Acsah to feed him. She had some good points, if only she wouldn't defy him about marriage.

He saw the top of the ridge looming before him and signalled a halt. Then, with another signal, the sound of 60,000 male voices all shouting at once resounded as men grasped their weapons and surged forward. Caleb led over the ridge and saw the enemy fleeing in disarray, armor deserted. "After them. Don't let them escape."

———

For a long time, Acsah and the other women watched as the men moved farther down the valley, then up the ridge on the other side. Two units of soldiers stayed behind to guard the camp. "But," she turned to Azubah, "that won't do much good if the other army gets past ours."

"Put your faith in the Lord, Acsah."

Acsah nodded, ashamed of her doubt.

After the army disappeared over the ridge, they waited in suspense. They moved back to the campsite. Acsah pointed at the thoroughly cooked barley soup. "You should eat with me. I made this before I knew Father wouldn't have time to wait for it."

"Thanks. I'll enjoy it. Let's see if the other women want to join us." Soon her sisters-in-law and the female servants joined them for soup and bread. As they sat in the dying light, they wondered how the men could see to fight.

Acsah sighed. "It's hard, isn't it? Every new battle tests our faith. We know the Lord has helped us miraculously in the past. We know we are obeying what he said to do, but we still doubt."

"I suppose we're afraid of hidden sin in the camp." Azubah's baby woke up, so she nursed him.

"You mean like the first battle of Ai, when we lost because Achan took the devoted objects from Jericho and hid them."

"Yes. Acsah, did you know your father planned a marriage between you and one of Achan's sons?"

"No. I didn't."

"It doesn't matter now, but I think you might want to know that."

Acsah sat thinking about how it didn't matter because Israel stoned Achan and all his family for his sin. She saw this as still another example of her father's blindness about choosing her a husband. Achan had a good lineage, no doubt, but he only pretended to be a godly man. She wondered what sort of husband his son would have been.

As though reading her mind, Azubah said, "I prayed about the one God would have me marry. I wanted a godly man above all. God answered that prayer by giving me Seraiah. He and Othniel are both genuinely good men."

"Azubah, would you pray for me, too? I want a godly husband."

"I will pray, Acsah, but you should pray yourself." Azubah stopped nursing to clean up the baby. Then she swaddled him again and handed him to Acsah to hold. A man came up to them then, breathing hard.

Acsah handed the baby back to Azubah and scrambled to her feet. "What's the news?"

The man gasped. "We have complete victory. Their armies have been routed and the king of Bezek, Adoni-Bezek, captured."

"You say armies. How many?"

"We know for sure both Canaanites and Perizzites joined together. We surprised them. I held the standard for your father, so I didn't touch any bodies. He sent me back with news."

"Here, have a bowl of soup." She dished a bowl up for him and watched him devour it.

Between mouthfuls, he commented, "We didn't kill Adoni-Bezek, but we cut off his thumbs and big toes."

"Why would we do such a thing?"

"We didn't want him to escape or ever use a bow or sword again. I understand it's common practice here in Canaan."

Acsah didn't want to hear any more details from the battle. Her stomach turned. "Thank you for giving us the news." She took his bowl, and he left for his own tent.

81

11

A csah ground barley all day to make plenty of bread for the men's return after the cleansing ceremonies. It had been a peaceful week since the battle ended, marred only by the billowing smoke pouring over the ridge where the men had made bonfires of the thousands killed. She understood better all the time what Othniel did during battles. Some other comments he had made began to make sense to her. How she longed to supply the comforts he craved.

She looked at the sun and then finished shaping the dough into loaves to bake on the pottery oven now heating over the fire. The loaves would soon rise, and the baking should be done as soon as the sun went down. Dinah brought out an assortment of raisins, dried figs, and cheeses to go with the goat stew simmering in the coals. "Will these be enough?"

"I believe so." Acsah looked critically at the array. "I don't know if the men will bring any plunder back from this battle. We'll see later."

In the past, the return after the cleansing ceremony was a wonderful moment for her because Othniel came back, too. He would not come today, perhaps not for a very long time. Her longing to see him choked her.

As the sun disappeared over the western horizon, she slapped the loaves onto the oven's hot surface, watching them rise, smelling their fragrance with pleasure.

A shout made her look up. Azubah and all her sisters-in-law appeared as Naam came into camp, carrying a sack over his shoulder. "We're back with plunder in hand." He embraced his wife Jerusha first and handed her the sack.

Behind him came Iru, Elah, and Seraiah, but Seraiah moved very slowly. She saw why. A man shuffled along beside him with a look of agony on his face with each step. Acsah wondered who he was, but a look at his feet told her—Adoni-Bezek, the king responsible for the attempted ambush. Not only his toes, but also his feet were black, and when he got closer, the stench from his gangrenous wounds made her want to retch.

At Seraiah's command, Adoni-Bezek dropped to the ground with a sob. Caleb came up, carrying the standard of Judah and a bag of plunder. "Well, the Lord won for us once again. We routed the enemy and lost no men at all."

Acsah couldn't stop her anger. "Since when did we take to torturing our enemies like this?" She gestured at the pitiful man on the ground.

"You wouldn't have wanted us to lose, would you?"

Acsah shook her head. "I hate cruelty wherever I see it."

Before Caleb could respond, the man gasped out, "Seventy kings with their thumbs and big toes cut off have picked up scraps under my table. Now God has paid me back for what I did to them."

Silence followed this speech for a few minutes before Acsah asked, "May I do what I can to ease his pain?"

"If you touch him, you'll be unclean."

"I know, Father, but surely something may be done."

"All right. Dinah, you assist her. Mehetabel can serve the meal."

Acsah fixed a bath of salty warm water. In it she placed the rotting feet and hands of the defeated king. He sighed in some relief. Poor man, helping him was worth the trouble of uncleanness. She bound up his feet and hands in oil and cloths and fed him some soup and bread.

Her father watched her with a look on his face she couldn't read, something combining guilt and pride.

The next day they packed up the camp and left to go farther south toward Jebus. It took them a few days of hard traveling. In order to bathe and be clean each evening, Acsah hurried before sunset to take the wrappings off Adoni Bezek's limbs and check for improvement, but by the time they camped outside Jebus, she had lost hope. The infection continued to spread, and his pain increased. That night, Adoni-Bezek died.

Her father would not allow her to touch the body. He ordered Asa to bury him and stay outside the camp for the prescribed week.

Acsah wept quietly in the back of the tent where her father would not see her.

Azubah came looking for her. Putting a hand on her shoulder, she tried to comfort her. "Acsah, I think I understand your pain; war is a horrible thing."

"I'm not crying just for Adoni-Bezek, but for all the heartbreak, pain, and death everywhere. I'm crying for Othniel." Then breaking out into fresh sobs of anguish, "I'm crying for my mother."

Azubah's arms went around her, and she crooned gently, "You're right. The world is not as it should be."

⸻

The battle of Jebus lasted less time than Acsah could believe. From their position east of town, Acsah, Azubah, Rahab, and her sisters-in-law spun wool and watched the two babies while smoke rose in the sky above the city.

"I don't understand why we attacked Jebus." Iru's wife, Mahalath, spoke up. "Isn't it part of Benjamin's land?"

Acsah adjusted her yarn on the spindle. "Maybe Father doesn't think the Benjamites can handle Jebus by themselves, so he's striking a blow on their major city to help them out."

"Well, we still have to wait a week for the cleansing ceremonies, even if the battle takes only half a day." Sela, Elah's wife, laid down her spinning and took baby Joab from Azubah. "Look how strong he is. He really arches his little back."

And with such female talk, the women carried on while Jebus burned. Acsah hated to admit she became a little more calloused with each passing day.

A week later, Acsah fumbled with the knots on the tents as she packed once again for a move. Sometimes it seemed they would go on forever, conquering city after city, waiting for the cleansing period to pass, and moving on to the next. Of course, she might not feel so frustrated if she weren't having her period. She had her usual work, plus she had to keep track of all her mats and blankets and keep any man from touching her or them. Last month at Shiloh, being settled had made things easier.

Once they started, she stayed back with the women of her campsite, who passed Joab around. Azubah nodded toward the mat she carried. "That time of the month?"

"Yes, not fun when travelling."

"I know. How are you, Acsah? Not just your period, but everything?"

Acsah looked ahead through the dusty haze created by the animals. "I'm better about some things. Right now, my period gives me an excuse to avoid Father. I'm afraid of what he might say about Nadab and Hamul."

"You can't avoid him forever."

"I'm trying to give Othniel more time."

"Even if he returned, would your father let him marry you?"

"It would take a miracle."

"That's what I'm praying for."

"Thank you, Azubah." Acsah pointed ahead to a pass between two hills. "Father said the journey to Kiriath Arba from Jebus would require three days if we really push."

Azubah shook the dust from her shift. "That's going to tax the children and elderly."

"And women who are unclean for one reason or another. I'm so ready to be settled."

"If you marry Nadab, you can settle sooner. I heard he plans to get land near Bethlehem."

"Where did you hear that?" Acsah wondered if someone had overheard their private conversation.

"He's always bragging about his plans, and Seraiah tells me what he says. He seems to think you'll secure him whatever he wants." Azubah accepted the crying Joab from Sela and opened her shift to feed him.

Acsah didn't reply, fearing what she might say. Nothing ever went right for her. Where was God when she needed him to intervene and protect her from the men who decided her life? Was Dinah right that a male god wouldn't understand a woman's needs?

That evening after she helped with meal preparations, she disappeared into the inner room. Although lonely, this kept her out of trouble. Sometimes her mouth betrayed her.

———◆———

Caleb knew they could meet Othniel at any time, and still Acsah hadn't chosen between Hamul and Nadab. In some ways, he couldn't blame her for hesitating. Both men irritated him. Hamul showed a decided tendency to question his authority. Nadab's demand for a high dowry was out of line with others' and his bride price offer was pitiful. Of course, Othniel's friend Salmon set that bar too high when he paid ten oxen, sixty sheep, and two sacks of gold for the Canaanite prostitute. What a shame Salmon wasn't still available for Acsah. She liked him, and his lineage ranked highest in Judah.

Sighing, Caleb headed for the tent. Acsah was avoiding him during her period, but he really needed to get this settled.

He went into the outer room and said, "Acsah, I know you are in there, and I want to talk about something."

"Yes, Father?"

"You've given me no indication which of the two suitors you want to marry. I thought by now you would have decided."

"I have decided, Father. Neither."

"Acsah, we've gone over this. You will marry someone from Judah."

"Othniel's in the tribe of Judah. You're in the tribe of Judah."

"But I do not have the blood. You must marry the blood."

"My desire to marry Othniel isn't the only reason I refuse these two. Can't you see that Nadab is a pompous fool and Hamul is a womanizer? If I can't marry Othniel, at least let me marry someone kind and true."

Caleb didn't reply to this diatribe, but he couldn't help thinking about it. Was it true that Hamul took advantage of women? He needed to investigate. No doubt Acsah exaggerated because she favored Othniel. If she did marry Othniel, they would gain nothing. The family would still be Kenizzite, and he had nothing to bring to the marriage. How could he settle this his way?

Othniel's goatskin bag hung empty. That morning he'd shaken drops of water off tamarisk leaves to soothe his burning throat. Now the sun blazed high in the sky. He was thirsty, so thirsty. He kept seeing mirages in the distance, but found only burning sand and hot rocks. What if he fainted? No one would ever find him. He must make it to Beersheba. He yearned for signs of the city. Finally the land began to green, and with relief he saw the walled city ahead.

A group of shepherds surrounded the well near the city gate. He waited in agony for them to finish, but they eyed him with suspicion. He spoke through dry lips. "Good day."

Instead of answering him, they pointedly took their time watering the sheep, as though daring him to complain. Othniel's thirst tortured him, but the soldier in him endured without flinching. Finally, the shepherds watered the last sheep and filled their bags. Othniel stepped forward for his turn, but one shepherd stood with his rod upraised. "Why should we let you have our water?"

"I'm sorry; I thought this was a public well. Is this your private property?"

"It belongs to the people of Beersheba. You aren't from here."

"True. I'm not from Beersheba, but would you condemn a man to death by thirst because he's not from your city?"

The biggest shepherd came forward. "I'll wrestle you for the right to drink."

Othniel considered his options. He could go looking for the other well, but he didn't know if he would have any more success even if he found it. Here at least he had a chance.

Setting down his bag and staff, he girded his loins, tucking his robe deeply into his belt, and stood ready to fight. The other man dived in, trying to hit low, but Othniel could move fast, considering his size. For several minutes they struggled, joints cracking and muscles straining. In the end, Othniel put the man flat on his back.

After that, the shepherds accepted him without reservations. Lifting the bucket from the well, he drank deeply of the cold, sweet water. He could feel his body respond, like a plant in a rainstorm after drought. Nothing ever tasted as good to him as that water. Then he filled his goatskin bag as tightly full as possible.

"Join us for our midday meal."

"Thank you, I will. You have more than one well in Beersheba, yes?"

"Yes, the other sits on the north side of the city. We have the best water in the Negev."

"I believe you. What kind of crops do people grow around here?" By making small talk, he gathered a wealth of information while eating some of their provisions. He considered the struggle worth the reward it gave him.

Othniel finished eating and gathering information. He bade the shepherds goodbye and walked through the city, continuing to get information in every way he could. As he worked, he realized that ever since his night at the springs, he had experienced a sense of hope even through his moments of doubt. It sustained him while he labored over the survey details, keeping such accurate and detailed records that even Uncle Caleb would be unable to find fault.

Finishing up his work around Beersheba, he headed north up toward Kiriath Sepher. As he got closer to that citadel, he saw people with bags of provisions along the road headed north, too. "I see you are headed toward Kiriath Sepher. Are you going to a festival?"

"Haven't you heard? The Israelites are coming closer."

"Israelites?"

The man shook his head in exasperation. "Where have you been? They have overrun our country. One tribe, I think they call themselves Judah, has burned Jebus. In one day. We have to get inside the walls of Kiriath Sepher. The Anakites will protect us."

As the man hurried away, Othniel smiled. Uncle Caleb remained undiminished in his vigor as a soldier and leader of men. If only he could have that same kind of vision when it came to his only daughter. Would Acsah already have married as Uncle Caleb promised, or should he continue to trust in the hope he'd received at the springs?

12

The battle at Kiriath Arba took much longer than the battles at Bezek or Jebus. Reports coming back to Acsah and the other women indicated a siege. Since no one handled dead bodies much, the men came out to the camp some evenings, although a three-watch guard stayed around the city every night and the full army set up siege during the day.

On the one night when he came into camp, Caleb's shoulders slumped. Acsah's pity rose. "Father, you're so tired. How can I help you rest?"

"Just listen to an old man ramble for a little while."

"I will."

"I think I'm getting too old for fighting."

"Don't say that." Acsah's security felt threatened. Her father had always been the strong one.

"My leaders aren't maintaining discipline with their men."

"Why do you blame yourself? What's changed?"

"I'm not sure. I changed two positions."

"Whom did you change?"

"I made Hamul the leader of Salmon's ten thousand after his marriage, and I decided to make Nadab the leader of Othniel's ten thousand since Othniel's away."

"You gave Nadab Othniel's position? Oh, Father, have you taken leave of your senses?"

"Acsah..." The note of warning in his voice stopped anything else she might have said. "Anyway, I'm not sure, but I think some of Nadab's troops are not fighting. His unit seems smaller than the others, and when I do my nightly inspection, I often find them asleep. That could cause serious problems. I've warned their leaders, but things haven't changed much."

She kept quiet, but she remembered now seeing Nadab among the leaders of ten thousand at the battle of Bezek. Why didn't she realize then what her father had done? And what could she have done about it?

If anything, Caleb looked more dejected than ever. She decided to speak up. "Father, if you could locate Othniel and get him back, he would get his troops back under discipline. You know he could."

"No. He's better off doing what he's doing."

Acsah became impatient. "This is all because of me, isn't it? Just because you can't accept yourself, why should you refuse to accept another worthy man? He's your own nephew and a great leader. Why can't you see that?"

Acsah's pleading seemed to have no effect on Caleb. He didn't answer her at all, as though he hadn't heard what she said.

❧—◆—❧

Late in the last watch one night, Caleb walked along behind the siege line, staring at the walls, which refused to budge. Not a sign of weakness anywhere. Why couldn't his leaders give him more ideas? In the past, someone would come up with something, a crumbling wall, a water gate, anything that would give them entry without the bloodshed a frontal assault would require. Whom could he ask? No, he wouldn't think about Othniel or Salmon. He had other good leaders.

Men bowed to him as he walked past, observing the troops. Something looked wrong. He had calculated having a man every eight feet, but here the men stood more than ten feet apart. "Soldier, who leads this unit?"

"Nadab, Sir."

"Where is he?"

The soldier shifted his feet and avoided his eyes. "I think he may have returned to the camp, Sir."

Anger threatened to make Caleb lose control in front of this foot soldier. Instead, he made himself speak calmly. "Who ordered you to stand at ten feet instead of eight?"

"We had to, Sir. We didn't have enough men to reach around the city unless we spread out more."

"I see. Have any of you men observed anything around the city that might give us an opening?"

"Pardon me, Sir?"

"Never mind, Soldier. Carry on."

Caleb turned away and kept walking. Why weren't his orders being followed? Nadab should stay with his unit. He looked up just in time to see an Anakite hurl a stone from the wall down toward the soldier he had talked to. The soldier dodged the missile.

The Anakite bellowed, "I am Sheshai. Tell your leader Caleb you will never breach these walls. Your god isn't as strong as our Baal. And no one in your army can compare with Ahiman, Talmai, and Sheshai."

As Sheshai continued to rant and blaspheme the name of the Lord, Caleb prayed for wisdom to take revenge on the enemies of God. Suddenly, he knew what to do. "Sheshai, I am Caleb, servant of the Most High God. I suppose we will never know if you are stronger than we, because you stay behind your walls like cowards instead of coming out to do battle as men. I challenge you to single combat. If what you say is true, you should manage to beat this 85-year-old man. If I defeat you, we will do what we want with your city. If you defeat me, you may do as you wish."

At this Sheshai shook his fist at Caleb. "Old man, how dare you insult an Anakite? When I kill you, I will take bits of you and feed you to the birds. You are a fool to wager everything on your own strength."

Caleb called to the nearby soldier. "Go into camp and find the leaders. Tell them to prepare to take the city within the half hour."

The soldier dashed away, and Caleb turned to watch as the gate opened to disgorge two people, an armor bearer and Sheshai. Caleb thanked God he had sharpened his sword the night before. Sheshai advanced toward him, a grin on his face. Clearly, he enjoyed this chance to become the city hero.

Caleb grasped his sword and moved to a spot where the ground leveled out before facing Sheshai, who towered over him by at least three feet. Caleb prayed for strength. The Lord promised to be with him. His strength came from the Lord.

Sheshai hardly gave him a chance to breathe before he attacked. Caleb coolly countered the blow and followed up with a swift strike at a vulnerable place in Sheshai's armor. The giant's expression changed from cocky to surprised and then fearful as Caleb's swordplay matched Sheshai's blow for blow, with power and accuracy. Finally, in desperation, Sheshai raised both arms to come down hard on Caleb's head. Before Sheshai could make the down stroke, Caleb saw a hole in the giant's armor below the armpit and thrust his sword in. Sheshai tottered as his sword slipped from his fingers. Then his huge body crashed to the ground.

Caleb had no time to enjoy his victory. The gates opened as Ahiman and Talmai rushed out to get revenge, followed by Canaanite soldiers who had no intention of giving up their city. Caleb and the small band of soldiers near him took the brunt of the attack, fighting for their lives, but soon Judah and Simeon's armies joined them, knocking the Canaanites back through the gates into the city, which they overran before noon.

Caleb found himself on the city wall, breathing hard and looking around at their accomplishment. All the people were dead. The bodies of the three Anakites hung from trees. The plunder rose in piles outside the city gate. Kiriath Arba was his. He turned to look out beyond the city at the lands he would possess. He had a week to look around before they could move on to the next objective.

All at once, Caleb felt his age as never before. Why this sudden weakness? He must come up with a better plan to overcome these cities than to bear the burden by himself as he had this day. How could he motivate the young men to come forward and take some responsibility for conquering? An idea came to him which made him chuckle. He could solve two problems at once.

———◆———

Acsah found out what Caleb had done after the men returned from their uncleanness following the winning of Kiriath Arba. "You did what?"

"I told the army that whoever could win Kiriath Sepher would have you for his wife. Since you can't seem to make up your mind, I decided to make it a military contest."

"But anyone could do that!"

"Well, you had the chance to choose between two suitable candidates. With both Nadab and Hamul as leaders of ten thousand, either could use his men to win the city."

"Oh, Father, how can you be so blind?" She burst into tears; then going into the inner room, she threw herself headlong on her mat and sobbed.

The next day, Acsah prepared for the trip down to Kiriath Sepher. She knew her father expected this battle to take as long as Kiriath Arba at least, especially since only part of the army would fight. Perhaps a long siege would give Othniel time to get back. But how would that help, since her father had promised her to the man who conquered the city? Othniel had no troops. Her father made everything impossible. She realized she hadn't prayed about this as she had said she would. She wondered again if the Lord God would answer the prayer of a young maiden who wanted to marry a certain man. *Lord, you are powerful. I believe that. If you care about me, you can make this work out somehow. Please, please let Othniel be the one.*

She could think of all the reasons this would never happen, but praying somehow lifted her hope.

13

O thniel approached the city gate of Kiriath Sepher with his mind on his survey work, but as a spy, he couldn't help evaluating the city for battle strategy. Caleb couldn't be far away now, and if Othniel could gather some information to conquer this city, he would. Perhaps Caleb would let him resume command of his troops and participate in the remaining battles.

Ahead he could see the city sitting atop a cone-shaped hill with walls all around—thick walls by the looks of them. Such walls would take years of siege to overcome. Deep valleys surrounded the hill on three sides, then spread out to rise into higher mountains. Yet in his direction, the south, the road appeared to go right up to the gate. Only when he got closer could he see this neck of land was dug away to form a moat. No doubt at night they lifted the bridge to provide them with protection. This would be a tougher city to conquer than he'd anticipated, unless he could find a weakness somewhere in those defenses.

Othniel left the path and started down a valley. Immediately, he noticed women carrying water pots toward a grove of trees in a side valley. So their main water source lay outside the city walls. That could prove helpful. He slipped out of sight behind some rocks, then made his way up to a point above the women. Here he could hear without being seen.

"Do you see that line in the side of the well?" said one young woman as she gestured to the cistern.

An even younger girl replied, "Yes."

"It leads to an underground passage that goes right up into the city."

"How would anyone get to it from here?"

"We don't want anyone to get into it from the outside, Silly. We want to open it from the inside and get to the water without being seen from above. We can survive if the Israelites come and lay siege to our city."

"That makes me nervous. I mean, what's the use of having a thick wall if anyone could just open that little door and come inside."

"They will discover the spring, of course, but they can't possibly see the door there. And besides, the passage leads right up into the barracks of the garrison in the wall. Even if an Israelite got into the passage, he couldn't get in to the city without being killed. We're safe enough."

"What about grain?"

"Stored in the caves under the city. We're ready, I tell you."

"Maybe, but I've heard such horrible things about what Israel has done to other cities."

"You make me tired. Here, let's get our water and go."

Othniel praised the Lord for this bit of information. He crept back down the hill and changed into the beggar's rags he kept for such times. Then he hobbled into the city, croaking for alms. Meanwhile his gaze took in everything. The thick walls contained the soldier's quarters. On the roofs stood lookouts, peering down the road to the south. He also noted the city's layout, the principal streets, and buildings. His mind churned as he planned a strategy based on the vulnerability he saw within the city. If only he could devise a way to get past the guardhouse through the passage, he could conquer this city with only a few soldiers.

He glanced ahead and started at the sight of two men approaching him, each at least nine feet tall. Othniel stood a head taller than most Israelites, but these men made him feel as short as a small boy. So these were the Anakites, the race of men who frightened the Israelites so much they refused to enter the Promised Land and wandered for forty years. For the first time, Othniel understood the other ten spies. He had always identified with his uncle and Joshua, but now he saw why those other spies refused the challenge of trying to defeat such people. Othniel wondered if he had enough faith to face the challenge, because he knew without a doubt only God could bring about victory.

One giant spoke to the other, "Do we have enough provisions to last through a lengthy siege?"

"Two years if we have to, but I don't think it will come to that. Our spies inform me the Israelites are becoming overconfident and are sending two of their weakest units against us."

"Weak in what way?"

"Leadership. Two new men command them, chosen for political reasons. Caleb seems to be losing his grip."

"What do you mean?

"He dismissed two of his best men and replaced them with these two."

"Nevertheless, I want the walls lined with soldiers on the lookout tonight, even if it means no one gets to sleep. We never know when these Israelites will come upon us. They can be tricky."

Othniel, the beggar, thought, "More than you know."

"What about guards for the grain supply?"

"We can post two in the east barracks to watch it, but it's safe in the caves." The two men continued down the street, but Othniel had heard what he needed to know.

As soon as they passed him down the narrow street, he hobbled his way to the gates and out. He needed to get to Caleb with his information as soon as possible. If only he could keep Caleb from showing his hand too soon, they might have a chance to end this quickly.

Othniel strode north for several miles, making good time. He started to circle around a promontory but sensed the presence of others. He pulled into the shadows and waited to see what would develop. He had never expected to see Salmon.

He hissed from the his position, "Salmon," ready to dodge any missiles thrown his way, but Salmon recognized his voice and hurried forward to him.

"Othniel, I need to talk to you. Something big has happened."

"Slow down, Salmon. I'm on my way to camp. What has happened?" Then his throat tightened in fear, "Acsah is married."

"Not yet, but she will be if you don't do something. Caleb has offered her hand to the man who defeats Kiriath Sepher."

As this news registered with Othniel, his face broke into a smile. "Praise the Lord. I can do that. I know exactly how. Let's go get my men. Hurry."

"Wait, you need to know something else. Caleb has given away your command."

Othniel stared at Salmon. How could he defeat the city without his troops? "Who commands them? Do you think he would let me lead him down and show him…"

"Caleb gave your command to Nadab, one of the two suitors he has handpicked. Nadab might accept your help, but he would take credit for winning the city to get Acsah for himself."

"Nadab?" The insult to Othniel was clear. He had left because of Caleb's orders. To demote him for following orders and to give his position to someone so inferior meant Caleb wanted to give Othniel no opportunity at all. His shoulders slumped. What chance did he have alone?

"Before you give up, I should tell you this. Nadab didn't like having aliens among his troops, so he put them on leave, including the Kenites. He didn't allow them to fight."

"Where are they?"

Salmon grinned. "On the other side of this rock waiting for my signal. I have three hundred of your most loyal troops."

"It is enough. Gather them together."

Soon Othniel was embracing his friends Jethro and Heber. "How can I thank you?"

"We're here for you, Othniel. Tell us what to do."

"Here's the plan that I think will work." He explained about the hidden door in the cistern. "Two men must slip in before the gates close and blend in with the crowd. Then after dark, we can let 100 men inside. We'll need to work by stealth to overcome the night guards and capture the tops of the walls. The rest will wait outside until someone inside lowers the bridge. From that point we will have them like rats in a pot, if we don't lose our heads."

He went on to explain about positions and to assign segments of the city to different groups. "Heber, you command the troops coming in by the well, and, Jethro, you command the outer force. Salmon and I will go in as spies. Any questions?"

Before they left for the city, Othniel made a speech. "Men, I won't lie to you. We're a small band against a much larger force, and the Anakites really are giants. We must put our trust in the Lord. Since he has opened this opportunity for me, I can trust he will give us the victory in an unmistakable way. He is our strength and our defender."

The men nodded before stealing away into the hidden wadi a distance away from Kiriath Sepher, while the two friends headed toward the city.

"What's the plan when we get inside?" asked Salmon.

"We'll pretend to be beggars in different locations until night. Then at the second watch, let's meet at the east wall. We can take the two guards there inside the barracks, go down in the secret passage to the cistern, and open the door for the others."

"It sounds so simple when you say it."

"You know we'll spend a lot of time waiting in suspense for a few minutes of action."

"Yes, but that's the nature of spy work."

"Speaking of that, shouldn't we turn aside and get into costume? We're beggars, you know."

Salmon grimaced, but put on the smelly rags Othniel gave him to wear before they continued into the city separately. For the second time that day, Othniel assumed the posture and character of an old beggar, leaning hard on his staff and hobbling. He made his way to a convenient station near the gate. His act was so convincing that he received quite a few coins. More importantly, he picked up additional tips about troop placements and how they raised and lowered the moat bridge.

Finally, night came on, and, like any beggar, he curled up in a corner of the wall, appearing to sleep, but actually listening and interpreting all the night sounds. He realized the moon would have set by the second watch. The Lord blessed in that as well.

As he lay on the cold stones, Othniel prayed, *Oh, God of Abraham, please help us as we do your will in this city. Protect the men outside from the eyes of the lookouts. Help Salmon and me to get the door open undetected and to find weapons for the men who come inside. Give us strength to overcome the enemy. And most of all, Lord, bless my beloved Acsah. Give her peace and rest and the desires of her heart.*

In this way, he passed the time, reaching out in faith to the God who had opened this way for him to win Acsah as his wife. Finally, he heard the changing of the guard to the second watch. The sometime beggar slowly rose to his feet and crept down the black streets, freezing in place at every sound.

At last he reached the east wall, relieved to see Salmon already there. He pointed out the door leading to the barracks. Inside, they found their task made easier because both guards were sleeping on duty. With their hidden daggers, the friends dispatched these two and propped up the bodies before opening the trap door to the hidden caves.

The caves were complicated, full of rooms, most with grain or jars of oil. But one contained weapons and armor. *Praise the Lord.* Othniel nodded and smiled at Salmon in the dim light. Finally, they found a passage that sloped steeply down into blackness. They crept down it. What would Acsah look like carrying her jar down this tiny passage to retrieve water from the well? The image made him want to laugh, but he stifled the impulse.

As the passage narrowed, Othniel took the lead, leaving Salmon behind with the torch so that light wouldn't be seen when he opened the door in the cistern. At the end of the passage, he found a ring. The door opened easily at his tug. He made a cricket noise, the signal to Heber, and a rope dropped in front of his face. Soon a soldier came climbing down. He helped the man into the narrow passage, where he squeezed past. He repeated this action over and over in the eerie silence. How many men did that make? Finally, Heber himself came down the rope. Othniel shut the door but left the rope. Even a dim light from above might give them away, but by the time the rope could be seen in daylight, they would either be victorious or dead. He prayed for the first.

Back in the cave, the men waited for direction. Salmon had already begun arming the men from the armory room. Othniel led the way to the trap door, where they slipped into the barracks room above. The next few minutes held the key to the operation. Some soldiers would spread out into the city, starting fires wherever they could. Five more men had orders to let the bridge down at the gate for Jethro and the rest of the troops. Everyone else would follow Othniel up on the wall to deal with the watch and distract the defenders from the soldiers on the bridge. Heber would start fires in the caves, burning the oil and grain. With fires below and behind and soldiers on two sides, the three hundred could be victorious.

Othniel led out and up the stairs to the wall. With their Canaanite armour, he hoped they looked like the relief watch. Once all his men stood in place, Othniel gave a signal, and the second watch of Kiriath Sepher lay dead instead of relieved. After flinging the bodies over the wall, Othniel and his men waited for the real third watch who marched up on the wall and stood at attention. The soldier in front of Othniel said, "I thought I heard a disturbance. Is everything okay?"

For answer, Othniel gave a signal to his men and then ran this soldier through, throwing his body down to the moat.

By now, the city residents surely knew the invaders had breached the walls. Fires burned throughout, and the bridge creaked down. Othniel caught a glimpse of Jethro and his men charging in by the gate before he spied a large Anakite soldier clambering up the stairs and swinging a huge sword as he bellowed the names of his gods. But Othniel took advantage of his higher position to lop off the giant's head before he could reach the top. He held his position there, meeting soldier after soldier with success. Then another Anakite came and engaged him in intense swordplay. For a few minutes, Othniel battled the huge man, dodging strikes that would have decapitated him but for his agility. Sweat broke out on his brow. Would he fail now when the Lord had led him this far? But the thought of the Lord lent strength to his lighter, quicker sword, and he overcame the other's powerful but slower movements. The Anakite's body soon joined his brethren's below.

Smoke poured out of the barracks from the fires in the caves. Othniel paused and looked around, breathing hard. They had taken the city. In only a short time, the Lord had given them the victory. His men knew their jobs and did them well. His heart filled with gratitude and joy. Acsah would be his!

It took the rest of the night to control the fires. Othniel carried the bodies to toss on the largest fire while it still burned, but other fires they extinguished. As dawn approached, Othniel and the men stood high on the wall and discussed the victory and what rewards Caleb would give them.

Heber, covered with soot, asked him. "Do you think Caleb will also give you the city, since you captured it?"

"As far as I know, he promised only Acsah to the victor. But perhaps he'll give me some land in this area." He looked out in the gray dawn at the vineyards on the hills and the fields of grain down in the valleys surrounding the city. "This area has good farms."

Jethro spoke up. "If I could have what I really want, it would be a metalworking shop."

"Really? I didn't know you did metalwork." Othniel looked at his friend in surprise.

"Sure. All Kenites do. But we haven't had many opportunities since we joined your group a while back."

Heber added, "We learned back in Midian. I don't think we'll find much ore around here, though. Deserts are the best for finding ore."

As they stared into the distance, Othniel spotted a dust cloud moving their way. Rank after rank of Israelite soldiers came into view and stood at attention below them. Salmon came over beside Othniel. "Obviously, they weren't planning a surprise attack."

"No, I think they will be the ones surprised today."

Othniel saw Hamul step in front of his troops and call out, "Who stands on these walls? Show yourself."

Othniel stepped to the edge of the wall closest to the gate. With blood, dirt, and soot covering him and the remnants of his rags showing under the Canaanite armor, he stood with pride and declared, "I am Othniel, the Kenizzite. The Lord has given me the city."

A shout of triumph erupted from the wall, soon joined by all the men below except Nadab and Hamul, stunned to see their ambitions slip through their fingers.

Othniel shouted again. "Send for Caleb. I understand he has vowed a prize of great value to the man who takes this city."

While they waited for a courier to go back to camp for Caleb, Nadab called up. "How did you do it, Othniel? No man could have accomplished this alone."

Without speaking, Othniel motioned for the men near him to move forward into sight. He wondered what Nadab must feel, looking at the men he dismissed from his unit, standing as conquerors on the ramparts.

99

14

Caleb paced in the area near his tent. Now rested from Kiriath Arba, he regretted not being in the action down at Kiriath Sepher. Had he made the right decision to give Acsah to the conqueror? Surely such a feat would show him the man with the most mettle and desire to win her. Of course, the city had Anakites and thick walls of its own, so it might take several weeks or even months before the man emerged who could win the battle.

"Caleb, Sir?"

He turned in surprise to see a soldier standing in full armor. "Yes, man. What do you want?"

"Your presence is requested down at the city." The soldier bowed low and stood waiting to escort Caleb.

So they needed help already. This could be a bad sign. He put on his armor, buckled on his sword, and headed down the road to Kiriath Sepher, with the soldier marching beside him. After a couple of miles, Caleb could smell the acrid smoke of battle. Could the city have fallen already? Impossible. They had only arrived. In a few more steps, he could see that someone had indeed taken the city.

He reached the spot near Hamul and Nadab, whose scowls and pristine armor showed they hadn't fought. "Who has done this thing?"

A familiar voice spoke from the wall. No. It couldn't be. Othniel stood above him. "I have conquered the city. And I understand you made a vow to give a prize of precious value to the conqueror."

How had Othniel managed this? "Yes. I made a vow. You have won. She is yours from this time on." His words sounded appropriate to the occasion, but his tone carried a very different message. Turning on his heel, he marched quickly back up to the camp. Somehow they must have planned this—Othniel and Acsah or Salmon or Seraiah. How dare they defy him? Someone had tricked him. By the time he reached the campsite, his rage ruled him. Let Othniel have her then.

———————

"Acsah!" Her father's voice contained both anger and command. She scrambled to emerge from the tent, where she was washing lentils.

"Yes, Father?" He stood looking at her with an expression she couldn't fathom. Was it anger or grief?

He asked, "What part did you play in this fiasco?"

"I'm sorry, Father. I don't know what you mean."

"Kiriath Sepher has fallen."

"So quickly? How wonderful! You thought it would take a long time."

His continued staring made her very uncomfortable. What could have happened to get this reaction? Her heart sank as she realized that now she must marry the victorious leader. She feared to ask. "Hamul or Nadab?"

"Come and see."

Acsah looked down at her old work shift in panic. Could she greet her victorious intended in such a state? But Caleb's expression gave her no choice. She followed meekly down from the camp to the valley containing Kiriath Sepher itself. The troops standing along the way moved aside as Caleb marched with military bearing to the gates of the city. Nadab and Hamul stood in front of their men, glowering at her father. Which would it be—the salacious Hamul or the arrogant Nadab? She trembled with fear as she faced an unthinkable future, no matter which way her father dispensed with her.

Then her father shouted. "Othniel! Come and claim your prize."

She turned in bewilderment to see Othniel standing above her on the ramparts above the gates. His bronzed face broke into a brilliant smile at the sight of her. In a moment, her feeling of despair changed to joy unspeakable.

Caleb declared in a voice loud enough for all the troops to hear. "Today I give my daughter Acsah to Othniel, the Kenizzite, as his prize for defeating the city of Kiriath Sepher, according to my vow. Othniel, do you promise to take Acsah into your tent and make her your wife?"

"I do."

"Then she's yours to provide for." Caleb then gave her one long look of grief and turned away from her without a word. The slump of his shoulders as he made the return trip to camp marked him for what he was—an old, disappointed man.

Acsah stood, uncertain of what she should do next. Then Othniel called down to her. "Acsah, I am unclean from battle. I cannot come to you for another six days. Go to Rahab and stay with her until then."

"All right. I will." She looked up at him, feeling such joy and longing, that she knew he must see what she could not say before all these men.

As she turned to walk back to the camp in the next valley, she saw both Hamul and Nadab turn their backs on her, but the foot soldiers smiled and gave other signs of approval. These men respected Othniel and agreed with the outcome, regardless of their leaders' feelings. Her heart warmed toward these who had served under Othniel and Salmon.

Othniel watched Acsah walk away from him, back up the road, with mixed feelings. The look of delight in her eyes when she saw him thrilled him as nothing had before. That no obstacles kept them from marrying was a miracle of God. On the other hand, Caleb's reaction dismayed him. He knew that look of bitter disappointment. Acsah had been his last hope for attaching his family line to Judah and thus to Israel. He wondered what effect this might have on relationships in the family. He sighed deeply.

He turned away and met Salmon's sympathetic gaze. "A week is quite a while to wait when you're anticipating something wonderful."

"Yes. But that isn't why I sighed just now."

"Caleb?"

"You see the problem. Thank you so much for letting Acsah stay in your tent. Caleb made it clear she could not return to his tent."

"Rahab will enjoy having her there. We'd better finish cleaning up and get on with the cleansing ceremony." Salmon waved at the unburned bodies and smoldering ruins of Kiriath Sepher.

After their long night, piling bodies for burning and separating out what plunder they could from the ruins of Kiriath Sepher made for grueling work, especially with only three hundred men. But at last they moved themselves and the plunder down into the valley by the springs.

The Levites who accompanied Judah and Simeon for this purpose met them there with hyssop branches that they dipped in a liquid made from water mixed with the burned and ground bones of a red heifer.

"Welcome to my tent, my friend. I am happy for you." Rahab reached out for her.

Acsah's eyes filled with tears as she fell into her friend's embrace. "Oh, Rahab, I'm so mixed up about everything. Do you know what's going on?"

"I knew Salmon took a group of Kenites down to find Othniel and tell him about your father's vow. I hoped he would get to him in time. Were they victorious?"

"Yes. And now I am Othniel's wife, or at least I will be when the cleansing ceremonies are over. How could Salmon take Kenites with him? Wouldn't they be in Nadab's unit?"

"They should have been, but he put them all on official leave."

"I see. You're saying Nadab didn't want the Kenites under his command." Acsah realized how everything fit together.

"Yes. You wouldn't believe the effect on morale. Salmon said the other men in that unit were angry, because the Kenites and Kenizzites were among the best fighters."

"Is that why they didn't obey Nadab's orders?"

"Probably. Anyway, after the speech about you, Salmon got this idea. He left with the Kenites yesterday morning."

"I will always be grateful. Salmon has been such a good friend to Othniel, and now to me." She looked around the tent. "I guess I'm really confused about why I'm here instead of with my father."

"I don't know the answer to that question. Salmon hasn't communicated much to me, but I assume you are here because your father doesn't want you in his tent."

Acsah wrapped her arms around herself. Would her father disinherit or banish her? He didn't want Othniel, but would he carry it that far? "I'm afraid, Rahab."

Rahab looked at her with compassion. "Do you trust God, Acsah?"

"I think so. He answered my prayer to give me Othniel. But if God will let me marry Othniel, why can't my father be willing?"

"I don't know, Acsah. I'll find out what I can about your situation. Don't worry. God will take care of you, and Salmon and I will stand by you, no matter what."

"Thank you, dear friend."

Over the next few days, Acsah did what she could to prepare for the arrival of her bridegroom. Frustrated, she thought of all the blankets and other household goods she had made and saved for this occasion. Would she get any of those things? All of her best clothing and jewelry were in her father's tent, too.

Rahab saw her pensive look one day near the end of the week. "I have something for you. I planned to save it until the day of, but you need cheering up." She opened her carved chest, the one that had belonged to

Salmon's mother, and brought out a garment. "I started making this for you not long after my own wedding. I've been saving it for you."

She held out a lovely linen dress, not blue like the one from Madon, but a creamy white. "Oh, thank you, Rahab. I wanted something like this so much, but I thought I would have to make do with my work woollen. I wanted to look attractive to Othniel."

Rahab smiled. "He will think you are lovely no matter what you are wearing, but I'm glad you like it." She looked over to where baby Boaz slept soundly in his nest of blankets. "While he's asleep, come and let me show you something else."

Acsah followed Rahab outside and across to the other side of the campsite. A newly-pitched tent sat in a space between two other tents. Rahab pushed the door flap aside and entered. Acsah came into the empty tent and looking around, suddenly realized its import. "This tent is for Othniel and me to... well, you know."

Rahab smiled again. "Salmon sent word to prepare this in case your father doesn't relent. Your wedding journey to your new home may be short."

Acsah could feel tears forming again, tears of gratitude mixed with all the other conflicting emotions of the big changes coming in her life. "I don't know what Othniel and I would do without you and Salmon. Your friendship means so much."

"I haven't forgotten how you befriended me when I came as a captive woman. I'm glad to call you friend." Rahab hugged her. Then the sound of little Boaz crying sent them scurrying back to Rahab's tent.

Acsah appreciated all the sacrifices Salmon and Rahab had made for them, but she knew that unless her father granted them some kind of dowry, they would be destitute. Othniel always turned all of his plunder over to his uncle. He had no wealth or animals of his own. Surely, her father would give them something.

15

------------◦◦◦------------

For the week Othniel and his men could not return to the camp, they spent the time exploring the country around Kiriath Sepher, looking at the farms. Othniel pulled a bunch of grapes from a vineyard in the farm that had caught his eye. "Are the farms north of here this good?"

Salmon, who accompanied him out in this foraging and surveying trip, pulled a luscious grape off the bunch and popped it into his mouth. "Mmm, delicious. I think the land here is somewhat dryer than the land up by Jebus and Bethlehem, but I wouldn't mind settling in this area."

"It's better than the land not too far south of here. The Negev is just desert." Othniel took out his sheets of paper and wrote down something. "I appreciate all your help in finishing the survey. I hadn't done this area yet, and I want it perfect to give to Caleb."

"What land do you think Caleb will give you? As conquering leader, you should get all of Kiriath Sepher and the surrounding fields, but those have already been designated as Levite. Still, now that you're his son-in-law, he should give you something good as a dowry."

"I don't know, Salmon. This piece of land looks perfect, especially with this vineyard."

"A good piece and well-maintained."

Othniel picked several more bunches of grapes to take back to the men at the cistern, at the place where they were camping. The camaraderie around the campfire gave him a sense of fellowship he had missed in his long trek south. But he still longed for Acsah.

At last the week ended, and they completed the final cleansing ceremony and took baths in water from the cistern. As soon as the sun dropped behind the hills, Othniel started walking toward camp. Salmon laughed as he caught up. "What's your hurry?"

Othniel smiled at him. "Actually, I want to drop these reports off to Caleb on my way. I'll come soon."

"Othniel, I didn't want to mention this before, but do you have a tent to take her to?"

"No, I guess I don't. I'm hoping Uncle Caleb will relent and allow us to have one of his."

"If he doesn't, I will have one ready for you when you come to get Acsah."

"Thanks, my friend. For everything."

◦—◦—◦

Caleb saw Othniel approaching as he sat under the canopy of his outer tent. He steeled himself, expecting Othniel to beg for a good dowry.

To his surprise, Othniel said, "I've come to report on my survey work."

He took the reports from Othniel. He should offer the man a seat, but he felt too bruised by Othniel's treachery for courtesy. The meticulously detailed pages gave him exactly the information he would need to allot land. He wouldn't let Othniel know he approved, however. "This will do. That will be all."

"Uncle Caleb, I need t...t...to ask you..."

Now he would hear the request. They needn't think they could treat his wishes with disregard and get anything from him. "Need to ask me what?"

"We...we...we haven't made any negoti...sh...sh...iations about bride p...p...price or dowry."

"Why should I negotiate with a man who never approached me and asked for her hand?" He made no attempt to hide his contempt for this stuttering, presumptuous traitor.

Othniel's brow furrowed in anger, and his voice came out fluently with an intensity Caleb had never heard. "I never approached you because you made it clear you wouldn't accept me no matter how I worded my offer. Yes, I am a Kenizzite, but so are you. You would rather have her married to a robber's son, or a miser like Nadab, or a lecher like Hamul than to me. Why? Because you want your grandsons to have Judah among their ancestors. Well, she'll have real love with me, and that's worth more than all the ancestors in Israel."

The words hung between them until the emotions cooled. Mumbling something about going to claim his wife, Othniel stumbled away.

Caleb sat still long afterward. For the first time, he saw his nephew as the powerful, capable leader others said he was. So why didn't he stay and see it through? Othniel should ask for what he needed to provide for his daughter.

The campsite grew quiet. All his sons and their wives had disappeared. Perhaps they went to the wedding feast that Salmon, no doubt, provided. Othniel should have invited him, if only so he could refuse. His bitterness rose in his chest again. Thwarted by everyone—his daughter gone, his nephew estranged, his battle plans in disarray. He was alone.

All the way to Salmon's campsite, Othniel berated himself. How could he have said what he did? Uncle Caleb's words filled him with anger, with a feeling like the adrenalin that powered him through battles, overcoming his natural timidity and making him the soldier he was. But what good could come out of such a speech? Would Caleb want to give him a dowry now? And how would he treat Seraiah and Azubah?

Somehow he must play the part of happy bridegroom. At least he had the cleansing ceremony bath. As he walked, he concentrated on forgetting what had passed and instead thought about the beautiful woman waiting for him.

Excitement filled Acsah. Earlier, she had bathed carefully and put on the new linen dress, just as attractive as the blue, but made for her without any stigma attached. Now as the sun went down, she sat on the floor of Rahab's tent, her hands idle in her lap. Was she ready for this step? Becoming a wife involved much she didn't understand. If only she had a mother to talk to.

Rahab touched her shoulder. "Are you nervous?"

"A little. How can something I've wanted for so long frighten me?"

"Othniel won't hurt you as some men might. I've had all kinds of men and experiences. Love transforms the marriage act into something wonderful. But like all changes in life, you'll have some adjusting to do. Just relax and enjoy being with the one you love."

"Thank you, Rahab. I wish my family would celebrate with us." A sob caught in her throat.

Then Rahab took her in her arms and held her close. "It will all come right, my friend. You and Othniel haven't done wrong, and the Lord has opened this way for you to be married. Trust him for the outcome."

Before long, a man's voice rumbled outside, but it was Salmon who stuck his head into the tent. "Othniel said to tell you he would meet with your father first and then come for you."

Acsah nodded. "I understand. That makes sense. Perhaps Father will come with him." The suspense made her anxious. How many times she had imagined this, but in her dreams, her father, brothers, and sisters-in-law celebrated with them. Rahab was cooking a small feast, just for the people in their immediate area, a gracious gesture. Outside the servants chattered as they put the last dough on the hot oven to bake. The food smelled wonderful, but for now, a knot ached in her stomach.

Night had fallen before Othniel came into the camp. Salmon greeted his friend. "Ah, the happy bridegroom. Congratulations, my friend. Your bride awaits you."

She could see him through a crack in the doorway. His shoulders slumped and the confidence of victory was missing from his voice. The interview with her father had not gone well.

Acsah concentrated on looking happy for his sake. And when she thought about it, she was happy. She would no longer be apart from the man she loved.

Othniel came into the tent and raised her to her feet. He bent down and whispered, "I'm so sorry. It's the best I can do."

She met his gaze in the firelight. "You are enough."

The feast tasted as wonderful as Rahab could make it, with roasted lamb, fresh bread, and plenty of raisins and pomegranates. Salmon rose to his feet. "May God bless this bride and groom and the seed of their union!"

Othniel responded, "Thank you, dear friends, for your blessing and for your generosity."

Acsah swallowed some of the lamb past the lump in her throat and made show of eating the hot wheat bread. Rahab looked concerned, so Acsah smiled at her. "Thank you for the delicious food, Rahab. I appreciate your hard work."

Finally, Othniel took her by the hand. "Are you ready, Acsah?"

For answer, she rose and allowed him to lead her to the borrowed tent.

As soon as the doorway dropped shut behind them, Acsah flew into his arms, clinging fiercely to him, all her pain, passion, and longing wrapped up in that embrace.

He lifted her up, his tears on her cheeks. "I know, Little One. We should be celebrating with our family."

His arms gave her such comfort. "Othniel, I'm so glad you're in this tent with me and not someone else tonight."

He released her and searched her face in the darkness. "Truly, Acsah?"

"Truly. I prayed for this."

"So did I." Then his head came down, and his lips met hers. "Oh, how I love you, Acsah." He kissed her again, and feelings of joy began to vibrate within her. Everything else disappeared into one reality. She was Othniel's wife at last, in every way.

The next morning, Acsah woke slowly to find she had fallen asleep with her head pillowed on Othniel's bare chest. She stirred as little as possible, but he woke anyway and smiled at her. "So, my precious one."

"So, husband."

"I'm still trying to believe you're mine. God is so good to give me what I've longed for." Othniel traced her face with his forefinger.

"He answered our prayers, didn't he?"

"Yes. He provided a way for me to win you."

"Tell me about the battle."

He told her all about the tunnel and the valour of the Kenites. "Anything could have gone wrong at any time, but the men executed every detail as if we had rehearsed it for days. Uncle Caleb used to talk about knowing God won the battle, but I understand what he meant so much better now."

The mention of her father's name made Acsah restless. She sat up and looked around the comfortable tent with its fine woollen blankets and woven matting. "Rahab and Salmon have been incredibly generous, haven't they?"

"We can never repay them."

"What's going to happen to us now, Othniel?"

"I don't know, Little One. I can't serve in the army for a year now."

"Did you get any plunder from Kiriath Sepher?"

"A little. We burned most of the grain supplies as part of our strategy to win the city. But what I had, I gave to Salmon and Rahab."

"Can we stay with them? After all, we aren't part of Judah, and we aren't servants either."

Othniel looked thoughtful. "Salmon mentioned one idea. He offered to go as the arbitrator with your father for dowry and bride price."

"Do you have anything for a bride price?"

"He's going to claim the city as the bride price, since he stipulated that for the marriage."

"If only I could talk to Father, I could convince him to give us some land."

"You know negotiations are between the men."

"He ought to give you all of Kiriath Sepher, but I heard it's been designated a Levite city."

"Kiriath Arba as well. Your father will have to live outside of town, too."

Acsah lay back down beside him and sighed. "I suppose we're unclean now."

They heard a sound outside the tent. "Othniel, Rahab has sent you two some breakfast. I'll leave it outside the door."

"That's Shamar. She cooks for Rahab and Salmon." Acsah slipped her linen dress on and went to the door for the generous meal of porridge, bread, and fruit with fresh goat's milk.

While they ate their breakfast, Acsah teased him. "You say you've wanted me for a long time, but I think I've loved you longer."

"I started loving you when you were only a tiny baby, and you couldn't possibly remember loving me then."

"I do remember how you used to pick me up and swing me in the air."

"You were the most precious little girl." Othniel picked up another piece of bread.

"I adored you. You filled a little of the vast hole my mother's death made in me."

"Do you know when I first realized I loved you as more than just a relative?"

"When?"

"When my own mother died and you comforted me so much. You were so womanly and caring. I think that's one of your best attributes— your ability to care deeply about others and reach out to them when they're hurting."

Acsah basked in the warmth of his praise. "And do you want to know when I first knew that I loved you?"

"After that kiss I gave you before I left for battle last year?"

"That was wonderful. But I loved you already. I started loving you as a man after the battle against Sihon and Og." Acsah thought back to those early battles on the other side of the Jordan. She didn't understand about war then.

Othniel prompted her to continue. "Why that in particular?"

"Some of the servants came into camp to tell us about the battle. They could talk of nothing but your valour and skill. Seeing you through their eyes made me realize you were more than a fun, big friend—you were a hero."

"I'm not sure that's quite..."

"Yes, it is. Besides, I'm telling this story." She winked at him before continuing, "When they told me you would have to stay outside the camp for seven more days for the cleansing ceremonies, I thought I could not wait. But when the time came, I felt shy, as though I hadn't really known you before."

"I remember sensing something different about you after that battle. I could never quite account for it."

"I suppose you would call what I felt then a crush, but combined with what I already knew of you and the passage of time, my feelings for you have developed into a deep love."

Othniel's expression went from interested to tender. She moved closer to him and wrapped her arms around him, snuggling her face into his chest with a sigh of contentment. Here in his arms, she was home.

Part II

16

For a week, Othniel and Acsah stayed in the borrowed tent, enjoying each other and becoming more intimate in their relationship. He described what he had seen in his travels and how much he missed her. She told him about the visit from the messenger of the Lord and what she knew about the battles of Jebus and Kiriath Arba.

Othniel shook his head, astonished at Caleb's challenge to single combat. "Your father is an incredible soldier, a man worthy of admiration."

"He didn't tell me much about it. I heard it from Seraiah. He said Father not only killed Sheshai, but Talmai and Ahiman, too. His body hurt after that battle. I think that's why he set up the challenge for my hand. He didn't want to go through winning a city singlehandedly again."

"God used that to give me my chance. I thought having you as my wife impossible, but here we are."

"Here we are." She smiled up at him and offered her lips for another kiss. He didn't refuse her.

They ate the generous and delicious food that Salmon and Rahab provided for them. Othniel prayed that one day he could somehow repay their friends.

Caleb saw Salmon approaching his tent. He should treat Nahshon's son with respect, but nothing would change his mind about the dowry.

"Caleb, Sir. May I have a word with you?"

"Of course, son of Nahshon. What brings you to my campsite, today?" He indicated a place beside him.

Salmon took his seat. "I'm here to act as arbitrator for Othniel in the matter of bride price and dowry. As you know, Othniel has very little of his own to offer as bride price. However, we believe you set the bride price when you offered Acsah for the defeat of Kiriath Sepher. Therefore, we offer the city as the bride price, to allot as you please."

Caleb nodded, but inwardly he scoffed. Kiriath Sepher? He would have done what he wanted with it anyway, but Acsah was married. Quibbling over the bride price wouldn't change that. "I accept."

Salmon continued. "As for dowry, we believe you will support this couple. Othniel has given you all he had. Acsah is your daughter."

Caleb answered as he planned. "I've selected a piece of land within Judah to give them. The land lies east of Arad in the valley of the Brook Besor where it turns southeast. The land includes the wadi below, not the surrounding mountains." Caleb watched Salmon's face to see if he knew this land lay in the Negev, but Salmon looked pleased.

"That's generous. What household possessions and servants?"

"The Gibeonite servants, ten sheep, one donkey, and a pair of oxen."

This time, Salmon's face reflected dismay. "Are you sure that's all, Sir? What about food, housing, and personal possessions?"

"Acsah may take her personal possessions. So may the Gibeonites."

"Including their tent and household goods?"

"I suppose so." He didn't like this part, but the Gibeonite servants caused problems with their surly attitudes and refusal to worship the Lord. Good riddance, even if it did mean losing his tent.

After Salmon left, Caleb tried to soothe his conscience by reminding himself of how Othniel had taken advantage of his offer in order to get his daughter. Now Othniel would understand how much he owed his uncle by seeing how he could make it without support in the Negev.

———

At the end of their bridal week, Othniel and Acsah both bathed and emerged from the tent at sunset. Othniel looked back at the tent with affection. Some of the happiest moments of his life had passed in it.

Salmon teased him. "Welcome back. So you've decided to rejoin society."

"Thank you again. Your hospitality has been wonderful." Acsah smiled.

"You probably want to hear about my discussion with Caleb."

Othniel nodded. "What's the news? Is it bad?"

"Caleb treated me with respect, listened to what I had to say."

"About letting Kiriath Sepher serve as the bride price?"

"Yes. In the end he gave you the section of land east of Arad in the valley of the Brook Besor where it turns southeast. Your land extends to the base of, but not into, the mountains. You may also have the family of

Gibeonites for your servants and one donkey, ten sheep, and one pair of oxen. He also allowed Acsah to have her box of personal possessions."

Othniel knew immediately that Caleb could give no worse allotment of land. He had seen that piece of land with his own eyes. True, the Brook Besor ran through the valley, but only during the rainy season, and in the Negev, that meant rain only four or five times a year. He'd seen no vegetation in that valley, and no ready source of water without the western mountain slope. Othniel sickened as he realized how little they would have. Ten sheep might sound like a lot for many men, but he knew that compared to the hundreds in Caleb's flocks, he meant it as an insult rather than a gift. And how would he feed even that few when his land had no food or water on it? He decided not to tell Acsah the state of things until he had no choice. "Thank you, Salmon. We appreciate your doing that for us."

"Now, I think you're going to need a few additional things to live. I want you to have this tent as a wedding gift from Rahab and me. I asked Caleb, and he will allow your servants to keep the tent they are in and their household goods. As for food, I saved out the plunder from Kiriath Sepher for you to take, Othniel. You've always given away everything you gained in battle. It's time you got to keep something."

"Thank you, Salmon. I can't ever repay you."

Salmon gripped his shoulder and smiled.

Othniel returned the embrace. Leaving Salmon again caused an ache in his heart, but they had to go. "It's time for us to leave and go to our new home."

"I will let Caleb know you are going. He can organize the servants to collect your things and have them ready when you say."

"Tomorrow, Acsah?"

"If you like." The trust in her eyes made his heart quail.

The next morning, Acsah tackled the familiar task of packing up a tent, but this time, she had very little to pack. Rahab insisted she keep everything already in the tent—some woolen blankets, a chamber pot, and a water jug. Just as they had the tent rolled into a tight bundle, Dinah and Mehetabel came into the area with the one donkey loaded with their household possessions. The tent was loaded onto this poor donkey's back, along with the plunder from Kiriath Sepher. The load looked heavy for the donkey, but Acsah knew it represented very little for the group of six people who had to make do with these things. For the first time, Acsah comprehended their poverty.

Dinah came over to her carrying her box of personal possessions. "Hello, Mistress."

"Dinah, I'm glad you're going with me."

119

Acsah looked into the box, which contained another dress, her spindle, combs, needles, and her jewelry. On impulse, she opened the box and took out a necklace of gold that had once belonged to her mother and took it to Rahab. "I want you to have this. You have been so good to me."

"Oh, Acsah. What a beautiful necklace. Are you sure you want to part with it?"

"I want to imagine it on your neck and know you're thinking about me and praying for me."

"I will pray for you. God does answer prayer; you know that now."

"I have received what I most wanted." Something inside of Acsah wept because in getting what she most wanted, she had lost her family and now her friends. But she tried not to focus on that for Othniel's sake.

She saw Salmon and Othniel talking earnestly together. Then Othniel clasped Salmon's shoulder in a gesture of affection and turned to her. "Are we ready?"

"I believe so."

"We'll meet Asa and Oren on the edge of camp with our stock."

Acsah hugged Rahab one last time and kissed the soft cheeks of baby Boaz. Then she followed Othniel as he led the donkey away to the edge of the camp. No one else saw them off. Tears threatened to fall again. This separation felt like death, except worse, for she felt rejected, too.

After they met with Oren and Asa, their tiny, vulnerable family group separated from the tribes of Judah and Simeon to begin their journey south to their new home.

At first the trip progressed pleasantly. They walked along smooth paths with farms on either side, many abandoned by owners who had fled to Kiriath Sepher for protection. They picked grapes and figs along the way, putting most into bags to dry when they arrived at their land.

As they walked, Acsah questioned Dinah. "How did my father act after he gave me to Othniel?"

Dinah pursed her lips. "He lashed out at us and at Seraiah, asking what we knew about this scheme to thwart his wishes. No one knew anything about it, and he stopped that after a few days, but we could tell he was still angry."

Acsah sighed. "I wonder if he will ever forgive us?"

Othniel called a halt before sunset. Acsah appreciated his concern for the poor donkey. She started cooking while the others set up the two tents and took care of the animals' needs. She made porridge and put out some bread Rahab had insisted on sending. They had plenty of fresh fruit, too.

Mehetabel came over to watch her. "You make porridge the right way."

"I learned from a Canaanite." Acsah wanted to laugh at Mehetabel's baffled expression. Thank God for Rahab's cooking lessons. She wouldn't have as many conflicts because of them.

After supper, they sat by the firelight, Acsah cradled in the curve of Othniel's arm. The five people she saw around her would be her only companions for who knew how long, and four didn't believe in the Lord God.

⸺ ❧ ⸺

Othniel gazed at the sleeping Acsah, marveling again. She belonged to him at last. So precious and womanly with her luxuriant brown hair flowing around her and her long eyelashes resting on her glowing cheeks. How he loved her.

His heart sank with the weight of responsibility he assumed by taking on a wife when he had few possessions and limited prospects. *Lord, what do I have to support this beloved girl-bride you have given me?*

He looked down at his hands, toughened by military training and hard work. God had given him strength. If the labor of his hands could make a difference, he would trust God for the rest. Hard times lay ahead, no doubt. Would Acsah cope with more hardship than she had ever known?

Acsah stirred then and opened her brown eyes. Reaching out, she pulled his head down to hers and gave him a thorough kiss. "That's for loving me enough to wait for me and to fight for me."

His lips returned to hers as his arms went around her. How he loved feeling her body next to his like this.

"Master, shouldn't we be getting started now?" Oren's voice outside the tent made him pull away from her.

"I'll be out in a minute, Oren." Leaning to give Acsah another brief kiss, he rose and began to dress. Unmarried men had no inkling of discretion at moments like this.

"I suppose I should get up, too." Acsah stretched daintily and rolled over, reaching for her clothes amid the tumbled blankets. Othniel could watch her all day, but duty waited outside.

⸺ ❧ ⸺

One day they came over a ridge. A barren land that caught Acsah completely by surprise spread out before them, though they had seen fewer fields and trees before. She remembered the story her father told

121

her about coming north into fertility. She was seeing what he saw in reverse.

After that, the going became much rougher. Instead of moving through sheltered valleys, they had to climb over hills because their way ran across the lines of mountains. Sand and pebbles constantly caught in her sandals, and all that day Acsah saw no source of water, only gray hills and red sand wadis.

Somehow Acsah expected that they would come out of this desert into settled and cultivated land again. Instead, they topped another ridge and looked down. Othniel gestured to the dry wadi. "This is our land."

Acsah stared in dismay. "The land my father allotted us? He's given us nothing, no water, no plants. How are we supposed to feed our animals and raise crops in this... this wilderness?" she spluttered.

Othniel stood beside her saying nothing. Then he pointed to the farther ridge. "Our land extends to the edge of those mountains, just where the soil changes color."

She peered at the place he mentioned and saw beyond it a shading of green in the hills. Why wasn't that part of their land? And further up, she could see another patch of green. "I think I see water and vegetation up in that valley between the hills. But from what you're describing, our land does not include those places."

"You're right. Our land does not include those springs of water."

"You knew when Salmon told you where we would be, didn't you? You surveyed this land."

"Yes, I knew."

"Then why didn't you say something at the time. This may be a death sentence for us. Who owns the land with the springs?"

"No one as far as I know. I believe we can carry water from them to our land without causing trouble."

"But we can't build there, can we?"

"No, we must find a place on our own property. But this location has one good feature."

"What?" She couldn't imagine anything good in this allotment.

"We're only a few miles from the Salt Sea. We can get salt anytime we need it."

"Yes, but the Salt Sea will not provide us with the water we need. Why didn't you tell me?"

"I wanted you to be happy. I didn't want you to dread the future."

Why didn't he trust her with information? She could have prepared better, but a look at his face reminded her to try for his sake. "Well, let's get on. We'll have to do the best we can."

17

Caleb saw Seraiah sneaking past in the dark toward his tent. "Seraiah, I want to talk to you."

"Yes, Uncle Caleb?"

"Tell me what you know about this scheme of Othniel's."

Seraiah squirmed under his gaze. Obviously, he knew something he didn't want to tell. "I didn't know anything about it. I doubt if he did before the day it happened."

"Why should I believe you?"

"I have no reason to bear false witness. I wouldn't break God's law."

Shame made Caleb testy. "You show more loyalty to your brother than to me after all I've done for you. I think you and your wife need to consider leaving my protection."

Seraiah gasped. "Where would we go?"

"You could join your brother in the Negev or go with those Kenites who helped him. Maybe you like them better than your own family."

Seraiah backed away. "May I take my tent and personal possessions?"

"Yes. Just go. The sooner, the better."

"We'll be gone before noon tomorrow."

Caleb came out of his tent the next morning to watch Seraiah and Azubah take their tent down and get their possessions ready to load.

Jerusha stood nearby holding baby Joab with tears evident on her cheeks. No one would look in his direction as Elah and Naam helped Seraiah load the donkey. "Where are you going?" Jerusha asked as she handed the baby to Azubah.

Azubah looked Caleb's way. The sorrow in her gaze threatened to melt the steel his heart had become. "We'll join the Kenites for now and go with them when their land is allotted."

Caleb watched as they moved away from him. Another family member estranged over this business. His daughters-in-law looked at him as though he were an Anakite. Why should everyone be upset with him? He had been wronged, not anyone else.

———

Othniel hitched the oxen to the plow he and Asa had constructed from bits of wood they found near the springs. It wasn't a good plow, but it would have to do.

His plan had Oren taking the sheep out every day, ranging far to find enough food for them in the surrounding hills. Meanwhile, he and Asa would prepare the soil for planting. The sandy ground broke easily, but even he could see it wouldn't hold water long.

"Master, you understand that to get plants to grow, we'll have to keep water on them constantly for the first few weeks," said Asa.

"We'll just have to bring water from the springs." Othniel's muscles ached at the thought.

Asa pointed to the other side of the wadi. "You'll want to plant to that point, but not too far away. If we have to carry water, we want to keep the field doable."

"Do we have enough seed to plant and to eat?"

"Maybe. I hope we can find some wildlife to eat to sustain us if the grain runs out."

"We can only eat certain animals. Many are forbidden for us by our law." He could see Asa didn't want to hear this.

"Well, your law won't keep my family from eating will it?"

"Actually, yes. The law specifies that servants obey, too."

Asa kicked a dirt clod. "Even if we don't believe in your god?"

"Yes."

"I hope you didn't bring us here to starve. That's all I can say."

"Asa, I want you to know I appreciate all you know about farming. I'm counting on your help to make this crop. For all of us."

In a week, they had the seeds in the ground. That evening Acsah approached him. "Now that you've planted, can we start building a house?"

"No, Acsah, I'm afraid not. We're going to have to water all the time to have any hope of raising a crop."

"Do you mean I have to live in this tent for several more months? I thought we'd have a house right away."

Othniel placed an arm around her shoulders. "If there had already been a house here, we could, but I can't build a house and raise food to keep us alive at the same time. You'll just have to be patient. You've lived in a tent all your life. Why should this bother you now?"

She didn't look convinced. Othniel sighed. With so much to do, he couldn't worry about extras like houses.

These springs in the valley, he realized, were the same ones he had visited during his desperate trip south, when God had assured him of his bigger plan. That knowledge kept him going in the next few weeks as he, Asa, Dinah, and even Acsah made endless trips back and forth from the springs to the fields, trying to keep the soil damp.

One day, they came out to see a glorious sight. The field had sprouted green overnight. "Look, Acsah. Plants!"

"I see."

He put his arms around her and swung her into the air as he had when she was small, but then he noticed that instead of laughing, she looked a little sick. He set her down. "Are you all right?"

"I'll be fine in a little while. I just need to eat a little bread or fruit."

Othniel could hardly take in what she was implying. "Acsah, are you with child?"

She looked at him with a weak smile on her face. "I think I might be. I haven't had my period since before we married."

Othniel didn't know whether to shout with happiness or tremble with fear. Instead, he took her gently in his arms and held her close to his heart. "No more water carrying for you, and you should eat more food."

"Othniel?"

"Yes, Dear?"

"Could I eat something right now?"

"Mehetabel, bring Acsah something to eat."

She came out with a piece of bread and a few raisins. "This will get you past the morning sickness."

"Mehetabel already knows?"

Acsah nodded. "I had to ask someone what the signs were, and she's the only person here who's ever been pregnant before."

Othniel went on to the fields to check on the new life there, considering the situation. Did he really want Acsah to deliver in this wilderness with their limited food and no Israelite midwife? But where could he send her?

———

Acsah swatted at the dreadful sand flies that swarmed around her, biting her to near madness. She had scratched her skin raw over the last few days.

Mehetabel looked up from grinding grain. "I can make a salve for that from mutton tallow and herbs."

"Thank you. That would help. They seem to like me." Acsah sighed. Why should the hardships of this new life bother her so much? She had lived most of her life in the wilderness. "You've been married. Did your husband make you happy?"

Mehetabel emptied the ground barley flour into a bowl. "Happy? I don't know about that. He worked hard and gave me two sons, so I really can't complain."

"Did you think marrying him would change your life in a good way?"

"My parents arranged my marriage. I didn't have expectations one way or the other. I appreciated that he didn't beat me."

Somehow Mehetabel's evaluation of marriage didn't help her much. She missed talking to Rahab, whose marriage seemed happy. Of course, Rahab married Salmon, who had plenty of wealth and servants. If she had married Nadab or Hamul, she wouldn't have to do without and live in the Negev. She watched Othniel out in the field, carrying jar after jar of water to the tiny plants. He would fall asleep too tired to talk to her again tonight. Well, he worked hard, and he didn't beat her. Maybe that was as much as she could expect from marriage, too.

◆—◆

For several weeks, Othniel was happy. The plants grew rapidly, and Acsah got over her morning sickness and began to show a little. Then one morning, a wind kicked up from the east. The unendurable heat smote their faces and made their tongues cleave to their mouths. Asa shook his head. "The sirocco, the hot east wind. We can't do anything about this."

Othniel carried water like a possessed man, trying to save the drooping little plants. Surely if he could just keep enough on them, they would survive. No matter how much he carried, the water evaporated when it hit the ground—without cooling anything. Finally, even his incredible strength gave out, and he returned to the tent where he sat glowering across at the scene of plants shriveling in the unrelenting heat and drying wind.

Acsah came and sat down beside him. "It just seems so unfair. We should have land in the hill country, if not at Kiriath Sepher, then by Bethlehem. There we wouldn't have all this trouble."

"The Lord gives and takes away. Blessed be his name." Othniel closed his eyes against the sight of the dying plants. Could he bless the Lord like Job?

"That sounds familiar. Who said it?" asked Acsah.

"A very wise man who suffered greatly, but refused to turn away from the Lord."

"The Lord has certainly taken away today. I don't understand why we have to suffer. You didn't do anything wrong to deserve this."

"Perhaps if I had just worked harder or understood farming better."

"Asa has farmed, and even he couldn't save the plants." She picked up her grinding stone. "So what do we do now?"

"Is there enough grain to plant again?" He knew the answer. Even if they could make a crop, they'd never last until it came in.

"We can try."

He turned to look in her eyes. "I love you, Acsah."

"Don't worry; we'll get through this somehow." Her tone didn't convince him she believed it.

18

In less than a week after the sirocco quit, Othniel had the new crop in the ground. Acsah watched him working from early morning to late night. She made smaller and smaller loaves of bread. Oren sometimes brought back an acceptable bird they could stew, but most of the time, she felt hungry.

Now Othniel and the men were digging a well with an improvised shovel. He told her if he had water closer to the plants, he could save more. A shout drew her attention.

"We've hit water already." Othniel came running over to her where she sat spinning. "The Brook Besor must run underground here. Now we'll have water close by."

"That's good." She watched him turn and go back to the work from her place in the tent's shade. The tents sat close to the fields and to the new well. Her frustration at living in a tent when the baby came rather than in a house and her fear of not having food made her irritable.

Dinah came and sat down beside her with the grinding for the evening porridge. "There isn't much grain left."

Acsah nodded. "We don't have enough to make it to the harvest, do we?"

"Probably not. We may not get a harvest. There are no guarantees in the Negev. Even in Gibeon, we didn't always get a crop."

"What did you do?"

"We tried to keep some grain in reserve always, and sometimes we went hungry."

"Dinah, I haven't told Othniel this, but I'm discouraged. I'm beginning to think we should give up. We could go back to my father and throw ourselves on his mercy. Othniel's trained as a soldier and spy. He's out of his element here."

"Why won't he?"

"Pride, I guess. He keeps insisting we trust the Lord."

"Perhaps he's trusting in the wrong god or not worshipping in the right way."

"What do you mean?"

"You could try putting up an Asherah pole."

Acsah knew she should forbid the naming of other gods, but her curiosity made her ask. "How could that possibly help?"

"Asherah brings gentle rains and fertility to earth and womb."

"I'm confused. You say Asherah. Is she the same as Ashteroth?"

Dinah kept grinding while she talked. "Well, some people say they're the same, and some say Ashteroth is Asherah's mother. We women worship her to get success and ease in childbirth."

"Who is Asherah's father, then?"

"El, the creator god. The same as your Yahweh, I think."

Acsah gasped. "You shouldn't say his name like that."

Dinah shrugged. "As you wish, Mistress. You say there's only one god, but if we're worshipping the creator, aren't we worshipping the same one? I can't see any difference."

Why did this idea sound logical to her? That couldn't be right, could it? "Then who is Baal?"

"He's El's son and the one who brings us crops, success in battle, and sons."

"I thought you said Asherah did that."

"Baal and Asherah are consorts. They work together to bring the same results."

"I find this very confusing. How are they consorts if they have the same parents, and why have Molech for success in war if you also have Baal?"

"We want to make sure we satisfy all the gods. We wouldn't want any of them against us. As for their behavior, they do what they want. We serve them, not judge them. Isn't Ya... your god the same?"

"The same as your gods?" Was he? Dinah's logic befuddled her mind. "About the Asherah pole, do you really think putting one up would solve our problems?"

"Just go ahead. When Othniel sees it, he'll be pleased you wanted to help in some way." Dinah pressed her. "It can't hurt anything. Why don't I have my brother carve and put one up? Then you can see what happens."

Acsah hesitated. Something didn't feel right. Shouldn't she ask Othniel about it? Of course, he insisted on keeping every detail of the law. But this wouldn't break a law, would it? Besides, she wanted to stop being hungry and seeing their crops fail. What if Yahweh and El were the same? What if their failure to worship correctly caused their problems? "Do it," she said in resignation.

———

Caleb sat on the mat beside his tent, waiting for a servant girl to notice and offer to bring food. How did he always manage to have food when he wanted it before? Nothing went right anymore.

True, they won every battle they attempted, winning not only the land for Judah as far south as Beersheba, but Simeon's lands as well. But the battles had not been smooth. A few men were injured because they weren't following his orders to the letter, and his troops complained bitterly about having to fight for the Simeonite cities after winning so many cities for the Levites. He thought the leaders had agreed to help Simeon after they fought with Judah.

He gave up on getting any food and called one of his male servants. "Nathan, gather the leaders of ten thousand."

"Yes, Sir." Nathan scurried away. He could count on Nathan.

As soon as they assembled, he looked around at them, really seeing them for perhaps the first time. He observed a weariness in some, resentment, even anger, in others, especially Hamul and Nadab. In a sense, he couldn't blame those two. Hadn't he promised one of them Acsah's hand? If only he hadn't made that vow about Kiriath Sepher. But he couldn't go back now and change things.

"Men, I've called you to discuss our next move. We've conquered all the hill country and Negev allotted to Judah and Simeon. Now we need to move against the Philistines of the coastal plains."

Instead of an enthusiastic reply, he saw an uneasy stirring among the men and furtive glances, as though they had discussed this out of his hearing.

"Well, have you nothing to say?"

Hamul stood up. "We've been fighting for a long time. Our families are tired of traveling, and we know we've conquered enough land now. If we don't hurry and settle, we'll miss the planting season."

Another man stood up. "Why should we try to defeat the Philistines? They have giants among them as well. At least I heard there are some at Gath."

Caleb felt again as he had that day at Kadesh Barnea when the spies stood against him and Joshua. Didn't they understand the Lord would be with them as in the past? Yet so many men were nodding in agreement with the last speaker, he saw his hopes for conquering all of Judah's allotted inheritance dashed. He sighed deeply and dismissed them. "If that's the way you feel, I will begin making allotments by unit tomorrow. Come back at this same time."

After they left, Caleb went into his tent, all the way into the inner room where Acsah once slept. He sat staring at the dark goat hair walls as his mind tried to make sense of the changes. Hadn't he trusted the Lord? He'd followed where he felt the Lord was leading. What had gone wrong?

He swatted at a sand fly biting him and sighed in frustration. He had to face it. His leaders no longer followed him. In all honesty, he admitted this hadn't happened all at once. At first he had noticed little things—troops in the wrong place, men missing at drills—but in the last few battles, he'd sensed this dissension more. Of course, the Simeonites fought without flinching. It was, after all, their land they were fighting for, but many of his own units held back and let others take the brunt of the battle.

Oh Lord, there is still so much land to conquer. His words fell flat. He could do nothing now. He had no one who cared. A keen sense of loss overwhelmed him as he looked at this small room—Acsah's room, and before that, the room in which he lay with Acsah's mother, Milcah. Dear Milcah. How he missed her womanly ways and cheerful chatter. Would he ever get over the sadness the thought of her gave him? She had died so young, but not before leaving him with his precious girl, his hope for aligning himself with the tribe of Judah. How would Milcah feel now if she knew their dreams of marrying Acsah to a Judahite had been usurped, and by his own nephew. As he sat brooding over his losses, a voice inside his head said, *How would Milcah feel if she knew you sent her little girl into the desert with too little to eat and drink and no blessing?*

Lord, are you speaking to me? He felt a tightness in his throat that had been building for some time. He could no longer hold in his pain. Tears fell from his eyes as his body shook with wracking sobs. "Oh, my little girl, what have I done to you?"

———◆◆———

"What's wrong? You seemed a little out of spirits at supper."

Acsah continued to brush her hair without meeting Othniel's gaze in the lamplight. "Nothing. I'm just tired."

"No, something's on your mind."

"It's just that all you men talk about is war." Acsah loosened the sash of her shift. "I get a little weary of hearing the advantages of a battle axe over a sword."

"We talk about other things."

"Yes. The best way to fertilize crops."

"You used to like it when I talked about my battles. What do you think we should discuss? Your pregnancy or how to get husbands and wives for the servants?"

Acsah squirmed under his gaze. He had gotten too close to the truth for her comfort. Hearing him say it that way made her concerns seem trivial. "Never mind. You wouldn't be interested."

She turned away from him, arranging her mat so she lay just out of arm's length from his. She didn't like her own behavior, but right now she felt miffed and wanted him to know it, even if her heart told her to stop acting this way. Was she upset because Othniel took so much pleasure in describing his military life or because she had done something without talking to him? Why should she feel guilty?

———◆—◆———

Othniel noticed the pole on a mound near the field and wondered, "Now how did that get there?" He moved closer to it. Seeing clear markings of an Asherah object of worship confirmed his growing suspicion. Anger rose in him as he surmised that one of his Gibeonite servants must have put it up in direct disobedience to his orders. What should he do? With his extraordinary strength, he walked over to the pole and lifted it straight out of the ground, then broke it into pieces for firewood.

Acsah looked up when he came to the tent carrying an armload of wood.

"One of the men must have disobeyed my orders and put up this abomination. I'm not sure which one did it, but when I find out..."

"I gave them permission." She raised her chin.

"You! How did y...you..? Why did y...you..." His stutter got worse as he struggled with strong emotions.

"I wanted to help," she said.

"Do you know what the Asherah pole rites are?"

"I thought it just sat there. I guess I didn't really think about rites."

"You're a married woman, so I'll explain. The worshipers of Asherah d...dance around the pole. They cut themselves with knives, and they have sex with each other and sometimes with the pole itself, spilling the s...seed on the ground."

"I didn't know."

Othniel calmed himself enough to speak again, "I've been trying and trying to teach my men about the Lord and his law. How am I supposed to teach them when they see my own wife defying me and breaking the law?"

"How have I defied you? How have I broken the law? I didn't do any of those things you talked about."

"You put up a worship object of another god. We're forbidden to worship any other god."

"I didn't bow down and worship it."

"What do you think worship is? Just the way you hold your body? When you worship, you believe in the god's power to make a difference, to provide everything you need. When you look to another god for those things, you're worshiping that god."

"What has the Lord done for us? Here we are stuck in the worst land in all Israel without water and with our crops failing." Othniel didn't miss her changing the direction of the conversation.

"Your father gave us this land."

"I don't understand why you won't go to my father and ask for a different field. After all, he owes you for all you've done for him."

"What does your father owe me?"

She sputtered, "Why, Kiriath Sepher, and the plunder from all those other battles where you excelled and he got the bounty."

"The Lord won those battles."

"But he used you! Why do you always have to drag God into these discussions?"

Othniel's heart almost quit beating at this point. How could Acsah say these things? He needed to calm things down. "I talk about God because he's my portion."

"What?"

"Do you remember in scripture when the Lord said the Levites would receive no inheritance with the other Israelites because the Lord would be their portion?"

"Yes, so?"

"I want that as well. Having the Lord as my true inheritance matters more than having good land to farm and pass on to my children."

"The Levites aren't without inheritance—they got Kiriath Sepher, which should have been yours. You fought for it."

"I fought for you, Acsah."

She didn't answer this, and her silence made Othniel's anger increase again. "You know why I can't g...go to your father. He has n...never forgiven me for marrying his daughter."

"Well, I guess maybe he was right about that."

Othniel couldn't believe what she said. He was breathing hard. "Acsah, after all we've experienced together. Are you really s..sorry you married me?"

She hung her head. "No, I guess not."

Othniel looked at her, wondering what he could possibly say to restore their relationship. "I know this time is wearing on you, but we'll get through it somehow."

"We can't get through it here without help. Why can't you see that?" She looked up with a set chin. "If you won't go to my father, I will. He wouldn't want me to suffer."

Beaten down by this conversation, Othniel simply put the wood down and walked out of the tent.

After that, a decided coolness came into their relationship. He spoke as courteously as ever, and he urged her to eat more food and drink plenty of water, but the tender intimacy between them was damaged.

———————

Caleb wouldn't have believed walking from Kiriath Arba to Timnah Serah could tire him this much. He stopped on a hill overlooking the village to lean on his staff and catch his breath. He needed to talk to Joshua. No one else in Israel understood him or what he had been through.

He had only to ask at the village gate to get directions to a home in the center of town. Joshua himself sat on a bench by his courtyard under a sycamore tree. "Caleb, my friend, nothing was missing from this day but a visit from you. How are you?"

Caleb sat down beside Joshua in the welcome shade. "I'm getting old."

Joshua laughed. "You will always seem like a youngster to me, though only you and I remember the Red Sea crossing now."

"You already served as Moses's attendant even then. Do you remember Miriam's song with the women?"

They reminisced about shared battles and miracles God had performed until Joshua called for a servant to bring some food. "Now, I don't think you came all this way just to remember old times. What's on your mind?"

Caleb took his staff and dug the end of it into the dirt at his feet without looking at Joshua. "I have failed in the tasks you set for me. The Philistines live with impunity near the Great Sea, and some Anakites escaped there."

"Do you think I hold you personally to blame for not conquering the large territory I gave you? Your young men should have come forward. What of Salmon and Othniel? They could have led the forces when you tired."

Caleb squirmed in discomfort. "They might have, but I dismissed them from their commands."

"Dismissed Salmon and Othniel? Why?"

"Salmon married and had to stay out for a year."

"Two years ago. Why didn't you reinstate him after the year?"

"Well, I put Hamul in his place, and I didn't want to remove him."

"Hamul?" Joshua's look of bewilderment mortified Caleb. Seeing his decisions through Joshua's eyes made them seem ludicrous. "And Othniel?" said Joshua.

Caleb told him about the challenge for Kiriath Sepher and how Othniel won it to get Acsah. "I didn't wait. I gave her to him right away."

"So he's out for a year now. May I ask who got his command?"

"Nadab."

"Son of Shammai? No wonder you haven't conquered the Philistines. May I ask what motivated you to do all this when you knew better?"

Caleb looked down again before speaking. "I wanted Acsah to marry Nadab or Hamul, so my grandsons could descend from the tribe of Judah." He hated hearing himself admit this to Joshua. What a fool he had been.

Instead of condemning him as Caleb expected, Joshua asked a question. "Do you remember how the Lord rejected the ten other spies at Kadesh Barnea?"

"Yes."

"God chose you and me, not because we come from pure lines of Israelites or have Levite blood. He chose us because we put our faith in him and were willing to do the impossible in his power and for his glory. I think a man who would go up against a walled city containing giants with only three hundred men to win your daughter has proven two things—he puts in faith in the Lord and he loves your daughter very much. I would be proud to have such a son-in-law."

"My daughter said some things like that to me, but I've been too stubborn to see."

Joshua smiled as he took the food from the servant. "It's never too late to ask forgiveness and make amends."

Caleb stayed with Joshua for several days, enjoying the good fellowship and regaining strength of body and spirit. At last one morning, he picked up his staff and headed south, praying as he went that God would allow him to make things right with Acsah and Othniel.

—◆—

Just when the grain lay in the bottom of the sack, and the plants in the field were ready to dry up again, a dark cloud came over the Negev, and in a few minutes rain started pouring down. Acsah went outside to let rain fall on her skin and hair. The drops ran down her face, and onto her parched tongue, cooling it. Othniel came over from the fields with a smile on his face. "Think of the water falling here. It would take me days to carry this much to the plants."

She started to answer him, but suddenly a shout from Asa made them aware of a growing sound, a threatening sound. "Get the women up the mountain. Flash flood!"

Acsah started to grab things from the tent, but Othniel urged her to run for the mountainside. She got just high enough to be safe when she saw a wall of water coming over the dry red sands, spilling over the banks of the streambed and rushing through the field Othniel had tended and watered in the hot sun. As she watched, the plants released their tentative hold on the sandy soil, and the water swept them away. Tears ran down her cheeks as she saw all their time and effort wasted again.

Othniel and the servants were trying to save the tents and their possessions before they washed downstream. From where she stood, she could see him, struggling to keep a foothold in the water as he gathered the tent around their belongings and started hauling them out in one bundle. She could imagine the pottery breaking. Suddenly, Asa lost his balance as he tried to do the same with the other tent. He went down, his head under the waist-high water. Without hesitation, Othniel dropped the bundle to grab the servant's arm before he washed away. The large bundle containing their personal possessions and food floated downstream.

Unable to stand still any longer, Acsah ran down to stop the bundle. For an instant she thought she could reach it when it snagged on a rock. She stretched as far as she could without losing her footing, but the current moved it away from her just before her fingers could close on the cloth. Standing wet and bedraggled, she watched it go as it floated down the wadi.

She trudged back upstream and found Othniel with the servants gathered around Asa above the spot where their tent once stood. Was Asa still alive? With a sudden convulsion, he coughed up muddy red water. She breathed a sigh of relief, but then looked around. Although everyone had survived, the collection of goods saved looked very small—one tent; two pots, which, though chipped, were usable; one water jar, and one basket of food—a pitiful amount to meet the needs of six people.

The flash flood diminished to a weak stream in just a few hours. The rain stopped, and Othniel took charge. "Oren, go downstream and come back with any items you can find. I'll survey the fields. Are the sheep all right?"

Oren nodded. "They were grazing up on the mountain."

Oren returned with a chamber pot and a dress of Acsah's, now caked in red sand. "Everything else washed too far away to get now."

Othniel came back from surveying the fields. "Our well filled back in with silt. I won't try redigging until after the rainy season. But not all the plants washed away. Some of the field survived." He turned again to his healthy male servant. "Oren, I want you to kill a sheep. You ladies can fix us a good mutton stew."

Acsah started to protest the loss from their flock, but a look from him silenced her. She sent Dinah to get fresh water from the springs, rather than the muddy water from the stream. She and Mehetabel cut up the meat when Oren brought it to them, and soon the simmering, savory stew made her stomach ache even more.

After that meal, everyone acted in better spirits, and Acsah felt physically better than she had in weeks. Othniel rose and spoke to the whole group. "We have suffered a blow. We don't have enough food left to feed all of us for any length of time without eating the whole flock. We are going to have to do something different." He turned to her. "Acsah, I want you to go back to your father, at least until we can get some kind of crop going. You can take Dinah and Oren with you. I'll keep Mehetabel here to cook for me and Asa, and I will see about the crops and the sheep."

"You should go, too. We've done all we can. Don't you think we should give up?" Acsah didn't want to leave him with so little.

"I cannot go to your father, Acsah. But you can, and you should. If we become desperate, we have the sheep. I don't want you to return until…" Turning away from them all, he moved into the darkness away from the fire. Acsah rose to her feet and followed him. She heard him sobbing beside the ruined well. She knew she should go to him, but she didn't.

That night, the three women stayed in the wet tent while the men slept outside on the ground. Acsah lay awake in the dark. What could she say to her father to make him understand their need?

Othniel put her up on the donkey the next morning and handed the rope to Oren. "You two take care of her on the journey. I've given you a goatskin of water from the spring and some cooked mutton. When you get to cultivated land, see if local farmers have anything to share."

After they ascended the ridge on the northwest side of the wadi, Acsah looked back to see Othniel still standing by the tent, looking gaunt, with shoulders slumped in a posture of defeat. The sight hurt her. She felt guilt and sadness and at the same time, a feeling she didn't want to name, something resembling contempt. Would he survive until she returned? Well, she would be safe with her father. She wanted to go, didn't she?

19

The trip to Kiriath Arba took less time with fewer people and no sheep. They soon reached cultivated land, settled now by people from the tribe of Judah. As they walked up the path, Acsah saw a man working in a field. "Could you offer help to some poor travelers?"

The man peered into her face. "I know who you are. You're Caleb's daughter, married to Othniel, the conqueror of Debir."

"Debir?"

"The Levites have renamed the city. They renamed Kiriath Arba, too. Now we call it Hebron. Of course you're welcome in my house."

His wife prepared a wonderful meal for them. Acsah had to restrain herself from overeating the wealth of foods. She had taken for granted having cheese, fruit, and bread at every meal before their time in the Negev. They gave her the softest bed and blankets. She thanked them for this respite before the next day's ordeal. The travelers left early the next morning with the family's kind blessings upon them.

The donkey bore her more easily than the load they had taken down to the Negev. Sometimes, she pitied Dinah having to walk the whole distance, but she remembered walking hundreds of miles herself, and now her pregnancy gave her the privilege of riding. She could feel movement in her womb now and contemplated the bittersweet knowledge that she carried Othniel's child. What had happened to the deep love they shared not long ago?

Caleb came home from visiting Joshua and recovered from the journey. One evening he sat on a stool by his door, thinking he should travel down to the Negev to take a proper dowry to Othniel. A group coming on the road from Hebron caught his attention. He could see a donkey with someone riding accompanied by a man and a woman. He rose from his stool as they approached. Could that be Acsah on the donkey? Yes.

The donkey stopped, and Oren helped her down. As he did, Caleb could see the swelling of her waistline. She was with child, Othniel's child.

Trembling, Caleb approached her. "What can I do for you?"

"Do me a special favor. Since you have given me land in the Negev, give me also springs of water." Acsah's gaze pleaded with him from sunken hollows in her skeletal face.

"Oh, my little girl. How I have wronged you." He drew her into his arms where he crooned, "How could I have been so blind?" He held her thus for a long time before he released her and looked into her face again. The pleading look remained. "Of course, you must have water. You may have the upper and lower springs and the mountains next to your land."

"Father, I thank you deeply for this gift."

"You need food and drink. Oren, put the donkey in my stable out back. You must stay with me for a while." He turned back to Acsah. "Come into the house. I will have some food prepared for you."

He led her in. "Do you have a house on the land I've given you?"

"No, we still live in tents." This admission cut him deeply. He couldn't help but see her eyes fixed on his ample supply of grain. "Zebidah, can you fix us a good meal tonight?" Acsah started toward the cooking utensils. "No, you have come on a long journey. You look very thin."

"Othniel has starved himself for my sake." She didn't want Caleb to think her starvation was her husband's fault. "We lost one crop to the sirocco and another to flash flooding. We have very little left."

Caleb closed his eyes. "I have sinned against you. I know that now. Othniel is a better man than I."

"Why do you say that?"

"I made a terrible mistake when I tried to keep you from marrying him, but the Lord overruled me. And I made a worse mistake by giving you that land in the Negev. In my anger I did a cruel thing. Can you forgive an old fool?"

"Don't, Father. Of course, I can forgive you. Can you do anything about the land?"

"We've allotted everything now. Only lands in the Negev are still unclaimed in Judah, apart from the lands of the Philistines, which we have not yet conquered. To tell you the truth, I just didn't have the heart to go on after you married Othniel. The younger leaders all ended up disappointing me. Once I gave them land, they began to leave until too few were left to lead attacks against the Philistines."

"Is that what changed your mind about Othniel?"

"That I missed his leadership in the army? That's part of it. Do you remember Nadab and Hamul?"

"How could I forget them? It's funny that now their names remain together in my mind, though they were so different from each other. I'll never forget the looks on their faces at Kiriath Sepher that day when Othniel won." Caleb waited patiently for her to stop rambling. "Sorry, just reminiscing. What about them?"

Caleb smiled. "A few weeks ago, I had a visitor, a stranger from the area around Jebus, I mean Jerusalem."

"Is that what we've renamed it?"

"Yes. Well, this man accepted the hospitality of my house, and we got into a conversation. As often happens with strangers, we tried to find mutual acquaintances. He knows Hamul and Nadab. They settled within an easy distance of both Jerusalem and Bethlehem. Not too far from Salmon."

"Is that where Salmon and Rahab are?"

"Yes. Anyway, he told me Nadab married a woman from Judah, but he also took a number of concubines, including some Jebusite women. And Hamul actually married a Jebusite woman. The man heard rumors that Hamul encouraged the worship of Asherah around that area."

"I'm not surprised that Hamul would want to worship an idol promoting unbridled sex. Did hearing their choices help you to understand what I said about them before?"

"Yes. It did. I knew Othniel would never do something like that to you or to God."

"No, he wouldn't. You're right."

Just then, Zebidah set food before them.

After dinner, he insisted on giving her his own sleeping quarters and providing her with plenty of warm bedding against the cool night air. He watched her snuggle down, content that their relationship had been restored at last, but he wondered whether Othniel had gone to sleep hungry.

———

After the little group went over the ridge, Othniel came to himself. Asa looked at him. "Well, Master?"

"I'll start hauling water from the springs. You shepherd the remaining sheep."

Othniel trudged back up into the valley, as he had so many times. The familiar cool shade there, the splashing water that never diminished soothed him. The last time he had felt this beaten down and alone, he had come to this very place and found reassurance and hope. He set the jar next to the spring and stood looking at the water. *God, you told me that you have a purpose for the events in my life. I see part of that now, because you allowed me to win Acsah. But why did you give us this land? Is this all linked somehow?*

No answer came to him, but he rose and filled the jar with sweet water and headed back to the tent encouraged.

He spent the afternoon working with the plants still standing. A third remained, but he praised God for that much. He also saw how the rain revived and nourished them in a way his watering could not. Already the plants looked hardier, as though they could withstand more hardship if necessary. He could hold on, too. But how he missed Acsah, not just away from him in the north, but far away from the loving companion she had been to him, before he brought her to the Negev.

—◆—

While Acsah stayed with her father for several weeks, her brothers and their wives came to visit. The servants fixed several feasts, and she began to settle into a life she imagined having with Othniel, living in a real house with plenty of food to eat, wool to spin, and her family for support. But where were Seraiah and Azubah? She asked her sisters-in-law about them, and they looked at each other uneasily.

Mahalath finally explained. "Your father didn't allot them land near here, but I don't know if he gave them land in the Negev. Since you don't know where they are, they must have gone with the Kenites."

"Where are the Kenites?"

Jerusha picked up a piece of lint from the floor. "After the break-up of the tribe, we think they may have gone back to Gilgal."

"Poor Seraiah. He has suffered because of my marriage to Othniel, too. Can we get in touch with them somehow?"

"Your father may have a way."

Later that evening, she broached the subject with her father. "Do you think Seraiah and Azubah are all right?"

Caleb looked stricken. "I should contact them, let them know I've changed and try to make things up with them."

"Do you have a way to do that?"

"I could find someone in Hebron traveling that way and send a message through them." He sighed. "So many people have been hurt because of my stubborn insecurity. I understand now that God has been working through everything to show me I am acceptable to him, not by becoming attached to the tribe of Judah by my grandchildren, but by having faith in Him. I don't know how I could have missed it before."

Acsah's eyes filled with tears. "All Israel has known you're not just acceptable, but beloved of the Lord. What convinced you now?"

"I visited with Joshua. He made me see. While at his house, I read and meditated on the law again. I realized that God commended Abraham and rewarded him, not for his parentage, but for his willingness to believe God and follow him into Canaan. And he commended Moses for believing him after the burning bush and going back to Egypt to get the Israelites, even if he didn't want to do it at first." His smile made Acsah think he might be remembering his friend Moses as he once had been.

Acsah prompted him. "What else convinced you?"

"Joshua reminded me no one considered us better men than the ten other spies, but when the time for faith arrived, we believed God. That's why we have lived so long and seen the Lord's promises fulfilled."

Acsah put her arms around her father's frail and aging body. "I'm so glad you understand what a wonderful person you are."

"What about you, Acsah. Do you think you're righteous in God's eyes because He commended your father, or do you believe for yourself?"

Startled, Acsah drew back from Caleb. Did he know about the Asherah pole? She said doggedly, "Of course, I believe. You know that."

"What have you done that shows your faith?"

"Done?"

"Faith isn't just something you say you have. The choices you make, especially choices requiring you to trust the Lord, show your faith."

"I still don't understand. What do you mean?"

Caleb replied, "Abraham went to Canaan because he believed the Lord told him to go. Moses returned to Egypt, even though he knew he might die for murdering the Egyptian. Joshua and I stood out against the rest of the spies, even when all Israel turned against us."

"Rahab protected Othniel and Salmon because she believed in the one true God. I see what you mean. So you're asking me what I have done to prove my faith, right?"

"Yes."

"But I've had no opportunities to hear from a burning bush."

"What would the Lord say he wants you to do right now?"

Immediately, Acsah knew the answer, though she didn't think her father meant to imply this by his questions. The Lord wanted her to show her trust by returning to Othniel and asking for his forgiveness. She knew this as clearly as if the Angel of the Lord stood in front of her and spoke aloud. Something inside of her resisted this idea, but her heart told her this recognition was her burning bush. She remembered how Moses argued with the Lord. Ironically, she had always thought Moses blind to argue with the one true God, but now she understood how Moses must have felt. She wanted to argue, too—to say that the Lord wanted hard things and that she didn't know how to start.

Caleb murmured, "I've made you think."

"Yes, you have. I need more time."

A few days later, only Caleb and Acsah were sitting on stools at his doorway looking across the valley at the flourishing vineyards and ripening grain. The peaceful scene didn't match the uneasiness in Acsah's soul. Why couldn't she be content now that she had plenty to eat and loving people around her? "Father, did you and Mother ever quarrel about things?"

Caleb said, "I won't say we never had words, but when we did, your mother always came to me first to make things right by asking my forgiveness. She understood my stubbornness. Why do you ask such a question? Have you quarreled with Othniel?"

Acsah told him about the Asherah pole. "I know now I was wrong. When Mother came to you and apologized, did that make things right between you?"

"Yes, but truly, I must say after she died, I regretted every cross word I ever said to her." He sat quietly for a few minutes. "Your mother was a precious woman, Acsah."

"I barely remember her. It comforts me to know you loved her so much, Father, but I wanted to know her, too. So many times as a young girl I needed a woman's help, not just a female servant, but a female relative who really loved me and could explain my feelings to me. If my mother had lived, perhaps I would handle my relationship with Othniel better. She would have taught me how to be a good wife and mother."

Caleb looked stricken at this outburst, so much so Acsah took pity on him. "I'm sorry, Father. I didn't mean to imply you haven't given me a good childhood and life. I knew you loved me."

Caleb replied, "But I abandoned you when you needed me. I had battles or strategy meetings or work as the judge for Judah. I left you for Zebidah to care for."

"And she did a good job. I love Zebidah."

"But she wasn't your mother."

"You don't think I'm blaming you, do you? You wanted Mother alive as much as I did."

"Who are you blaming then?"

This question caught Acsah by surprise. She would normally have said she blamed no one, but the question's assumption, that she did blame someone, made her think.

Caleb pressed her. "Do you blame the Lord for your mother's death?"

"Yes, I believe I do. I never realized it before."

146

Caleb's look became more intense. "Is that why you're angry with Othniel? Because he continues to press you to serve and worship the God toward whom you feel bitterness?"

His relentless questions were breaking through her carefully constructed world—the one in which she felt justified in demanding more of Othniel than he could deliver, in blaming her father for giving them inferior land with no water. She wanted to fight back, but she could not ignore the truth of what he said.

As the sobs overtook her control, Caleb's arms came around her. "I know, my daughter, I know. The horrible pain makes us want to lash out and hurt someone to make things even. We can't hurt the Lord, so we hurt everyone around us."

She gasped out, "Oh, Father, how can I change? What can I do?"

"Tell the Lord what has made you so angry. He will not mind if you list his wrongs against you. But prepare for his reply."

"What do you mean?"

Caleb released her and gently wiped the tears from her cheeks with his hand. "We have a very ancient text which I read in my youth. I believe Eleazar has it among the sacred writings. It tells the story of a man named Job. At first, he had a very good life and worshiped the Lord faithfully, but suddenly, all he cared about was swept away from him—his animals, crops, even his ten children—all destroyed suddenly in one day. Later he himself suffered terrible boils. His own wife told him to curse God and die."

"Did he curse God?"

"Would you have?"

"I don't know. I might have."

"Well, he didn't, but he did complain and tell God his troubles."

"And God replied?"

"Yes, God asked him who he thought he was to question the grand plans of the creator, to question the actions of God based only on his own suffering without knowing all God was doing."

"Do you think God would say that to me now?"

"I think you can trust the Lord's wisdom and goodness. He had a reason for allowing your mother to die."

Acsah thought about what her father said. If God had a reason for her mother's death, then He also had a reason for her marriage to Othniel and for putting them in the Negev. "Did this man say, 'The Lord gives and the Lord takes away; blessed be his name.'"

"Yes, he did, as a matter of fact."

"Father, I want to go home now. Will you return with me?"

"Yes, daughter. I think that would be wise. I need to go to Othniel and ask his forgiveness, too."

20

Asa and Othniel walked side-by-side one afternoon looking at the wheat, now growing heartily and ready to ripen. The roots had gone deep enough that the plants didn't wilt easily. Asa pointed at the plants. "I think another two weeks will see us harvesting."

"Praise the Lord. He has come to our aid. And I appreciate all you know about planting and harvesting, Asa."

"I have to survive, too, Master."

"We may have to kill another sheep to make it to the harvest. I'm afraid I haven't provided very well for you."

"You have shared your food equally with me and given more to my mother. We know this. We are starving less than you are, and I'm sure Dinah and Oren are doing well with Caleb."

"I hope so." Othniel glanced up to the ridge as he often did, as if wishing for Acsah would bring her home. Today, he saw something move. He stared and walked in that direction, then ran. Coming over the ridge, a donkey carrying a person was led by one man and accompanied by another. Then as the group began their careful descent down the side, he noticed more people coming behind, driving animals: sheep, goats, cattle, and donkeys laden with packs.

By the time they reached the wadi, Othniel could see them and hurried to their group. Without noticing anyone else, he lifted Acsah off the front donkey and held her in his arms, tears of thanksgiving running down his cheeks. For a long time, he squeezed her without speaking. She trembled in his arms, and he finally set her on the ground and took a good look at her. She looked beautiful, more beautiful than he ever remembered before. She had gained weight, not just in her middle, but in her face. Neither spoke, and, finally, Othniel looked around and realized other people were waiting.

Caleb came forward. "Othniel, my son. Can you ever forgive me for my foolish pride?"

"Of course, Uncle Caleb. I forgive you." He moved forward on impulse and gave his uncle a manly hug.

"I've brought you a better dowry than the one I gave you months ago."

Acsah spoke at last. "And Othniel, he has given us the mountain with the springs as part of our land."

This complete reversal of fortune overwhelmed Othniel. Putting Acsah back on the donkey, he walked beside her with one hand clinging to her foot as Oren led the donkey to the tent.

Before he could take it all in, Othniel saw tents going up all around the campsite, reminding him of the years of travel in the wilderness. He had never been afraid of starvation then.

Caleb took charge, while Othniel watched, relieved to have someone else responsible. "Nathan, Elidad, let's slaughter a sheep for dinner. Zebidah, you and the other women grind up some of this wheat for bread."

Acsah helped Dinah with the food preparations, taking joy in being able to feed Othniel good bread and fruit again with the meat. When she had seen him coming toward her donkey looking so skeletal, her heart had broken. She tried to imagine what she would say to him later. Would he forgive her? She shook her head as she realized how much her thinking had changed since she left. Before she thought of him as an ineffectual provider; now she realized what hurt she had caused him and marveled at his patient endurance.

When all the others had entered their tents after the feast, she couldn't put off facing Othniel any longer and slipped into the tent designated as theirs.

"Othniel, can we talk?"

He looked up from removing his outer garment. "Certainly, my love. What about?"

Realizing her hands were trembling with emotion, she placed them firmly on her rounded belly and began. "I was wrong not to discuss putting up the pole with you before giving them permission. And I said some unkind things I didn't mean. Will you forgive me?"

Othniel gazed into her eyes and then held out a hand to her. "Come here, Little One." He pulled her into his lap and held her close against him. "I do forgive you." He held her for a long time, and gradually, Acsah's heart eased.

"Acsah?"

"Yes?"

"What possessed you to think you should approve one of those poles?"

She sighed. How could she explain how she felt then? "Dinah and I were talking about how to improve our chances of making a crop."

"I see, and she recommended a pole, right?"

"Yes, that's right."

"What else did Dinah say to you?" His gentle voice didn't accuse her.

"Dinah thinks the Lord and the god El are the same."

"Why?"

"She says they're identified as creator gods, so they must be the same person."

"What do you know about the god El?"

"Well, it's all very confusing. She says he has a wife and children, and he sleeps with both the wife and the daughter. For that matter, his children Baal and Asherah are siblings and lovers. Somehow it's all tied in with fertility and power." Just talking about it again brought back her doubts.

"Does that sound to you like the God you've learned about since childhood?" Othniel's probing really made her think. Was God like that?

"No. He's very different."

Othniel smiled at her. "Acsah, you're intelligent. You know if there's only one God, then men made up all the others. Do you remember a conversation when I told you people will give their objects of worship whatever characteristics they want them to have? That's why the Canaanite gods are so sexual in their behavior and worship demands— men wanted that."

"How do you know our God didn't come out of someone's head?"

"I know because I've seen his power at work. You have, too. Could an idol of stone or wood have made the Jordan part just when we arrived? Could a brass ox make the walls of Jericho collapse just when we shouted?"

"No, you're right." Acsah's doubts flew as she remembered miracles she herself had seen. "I sometimes forget everything the Lord has done for us."

"I also believe because the laws Moses wrote down reveal a God who shows himself directly to people and asks them to do things against their nature, but which are good for them."

"While the other gods demand things that are bad for people..."

"...but appeal to their lowest nature. I'm saying our God is who he is, not what we try to make him by our imagination or reasoning. He defines himself to us. I think trying to say God must be this way or that way is a form of making our own gods. We can choose to worship him or not, but we cannot make him into our version of what we want him to be."

"How do we get to know the real God?"

"By studying the law and the stories about what he has done and thinking about that. Pondering God's faithfulness to me in the past keeps me going."

"You trust him, don't you?"

"Yes, because I love him. When you love someone, you trust him, even when you can't see what he's doing."

Acsah thought about how many times she had shown she didn't trust Othniel. "I don't understand why you still care for me after all I've done to hurt you."

"I love you, Acsah."

"But I haven't done anything to deserve your love; in fact, my actions and words should have destroyed your love." Acsah remembered what her father said about regretting every unkind word he had said to her mother. She understood what he meant now.

"My love for you rests in who you are. I love you. Not what you can do for me."

"I don't understand."

"I believe my experiences here in the Negev, when I knew God controlled everything happening to me and always took care of me, gave me the wisdom and—oh, I don't know how to say it exactly." He paused and thought for a moment. "Being loved by the God of creation makes me able to love you without needing your love in return. He showed his love by giving me what I wanted most."

"What did you want most?"

"You as my wife."

Acsah lifted her head from his chest for a most satisfying kiss.

21

The next day, Othniel marveled at how much activity could occur when Caleb became involved. Caleb got Acsah organizing her women servants, Mehetabel, Dinah, and Zebidah, to help her sort and store the food and to see that all the tents had what they needed. He sent two male servants out with the animals to forage for food. Then Othniel saw Caleb coming toward him. "You have at least two weeks before your wheat harvest. What do you think of starting a rock home over by the springs?"

Othniel considered that. "How long will you stay?'"

"Until after I hold my grandson on my knees and bless him. That will be after your wheat harvest, so we'll help you with that as well."

"All you are doing for us, Uncle, it's too much."

"Long overdue and much deserved. I'm only sorry I took so long to see."

In a few minutes, Caleb gathered the male servants not herding animals. Othniel followed them into the valley of the springs. "I think a good spot for a house would be just above the first spring with one wall against the mountain."

Caleb nodded. "How about you have two rooms, a courtyard with a stable, and a flat roof for entertaining?"

This last idea made Othniel smile. He didn't expect to entertain much here in the Negev. Soon two men were digging down to find a rock foundation, and Asa and Oren were showing a third man how to pick good rocks for building, which they piled up ready for the time they would need them.

Caleb pointed up the mountain. "Walk with me. I want to talk to you a bit." They went farther up, where the upper spring emerged before cascading down to the lower spring below. "Here in this valley, one almost forgets the desert beyond."

"Yes, I love this place."

"Othniel, I've thought a lot about something Acsah said to me before she married you."

"Sir?"

"She said I didn't accept and love you because I didn't accept and love myself."

"I'm sorry; I don't understand." Othniel wondered what Acsah meant by such a statement.

"She was right. You remind me of myself as a young man—a good warrior and spy, relatively quiet around others."

Othniel's heart began beating with the uncomfortable feeling before he stuttered. "Th...thank you, Sir."

The look of compassion on Caleb's face differed from his usual impatient glare at Othniel's stuttering. "Don't thank me yet. Your being like me made me treat you the way I treated myself—always expecting more, never satisfied with what I'd accomplished. I wanted you to succeed, and that isn't bad." He paused and looked down at the splashing spring. "I think I never believed I'd succeeded because I could never stop being an Edomite."

This label startled Othniel. Usually they referred to themselves as Kenizzites; somehow that seemed closer to Israel because Kenaz was Judah's friend, but Esau! He had been Jacob's brother—and enemy.

As if reading his mind, Caleb continued, "Yes, we're descendants of Esau, but something reminded me recently that the story doesn't end with hatred. It's true that Jacob and Esau quarreled and that we consider Edomites our enemies now, mostly because they wouldn't let us go through their lands forty-six years ago. But one part of the story we sometimes forget."

"What part, Uncle?" Othniel struggled to remember the stories told about his ancestors.

"Esau heard about Jacob coming back to Canaan after his sojourn in Haran. His anger over Jacob's trickery hadn't cooled."

"Stealing Esau's birthright and taking the blessing of the firstborn?'

"Yes. He held onto his anger all those years, so when he heard of Jacob's coming, he decided to get revenge."

"Is this the story about his raising an army of men and heading east to kill Jacob?"

"You do remember it."

"I remember Jacob kept sending gifts of animals ahead with servants to try to appease Esau." The idea of gifts made Othniel smile.

"Right. Esau couldn't help but soften at Jacob's obvious desire for reconciliation."

"Uncle Caleb, is that why you brought all those animals with you?"

Caleb laughed a hearty laugh. "You see into my mind, don't you? I told you we're alike. But I do want to say this, Othniel. I am proud you're my son-in-law and will be the father of my grandchildren. You're a good man."

"Thank you, Uncle Caleb. Maybe I'm like you in that as well." Together the two men walked back down the hill toward the building site. Othniel's heart felt like it might burst with joy. God had answered his prayer to please his uncle and to receive his blessing.

Two weeks later, Othniel eyed the walls of the house, which already stood four feet high all around. He could hear Asa and Oren telling the other men how to build. Asa picked up a rock. "You can't pile them on without paying attention to how they fit together. See? Look at how this one has a lump. That will have to be knocked off." They clearly enjoyed giving advice to the other servants, who had never built a house, having always lived in tents.

Now that the wheat was ripening, Othniel no longer had to give constant attention to watering. Every day, he, Asa, and Caleb looked at the wheat crop before going to the valley. One day, Caleb pointed to a flatter place on the hillside. "You might want to let the men stop work on the house now and begin making a threshing floor. That spot looks like it might work."

Asa agreed with Caleb's assessment, but added. "Many of those rocks would work for the house. We could do some of both. Let's use the oxen to drag some stones over."

In two days, they completely exposed the flat rock surface and swept it off in preparation for threshing. They also gathered enough stones to finish the walls of the house when the harvest ended. Othniel couldn't believe how much people working together could accomplish.

Finally the day came when Caleb said, "It's time to harvest." Othniel joined the others under the supervision of Asa and Caleb. Even Caleb admitted the harvest would be small, but Othniel thanked God any of that year's crop had survived. Oren cut the first sheaf and set it aside. "What are you doing? That needs to dry some more."

Othniel had picked up the sheaf and started away with it. "We have to save this one for the first fruits festival at Shiloh."

"You save it as a sheaf?"

"Yes, we take it to the priests as an offering to the Lord."

"You're not going to have any grain to spare this year. Why not wait for another year to make an offering?"

Othniel shook his head. "No, we will take this, and ten percent of the total, too."

Oren shook his head and went back to the harvesting. Othniel could see he didn't think much of God's laws. But what was sacrifice if it didn't cost him something, maybe even hunger?

When they finished cutting the grain and stacking the sheaves, they took them to the threshing floor where the oxen walked around and around in a circle treading out the grain from the straw. Othniel thought the oxen looked happy to have the opportunity to eat mouthfuls of the straw, a much better food for them than the rough desert scrub they had been getting.

The women helped by tossing the separated grain into the air to let the chaff blow away. Othniel watched Acsah doing this with anxiety. Her time was approaching, but other than having to work around her protruding middle, she seemed well, even happy.

The harvest took several days. At the end of that time, the amount of grain amounted to only a few bags, but Asa observed, "For the amount of acreage, we have a good return. You have been blessed."

"Praise to the Lord." Othniel raised his hands. "We can plant and water, but only God can give the harvest."

Asa looked at him curiously. "You talk about your God all the time, as though he were standing by us here in the field."

"Well, in a sense, he is. He has been with us through all of our difficulties and has taken care of us and blessed us."

"How can you know that? What makes you think he's the one blessing us?"

"Because he told me he would before any of this happened."

"How?"

"I came once to this very place full of despair. I had a dream or a vision, I'm not sure which, but in it, I heard the Lord say everything happening then would work out for my good, and not just mine, but all of Israel."

"And you believe that?"

"God has answered so many of my prayers, and I have seen how he has used bad things before to bring about his plans, so I trust him."

"Well, it doesn't make sense to me. But unlike you Israelites, we Canaanites let people believe whatever they want."

"No one can force someone else to change his beliefs, but if I know what I'm saying is real, then I'm going to state it that way and doubt everything else."

Asa shook his head and turned away. Othniel thought about that conversation long afterwards.

One evening after the harvest, Othniel found Caleb working with some sand near the tent where he slept. "Othniel, I want to talk to you about something."

Othniel watched him pushing the sand around in a random pattern of mounds and trenches. "What do you want to discuss, Sir?"

"I can see the land I've assigned you here in the Negev isn't working out very well."

"No, Sir. Getting enough water to the plants has proven difficult, sometimes impossible."

"Have you thought about irrigation?"

"That's how you raised crops in Egypt, isn't it?

"Yes, we used the Nile. We had rich soil there, too."

"Well, the creek bed in our valley has water below the surface; we dug down and found that out. We tried to use the water from those wells to water the crops, but a flash flood came through in late summer and took out most of our work." Talking about his losses hurt.

"I have a suggestion." Caleb pointed to the mounds. "Let's say these are the hills above your land. I have now given them to you with the upper and lower springs, right?"

Othniel nodded, looking at Caleb's work in the dirt.

Caleb continued, "Do you see the upper springs in my model here?"

"Is this the spot?" Othniel pointed to a place about two-thirds up the hill.

Caleb continued to work with the dirt, now placing some pebbles in little rows across his miniature hillsides, then adding more pebbles to make walls. "You see, if you build some retaining walls from the rocks on the hillside, you can fill them with the clay from the hillside mixed with some sand from the valley and some animal dung. In such a soil, you can grow anything you want."

Caleb then dug trenches leading from the upper spring across and down into each level. "Build little wooden gates to hold back or release the water into each level as needed. As long as the spring continues to produce water, you'll have crops."

Othniel stared amazed at Caleb's plan. He could see how to make it work, but he could also see backbreaking labor. "Thank you for your advice, Sir. Do you think my men can help me?"

"Your men are Gibeonites. They have lived in hill country all their lives. They know how to terrace. But they never had to irrigate because regular rains fall in the hill country, unlike in the Negev."

"I think this will work. We can get started on this and have at least some ready before the next planting cycle."

Now he faced a dilemma. The Passover and First Fruits festivals were taking place in Shiloh. All of Israel's male population should attend according to the law, but this year, that would mean leaving Acsah here with her baby due soon. He knew Caleb would go. He discussed the problem with him. "We might be away three weeks or more. Do you think we can leave Acsah with my two male servants as protection?"

"We don't need to leave for another week. Let's see if we can get the house finished enough for Acsah to move in. The valley of the springs is highly defensible."

So for a week, Othniel rejoiced to see all the men, and women too, working hard to finish the house. The female servants returned from ranging far and wide, carrying brush to lay across the roof beams that the men had ranged even farther to find. Othniel didn't want to cut down any trees in the valley itself unless they were already dead or dying. Meanwhile, the walls grew until they reached the proper height. Every day, Othniel checked them, marveling at their speed. "Oren, you've done a marvelous job putting in those windows."

"Windows take skill, Master. Not everyone can do them."

"I'm glad we have you and Asa to help us." Othniel kept reaching out to the two Gibeonites, praying sometime they would want to obey the law, not because he made them, but because they loved the Lord themselves. Would that time ever come?

When the men had finished setting the beams and rafters, the women mixed dirt and clay from the hillside with water and straw to make a covering for the roof. On the last day they could possibly stay in the Negev before going to Shiloh, Asa applied the last of the mud, and the house stood ready for occupancy. Everyone gathered around the house, and Caleb said a blessing. "God, bless this house, all who dwell therein and their seed. Keep them safe from all harm and make them prosper."

Afterwards, everyone ate another feast, which Othniel knew Acsah had prepared while the others worked on the house. As hungry as they all were, he saw that she had baked enough bread for the men to take on the trip with them. "Acsah, you're a wonder. Thanks for all this."

"You're welcome." She wrapped the fresh bread in cloth and put it in his bag.

"I don't feel right about leaving you here in the tents. Can't we go ahead and move you in before we leave?"

"I have two men and three women to help me. We can move into the house all right." Her eyes twinkled at him in amusement.

That night Othniel held her in his arms, feeling again the tenderness this small woman brought out in him. He knew the separation this time would not last long, and she had plenty of food, but still, uneasiness plagued him.

She turned to face him in the dark, putting one hand on his cheek. "I will miss you, my love." His lips covered hers in answer.

———————

The next day saw the men taking off for the north with only provisions for the journey and the first sheaf and tithe of wheat to burden the one donkey. Acsah saw them go with a sigh. Having everyone here these days had been delightful, and she would miss Othniel terribly. Perhaps she should worry about giving birth early, but on this glorious spring morning, she had a new house to move into.

All morning, Acsah and the other women swept out the building rubbish from the little house. She laughed. "Othniel wanted me to move in last night. Can you imagine the mess?"

Zebidah chuckled. "Men probably don't consider sweeping necessary for moving in."

"I'm glad we have leisure to do it properly." When Caleb had insisted on bringing Zebidah down with them, Acsah had worried about how she and Mehetabel would get along, but they seemed to be friends now. Perhaps Mehetabel missed female companionship of her own age. The thought made Acsah sigh. How she missed her friends Rahab and Azubah.

Mehetabel picked up some loose branches left from the roofing to put with the firewood. "Dinah, I've seen you flirting with that Nathan. Are you interested in him?"

Dinah giggled and went back to her sweeping with a red face. Acsah paused and stared at them both. Nathan belonged to her father. As an Israelite, he would worship the Lord. Dinah believed in other gods, even if forbidden to worship them, and God forbid that type of intermarriage. Should she intervene? *Oh, Lord God, how will Dinah marry unless she becomes a believer in you? Give me wisdom to help her know you.*

That afternoon, they arranged everything else in the house from the tents. Acsah opened a sack she had brought from her father's house. In it she found the blankets and other household goods she had made so lovingly with Othniel in mind over the last few years since Rahab taught her to spin and weave. Now at last she had them for her home, new and beautiful.

When she had everything in place, she sat down in her courtyard and rested for a few minutes. The lower spring pooled conveniently below the house, and the delightful sound of falling water from the upper spring filled the air with soothing peace. After living all her life in tents, mostly in deserts, Acsah basked in the comforts of her home.

But she couldn't stay idle for long. She had so many things to do and wanted to finish them before the little one came. "Mehetabel, could you ask Asa to bring the sheepskins?"

He brought them in to her, and she spread them out in the courtyard. "I'm going to keep this one with the wool still on it as a soft place to lay the baby. Later we can use it as a rug." She turned to Asa. "Have we sheared the sheep yet?"

"Oren is doing that now."

"Take these sheepskins and have them sheared as well. We need to start working with our wool soon. And we can also use the leather."

In a few days, they had sheared the wool, washed it in the spring, and dried and combed it. Acsah took some wool, and, borrowing Zebidah's spindle since hers had washed away in the flood, spun the finest yarn she could manage. "I want to make a blanket for the baby."

Zebidah nodded from where she sat cutting the sheep leather of the shorn skins into sandals, belts, and leather pouches. "You may have enough time, if you hurry."

Oren and Asa came together to see her one day. Oren pointed to the wheat field. "We can turn the animals loose now to eat the straw stubble. That frees one of us from shepherding."

"And we have no crops to tend right now. We heard about Caleb's idea for terracing. Could we have permission to begin gathering stones together from the hillside to make the walls," asked Asa.

Acsah nodded her head without stopping her steady spinning. "That's a good idea. Thank you for thinking of it." In many ways they were great workers. Managing five servants alone would be miserable if they didn't cooperate so well.

She watched the men working one day. She could see the work required would overwhelm two or even three men. How could they terrace enough fields by planting time to make a crop the next year?

Dinah and Mehetabel began weaving some straw left from the wheat harvest into baskets and window coverings. Acsah saw the beauty of the weaving. "Could you teach me how to do that?"

Dinah grinned at her. "How will you finish your blanket if you start this?"

"If I learn to do it well, I can weave baskets and you can finish the blanket." She fumbled at first, but soon learned to make a tolerable basket. So in doing what she could with the servants' help, the last few weeks of Acsah's pregnancy were passing pleasantly.

22

The trip north was long but quick for the men. Without flocks or women, they could cover longer distances every day, especially since they didn't bother putting up tents at night. On the way, they stopped in Hebron, where Caleb's sons joined them, bringing the first sheaves and firstborn lambs from their farms and Caleb's.

Naam greeted Othniel. "So good to see you again." Othniel noticed that everyone acted as though nothing had ever come between the families. He decided not to comment, though he wondered if anyone knew where Seraiah had gone.

After that, the trip became noisier with the bawling year-old lambs. Elah teased him. "You might as well get used to the sound of a baby crying. You're going to have a lot of that in your house soon."

Finally, they arrived in Bethlehem, where they found Salmon's large beautiful home. Othniel embraced Salmon. "My friend, you don't know how good it is to see you."

"And you. Did you bring Acsah?"

"Acsah didn't come. She's with child."

"Congratulations, Othniel. Your life's about to change."

"In a good way, I hope."

Salmon laughed and gripped his shoulder. "Rahab will be disappointed Acsah couldn't come, but excited about your news. We have much to discuss." He turned to greet the others and to have his servants wash their dusty feet.

That evening they sat in his courtyard around the cooking fire, eating the large stew Rahab prepared for them and talking. Little Boaz was toddling around the courtyard with one young servant girl assigned to keep him out of the fire and animal dung. Othniel looked at the child with affection and anticipation.

Salmon asked Othniel, "Did you hear what happened with the two and a half tribes?"

"They went back across the Jordan, didn't they?"

"Yes, but on the way, they built an altar at Geliloth."

Caleb spoke up. "I thought I'd told you about that."

"I hope someone tried to stop them. Did you tear the altar down?" Othniel couldn't believe the tribes could go wrong so quickly.

"My reaction exactly. Men came from all over Israel when word got out. We prepared to go to war," said Salmon.

"Why didn't I hear about this?"

"You've been so isolated down in the Negev, and besides, you couldn't have fought anyway, you still haven't been married a whole year."

"Did you go to war?" Othniel looked around the group.

Caleb answered. "It's a serious thing to start a battle against your own people. We decided to give them a chance to explain. Phinehas and the other tribal leaders and I went down to Gilead. We met with the leaders from Reuben, Gad, and Manasseh."

"How did they explain it?"

"The leaders from those tribes said they built the altar to remind us and them of the bond between us so we wouldn't forget they were part of us. They still want to worship together at the tabernacle altar. They never planned to offer burnt offerings on it."

"That's a relief."

"Yes, I think we were all relieved not to kill our fellow Israelites." Salmon stirred the coals.

"Has anything else happened I should know about?"

"I've heard some northern tribes, Manasseh and Ephraim in particular, complained to Joshua that their land wasn't adequate for their needs."

"Why?"

"The Canaanites in that area stood strong against them. They failed to drive them out, so they were asking for more land somewhere else."

Othniel wondered if only he didn't know the news around Israel. "What did Joshua say?"

"He told them to go up and clear land in the forests of the Perizzites and Rephaites."

Elah spoke up. "Then they complained about the Canaanites in the plains having iron chariots. As if we hadn't beaten a large army with iron chariots earlier. I think they wanted an easy way out."

Caleb sighed. "Son, we shouldn't be too quick to judge. We never finished conquering all our lands either. Judah should extend all the way to the coast, but those Philistine towns stand, undisturbed."

The cooking fire burned down to coals. The men sat near it as a chill came with the sunset. Rahab came to claim Boaz and to say good night to the men.

Othniel listened to all this with consternation. For some reason, he assumed the conquering continued. Now it appeared unconquered peoples surrounded them, no doubt with a vendetta against them.

Salmon understood his silence. "You're thinking about how all this will affect our future."

"And our children's. I'm really concerned about this, Salmon."

"You should be. But tell me something. I didn't want to mention it before, but you're looking mighty thin, my friend."

Othniel spoke softly to Salmon only. "We've had a rough time, but God has been with us. We're reconciled with Caleb now, and he's given us water on our land and provided us with a much better dowry. I'm trusting God will bless us, even in the Negev."

They continued talking into the night, finally rolling up in their traveling cloaks and sleeping under the stars in the courtyard.

The next day, on the eve of the Passover feast, Othniel had the opportunity to celebrate in an actual house with a real doorway for the first time in his life. Salmon splattered the lintels with the blood of the sacrificial lamb. Such a lamb had provided salvation for those inside each house in Egypt from the Angel of Death. Somehow, he felt closer than ever to the meaning of the Passover, the reminder of God's care for his people.

A few days later, the men headed north to Shiloh for the first fruits festival. Othniel couldn't help noticing how much more grain the others had to take, but, he thought, no one could have worked harder or sacrificed more to bring his offering than he had.

As they walked, one of Caleb's servants, a young man named Nathan, sidled up to Othniel. "Sir, I'd like to ask you a question about one of your servants."

Surprised, Othniel tried to think who Nathan might mean. "Yes?"

"Is your female servant, Dinah, promised to anyone?"

"I don't believe she is. Why do you ask, Nathan?"

"I would like to marry her if you can make arrangements with Master Caleb."

"Nathan, let me ask you a question. Are you a believer in the Lord?"

"Yes, absolutely."

"Dinah isn't. I'm not saying we let her practice her worship of other gods; we don't. I cannot sanction a marriage between you because it would break God's law regarding marrying Canaanite women."

"Master Salmon married a Canaanite woman."

"Yes, he did. But she believed in the Lord before he married her, before they even met."

"Are you saying that if Dinah became a true follower, you would allow her to marry me?"

"How could we know? She might say she believed just to get a husband. No. I think you should forget about her, Nathan. I'm sorry."

Nathan hung his head. "It is the law." His expression made Othniel sad. He knew how it felt to be denied the woman he loved.

—◆◆—

"You've changed, Mistress."

Acsah looked up from her weaving in surprise at this comment of Dinah's. "What makes you say that?"

"Before, you would criticise your father and then your husband to me, and you worried all the time about how we would have enough to eat and when we would get into a better shelter. Now you hardly complain at all."

"We have plenty to eat now and a wonderful house to live in."

"Yes, but you changed before, when we went to visit your father."

Tears pooled in Acsah's eyes as she remembered her spiritual struggles, but she smiled, "Yes, that trip changed me, but not just from talking to him."

"What, then?"

"I had an encounter with the Lord. I understood as I never had before what it means to have faith—to really believe in God and to trust Him."

"But how could that make you different?"

"I learned that obeying God proved my faith."

"What did God want you to do?"

"Trust and love my husband, because he loves and trusts God. I had trouble doing that before because I blamed God for taking my mother away from me at a young age. When I understood that, I saw how ridiculous it was to blame my husband for everything."

"I'm afraid that doesn't make sense to me."

"When I forgave God for letting my mother die and accepted that life is difficult, I could learn to respect and love my husband because I no longer expected him to do what only God can do. I could trust God to take care of me. And he has, but in his own way and his own time."

"I feel bitter against the gods, too."

"Because of your enslavement?"

"Yes. I can't make sense out of that."

"You worshiped your gods faithfully, but in the end, none of them kept Israel out or saved anyone from death or enslavement."

"Your god is more powerful than our gods."

"Our God is the only one. The others are just created by men."

"Even Ashteroth?"

"Yes, even she."

"I want to know more about your God. Would you teach me?"

"I would like that very much."

———❦———

They arrived in Shiloh, where a confusion of men and donkeys reminded Othniel again of the Israelite camp all the years of his growing up. Did the Lord want them to come together like this to remind them of that time, a time when they were all united and obeying his leadership without question? He unloaded the sheaf and his small sack of grain and went immediately to present his offerings at the tabernacle. He experienced the familiar awe in the presence of the holy things. His was the God who had spoken to him personally and answered his prayers. *O Lord, help me to be a man totally dedicated to you and to following your law.*

As he turned away from the tabernacle, he spotted some familiar figures in the crowd of men standing just outside the outer courtyard.

"Seraiah, Jethro, Heber!" Othniel choked with emotion as he embraced his dear friends and his brother. "I wanted to see you. Are you all right?"

"We're managing. We've gone back to Gilgal, but we aren't settling in well there." Jethro didn't meet his gaze.

"You look starved, Othniel." Seraiah touched his thin arm.

"I'm going to be all right. How are Azubah and baby Joab?"

"He's beginning to get into everything now. Azubah stays on the watch all the time. He tried to run away from the tent a few days ago. But she caught him before he could get far."

"Acsah's expecting."

"That's wonderful. Is she all right?"

Othniel knew Seraiah was looking at his weight loss as he asked this. "She stayed with Uncle Caleb for several months. He's changed, Seraiah. You should talk to him before you leave. We came up together."

Seraiah looked a little unsure at this, but nodded his head. "Perhaps I'll seek him out."

"Do you remember how we told you at Kiriath Sepher, I mean, Debir, that we wanted to be craftsmen? We thought we could do something like that at Gilgal, but so far we haven't had enough raw materials to work with, and since we've received no land..." said Heber.

"Why don't you have land of your own?"

Seraiah kicked at a stone near his feet. "Caleb gave Nadab the power of allotment for his unit." He gestured toward the Kenites, "When we came to Nadab to have lands allotted to us, he refused to give us any land, saying we weren't really Israelite and couldn't inherit with the descendants of Jacob."

Othniel felt his throat muscles tighten with anger. "But Uncle Caleb had an allotment."

"Yes, by Joshua himself. He divided it among his sons, but he didn't offer to give me any land."

"Because I married Acsah."

"He didn't say that directly, but..."

"I'm so sorry." Othniel turned to the Kenites. "Didn't Caleb give you any land?"

"He offered us some in the Negev, but we can see how that would work by looking at you."

"Talk to Caleb. He may help you out more now."

"How long are you staying here, Othniel?" Jethro's question reminded Othniel of his need to get back to Acsah.

"Just until after the festival."

"We'll try to see you again before we leave."

At that, they went into the outer court with their offerings, small like Othniel's, which made him wonder how they were surviving.

———————

That night Caleb sat with his family around their campfire. He looked up to see Seraiah approaching. Nervously, he rose to his feet and went right up to Seraiah. "Can you ever forgive an old fool? I was wrong to send you away and give you no good land in the allotment."

Seraiah looked a little dazed. "Uncle Caleb, of course I'll forgive you."

"Tell me about your situation now."

Seraiah told about his life with the Kenites. "They've been teaching me how to blacksmith, make things with metal. I really like metalwork, but where we are now doesn't provide us with enough ore and business to justify so many of us. I'm not sure where to go next."

"Come aside with me. I want to talk to you privately. They walked away from the campsite into the dark. "I have no more land to allot now, but my offer still holds for the land in the Negev."

"But Uncle Caleb..."

He held up his hand. "Before you panic, let me tell you what Othniel plans to do down there." Caleb explained about the terracing and the irrigation. "He can't do it without some help. But the springs will provide enough water for all of you, even the Kenites. If you join him, you may find resources in the area to pursue your metalwork. You don't need arable land for that, and you can trade for food."

"Well, I want to help Othniel out, and having some land is better than living on the charity of Israelites who treat us with disdain. I'll talk to Heber and Jethro. Don't tell Othniel. I wouldn't want to disappoint him. If we decide to do it, we'll just go there."

"Fair enough."

They went back to the campfire where they visited until the coals began to glow uncertainly. Then Seraiah gave Othniel a brotherly hug and headed back to his own campsite.

The next day, the first fruits festival ended. The Kennizites left early to return south toward Hebron and on to the Negev. Caleb could see that Othniel could hardly stand the suspense. Would Acsah have had her baby?

23

As the morning sun grayed the sky outside her window, Acsah woke with the most uncomfortable ache she had experienced yet. The last week or two, her back hurt more, and she waddled when she walked, but this felt different. She waited. Would the pain pass or keep going? She stroked the large roundness that perched on top of her and stirred around inside of her.

She knew when the time came, she would have Zebidah and Dinah and Mehetabel, not Othniel, but she still wanted him to come home. What if he didn't get here? Could she trust in the Lord the way Othniel did—that everything happened for a reason?

Dinah came in to check on her as she had for so many mornings as her personal maid. Dinah had come a long way in her understanding of God, but in this one area she still resisted. Just two days before, she said, "Your male God gave women pain in childbirth. A female god would never have done that. Why can't I keep a female god for childbirth at least?"

Acsah had no answer except to say, "There's only one God."

Today, Dinah looked knowing. "I think something will happen soon. Let me fix you some porridge."

Acsah got up and used the chamber pot before going out to splash her face in the pool. It seemed much hotter now than when Othniel had left with her father and the other servants. Then she gasped as the pain hit her again. But, as before, it passed in a few minutes.

Dinah brought her the bowl of porridge, which she ate sitting on a stool not too close to the cooking fire in the courtyard. She ate hungrily, but afterwards another pain came and she wondered if she could be in labor.

169

The morning dragged by as she wove a basket and spun some wool, trying to distract her mind from the intensifying and more frequent pains.

Finally, Zebidah and Dinah made her go into the back room, where she lay down and let Zebidah check her.

"Well, my girl, I think you will have this baby in a few hours." Acsah didn't know whether to feel relieved or disappointed. Several hours seemed like a long time, but at least she knew she was progressing.

Before long, the pain became so overwhelming that she no longer knew how much time passed. In the brief respites between contractions, she swallowed sips of water Zebidah gave her. Then the agony would overtake her, and she would be drowning in pain, trying to stay focused on anything that would give her the strength she needed. Othniel wasn't here. The baby. She had to finish this to have the baby, but what if she died? What if this pain killed her? *O God, give me strength to make it through this!* Her cries of anguish came between lips dry from the work of labor.

Finally Mehetabel said with maddening calmness, "You can push now, Acsah."

Just then a disturbance at the doorway caught her attention. "I must see if she's all right."

Another voice, Dinah's, replied. "Othniel, we're having this baby right now. Just wait here."

Then Acsah pushed. What a relief to do something, instead of just enduring the pain. With each push, the baby moved a little. Then with a tearing, burning release, the baby's head came out. She panted as the pain built once more. One more push, and the body emerged.

She heard the cry. "It's a boy!" Then somewhere she heard a man sobbing, whether from relief or sorrow, she couldn't tell, for she lost even that bit of consciousness.

———◆———

Othniel, Caleb, and two servants had left Hebron that morning, traveling quickly with only another donkey-load of grain, which Caleb insisted on bringing along to supplement what he had brought before. Heat rose from the sand and rocks when they left the cultivated country and started the arduous up and down of the Negev landscape. Othniel had stopped talking several miles back. He could think only of one thing. Would Acsah be all right?

Finally, they topped the ridge looking into their wadi—his land, which he tilled and harvested with his own hands. The area seemed strangely quiet. The animals grazed in the wheat stubble, but no one was around. His heart raced. Wouldn't Acsah be watching? Somehow he expected her to come out to him.

They reached the valley and started up. Othniel left the donkey with Caleb and the servants and ran toward the house. He heard a woman cry out with such pain and despair in her voice his heart froze. Acsah! He raced across the courtyard and into the first room. He strode to the door of the bedchamber, but Dinah stopped him. "Please let me see her," he begged.

"You can't come into a room of childbirth." She thrust him back into the first room, where he could do nothing. Caleb came in and put an arm around him. How long would he have to wait for news from the next room? The sound of Acsah's screams tore at his heart and made him want to hurt someone. How could he stand to do nothing while she suffered?

"It can't be long, my son. She is in the Lord's hands." Caleb's words couldn't penetrate his agony.

After a long period of waiting, he heard the sounds in the next room change to grunting moans. "What is happening? Why can't I be with her?" Then another sound pierced the air—the sound of a baby wailing. Zebidah called out, "It's a son." But immediately after, Othniel heard her exclaim, "Oh, we're losing her."

He didn't realize he was sobbing until Caleb put his arms around him and held him in a tight, comforting embrace. How could they go on living without Acsah? Was this part of God's plan, too?

Then just when he thought he couldn't survive this pain, Dinah called to him from the door. "Here's your little boy." She handed him a small bundle he could hold in one of his large hands. He looked through eyes so blurred with tears that at first he couldn't make out the tiny features of this new human being.

Then another voice changed his despair to joy. Acsah spoke. "Where's my baby?"

"She's alive."

Dinah took the baby back from him, "Yes, she lost consciousness for a while, but she's okay. They're almost finished with her. You may talk to her in a few minutes, but she'll be unclean for two months."

Othniel looked at Dinah in surprise. When did she learn the cleanliness laws?

—◆◆—

As Acsah held her small son in her arms for the first time, she couldn't stop babbling. "He has real hair and toes and little eyes."

Zebidah laughed. "What did you expect, my girl?"

"He's just so perfect. Oh, Zebidah, I've never worked so hard for anything in my life, but he's worth every bit of the trouble."

"So I've heard."

Acsah realized only Mehetabel had ever actually given birth. "You know, I think I understand something that I didn't before."

"What's that?" Dinah looked at her with curiosity as she rolled up some bloody bedding to take for washing.

"The reason God gave women pain in childbirth. I can never take this baby for granted. What I have experienced was too intense for that. He will always be precious to me because he cost me so much. I think we humans value things more when they cost us more."

Dinah put the bedding aside. "That makes sense to me. In Gibeon, the women never really wanted to give up their babies to Baal once they gave birth. The men didn't mind so much. But from what you are saying, that's because they didn't suffer as much to bring the children into the world, so they didn't value them as much."

"Perhaps the fathers value them more later, after they've spent a lifetime working to support them and to help them grow into men."

Mehetabel said, "I don't know, Acsah; I think Othniel suffered a lot on your account. Do you want to talk to him now? He's waiting outside."

"Yes."

Othniel came into the room, now tidied by the three women so no sign of blood or afterbirth remained. "Acsah, are you okay?"

"I'm fine, Othniel. Did you see your beautiful son?"

"Yes, you've done a marvelous thing."

"God has brought us a miracle."

"Yes. I praise him." He hesitated. "I wish I could hold you, Acsah. I want to feel you're still alive."

Acsah smiled. "I'm here, dear. I'm real."

Seven days later, Caleb took the baby on his knees and gave him a blessing before Othniel had the painful duty of circumcising his little son. "His name will be Hathath."

The baby cried for a little while, but Acsah took him quickly to her breast, where he settled down to eat. Othniel wiped his brow. "That's the hardest task I've ever performed."

Asa, who watched this ceremony with interest, spoke up. "Why do you Israelites do that?"

"It represents the blood covenant between us and our God, established with Abraham."

Caleb observed. "You know, I never had to circumcise a baby. My sons were all born in the wilderness, and we didn't circumcise any of them until we came across the Jordan at Gilgal."

"That's when I was circumcised, too." Othniel remembered the pain and vulnerability of that time. That had taken trust.

Asa asked. "So if someone wanted to follow your God. He would have to be circumcised, right?"

Othniel nodded. "Right."

24

Once things settled down some from the birth, Othniel turned his attention to the terraces. Asa showed him how. "You start at the bottom of the hill building a wall, then bring down clay from the hillside to fill in behind it. We can mix sand and animal dung in the top few feet." After they filled the first level to the top of the wall, they began building the next wall at that level.

Othniel didn't see how they could get enough land prepared before spring planting with just the six men they had now. The work taxed them, and Caleb in particular lagged some in the afternoon heat.

He was thinking about that one evening in the twilight after dinner. He looked up and saw an amazing sight. Who could all those people be?

He walked closer and saw his brother Seraiah leading a donkey with Azubah riding and carrying little Joab. Then he could see Jethro, Heber, and all the other Kenites who helped him at Debir as well.

After some greetings and backslapping, Othniel asked. "What are you doing here?"

Jethro spoke for the group: "We've come to help you, if you'll have us."

"You're more than welcome, but I don't know how fair it is to ask you to share my poverty."

Heber spoke up. "If willing hands and backs can end your poverty, then you have them."

His heart bursting with joy, Othniel embraced his comrades. "Did Caleb tell you our situation?"

Seraiah nodded. "We have more than backs and hands—tools. They've taught me how to make them, too. We've brought shovels, picks, and plows."

Othniel said, "If this works as Caleb predicted, we'll repay you soon."

Jethro's tone turned serious. "Before you give us too much credit, you should know we haven't been thriving either. If your plan here works, it may be the saving of us all."

The Kenites put their tents up around the wheat field. It looked like a city, three hundred men with their families and children. The very next day, the men joined Othniel and his servants in constructing walls, moving dirt, hauling sand, and contributing their own animals' dung to the mix.

After about a week, Caleb announced one evening before the family that he needed to return to his own home. "I have responsibilities as head of Judah I can't do very well from here and my own farm to supervise. Before I go, I want to give you one more gift. You must keep my servant Nathan as your own. I believe from what I've observed that at least one of your Gibeonite servants has become a true believer in the Lord God." His eyes twinkled.

Acsah's heart wrenched at her father's plan to leave. He was 86 years old now, and not as hardy as he had been. Yet she knew his faith and wisdom as well as his generosity had strengthened them and made what was happening here in the desert possible.

On the day that Caleb, Zebidah, and his remaining servant left, Acsah walked to the edge of the wadi with them. First she hugged Zebidah, the nurse who had raised her in her mother's absence and now had delivered her first child. "You've been like a mother for me. I love you."

"And I love you. Take care of little Hathath and Othniel."

Then she turned to her father and held him for a long time. "Oh, Father. We can't thank you enough for everything you have done for us. I really think we'll be able to make it here now."

"I should have helped you more at first, but I was too stubborn. I'm glad God finally made me understand some things."

"He made me understand some things, too." She hugged him again before he turned and headed up the hill. She watched his donkey until they cleared the ridge. Would she ever see him again?

But she didn't have time now for grieving. Young Hathath really did need caring for, and she had women in her courtyard nearly every day. She loved the company, especially having Azubah and little Joab nearby. Her own brothers were so much older than she that they seemed more like uncles, but she had grown up with Othniel and Seraiah. She and Azubah were around the same age, so they had a lot to share, especially with their babies.

Azubah told a little more about the time they spent in Gilgal. "The Kenites got a little ore from traders coming through, but by the time they made something, they couldn't get enough for the implements they made to pay for the ore and their time. They really need access to their own ore."

Acsah opened her shift to feed the ever-hungry Hathath. "The people of Gilgal wouldn't share the rich land near the river with you?"

"We had small gardens near our tents. The Benjamites there all had land close to the Jordan. We had to take our flocks south into the desert to feed. Even after all the fighting and worshiping we had done together with the Israelites, they never exactly accepted us."

"I'm sorry you've experienced so much trouble."

Azubah smiled. "This situation works better for all of us. If only the Kenites could pursue their smithing, I think we could remain here, even after the men finish your terracing."

"Didn't Caleb give you and Seraiah some land down here, too?"

"Yes. It isn't too far from here, but I don't think it has any water on it."

"Water is always the problem, isn't it? But we can all live here and use your land for shepherding."

"I like that idea just fine. Now, tell me about Dinah and Nathan."

"Well, they've been attracted to each other since he came down here with Father, maybe even before; I don't know. But Othniel wouldn't give them permission to marry because Nathan believes in the Lord, and Dinah didn't. But while the men went to Shiloh, she began asking me a lot of questions about the Lord and his laws. Then when I had my baby, the last of her reservations dissolved. I think they can marry as soon as Othniel gives them his blessing."

Azubah ran to catch Joab before he fell into a water jar. She came back carrying him and sat down breathless. "Enjoy Hathath while he's small. What were we talking about?"

"The Gibeonites?"

"Oh, right. Do you remember our conversation so many months ago right before Joab was born?"

"I'd forgotten, but yes. We wondered then if we could get the Gibeonites to believe. At least one has now. I don't know about the other three."

Just then Dinah came out bringing them some lunch, so they changed the topic to something else.

Not too many days later, Othniel was leaving the house to check on the terracing when he heard a shout outside.

"Othniel, you won't believe what I've found today." Jethro's voice vibrated with excitement.

Othniel went outside to the courtyard to greet the panting Jethro. "Slow down, my friend. Let me get you some water."

As he got the dipper of water, Jethro kept talking. "I was herding the sheep southeast of here, not too far from the Salt Sea, when I noticed a green color in one of the hills. When I checked it, I found copper ore, not just a little, but a whole vein, easily accessible."

Othniel handed him the water.

Jethro took the dipper and downed it with one gulp. "Thank you," he gasped. "This means we can make things here in the Negev? We could make helmets, armour, outfit a whole army if we needed to."

"That's wonderful news, Jethro. Now you can pursue your craft."

As soon as they finished the terracing, which to Othniel seemed miraculously fast, the Kenites moved their camp farther east and began mining the copper down near the Salt Sea. They bagged up salt for barter, too, and supplied Acsah with as much salt as she could ever use for preserving and seasoning. Othniel went at Seraiah's invitation to see their industry as they began to work on smelting the copper into implements. He watched Jethro pushing on a leather bellows, pumping air into a beehive furnace with smoke rising from the top.

Jethro wiped the sweat out of his eyes. "I have a clay crucible in there melting copper ore into pure copper with a little tin to make it a stronger metal." He went back to pumping. "I have to keep it hot."

Jethro opened the oven door, and the heat smote Othniel in the face 20 feet away. What hot work, but Jethro thrived on it.

"See here. I'll just pour this out into a mold."

Othniel waited to see what the result would be. Jethro opened the mold, and a spearhead came out with a space for a shaft in its base. "Jethro, just who are you selling these to? Nobody close by, I hope."

"Traders going north and south mostly. Nobody we need fear." He looked a little defensive. "We're not selling to Philistines, if that's what you're worried about."

"No. I hope you're making some plowshares and tools, too."

"Of course, more of those than the weapons. But Othniel, if we ever need weapons, you'll know where to get them."

"Let's pray we don't need them."

Seraiah came over then to show him how he used cold hammering to make some pure copper into bowls and cooking utensils. "I've really found what I love to do. And the Kenites know how to make this pay."

⸻

On the day Dinah wed Nathan, Acsah and Azubah joined together to help Mehetabel prepare a grand feast. So many people crowded the courtyard they spilled out onto the roof. Dinah looked radiant and Nathan shy, as though he hadn't expected such a big affair for a servant's wedding. The men had joined together to build a small rock home for them down near the entrance to the valley. Asa and Oren toasted their sister the bride until she blushed. Acsah looked at all this with deep satisfaction. After all their work, she could see God had given them his peace and prosperity, even in the desert. Othniel came over to her carrying the sleeping Hathath. "You look beautiful tonight, my love."

"And you look handsome. I think they'll be happy, don't you?"

"Yes, but not as happy as we are. God has been so good to us. I continue to see how everything works out, not just for us, but for all these other people as well."

"And the story isn't over yet. He's still working."

Part III

Twelve years later

25

O ne noonday after a morning of working in his fields, Othniel stood looking at the healthy stands of golden barley, green-gold wheat, and winter vegetables beginning to show green in the terraces closest to the top. The olive trees and fig trees near the lower spring had produced well for the past two years and promised to do the same this year. He could hardly realize all the abundance they had in this desert! He lifted his hands into the air. *Oh, Lord, I am unworthy of your blessing, but I praise you for your kindness and mercy to me and to my family. I want to serve you with my whole heart.* Then he bowed his head and worshiped.

Why had God given them so much when the rest of Israel suffered so? Each year for the last twelve, Othniel had gone north three times for the required festivals. His offerings got progressively larger while those of other men grew smaller. He noticed the number of men attending the feasts decreasing over time, especially after the invasion of Cushan Rishathaim seven years before.

Every year he heard rumors of worse abominations happening in Israel. At first he wasn't alarmed. Even in the wilderness, people stole or blasphemed, but, of course, judges would mete out justice according to the law. Now the whole legal system was in jeopardy.

When they sat around the fire in Salmon's courtyard on the way to or from Shiloh, the state of Israel occupied the men's conversations. In particular he remembered one conversation with Salmon's cousin Elimelech several years back. Even before, Elimelech hadn't believed in a strict interpretation of the law. "We should compromise with local customs and beliefs. These Canaanites had a thriving market economy. We should learn from their sophistication."

Salmon's embarrassment over his cousin's words made him irritable. "We don't need sophistication if it means compromising with God's word."

"You'll find out how few of your neighbors agree with you soon, Salmon." Elimelech's words proved true. The majority of Israelites embraced the sensual, materialistic Canaanite culture, rejecting the God who brought them safely out of slavery into this prosperous land. Othniel hadn't really shared his concerns with Acsah, but sooner or later she would find out that Israel had quit following the Lord. Sighing, he took his tools down to the storage shed beside the new grain house. Acsah would have a good meal ready.

—◆—

"The crop this year will be unbelievable." Othniel kissed Acsah before sitting down to eat.

"Praise the Lord for his goodness to us."

"Yes. But somehow, I think it means something. You know I am planning to take an offering to Shiloh for the Passover and Festival of First Fruits this month. I sense the Lord has something special in mind for this bounty, that it isn't ours to hoard."

Acsah's stomach dropped a little. She admired the way Othniel trusted the Lord. But after their earlier struggles, she wanted to beg him to lay everything extra aside for the lean times. Instead, she said calmly, "The Lord has given us plenty for the upcoming sabbatical year."

"You're right, of course; even then our needs will be less than we will have. I wonder…"

Acsah ate the goat's cheese and fresh fruit in front of her and thought about the last few years. She had given birth to Meonothai and Rachel. But there had been deaths, too. First Mehetabel died. Then in one year, Joshua, Eleazar, and her father died. How she missed her father. But hardest of all, six years ago they hadn't planted anything because it was a sabbatical year. It had taken all her self-control not to argue with Othniel about this. The farm had finally started producing, and the idea of going hungry again terrified her. But God had provided that year as well. They had enough to make it, without going hungry. Othniel had never missed taking an offering to the Lord, no matter how small. "Othniel, what would you think about all of us going to Shiloh this year?"

Othniel stopped in mid-bite. "I hadn't really thought about that. Do you want to go?"

"Yes. I'm not pregnant or nursing now, and I haven't seen my brothers or their families in years. We might even get the chance to visit with Rahab and Salmon."

"Meonothai can help now with the animals. And you and I will not have to be apart." He smiled into her eyes. "Let's plan on that."

But a few days later, something happened that changed their plans.

Occasionally, some Kenites would take a string of donkeys loaded with salt and copper implements north. They would return with a variety of objects, but mostly tin to make bronze. With the Kenites making these regular trading trips, Othniel became less cautious about traffic on the winding path into their wadi. For that reason, he didn't pay much attention to the very small band of people coming down from the northern ridge. His chest tightened in surprise when Salmon's cousin Elimelech and his wife Naomi appeared on the doorstep with their two sons. He didn't remember Elimelech's being so thin and old looking, and Naomi had lost weight, too.

"Welcome, Elimelech. You look travel weary. Come into the courtyard and seat yourselves." He held back his curiosity about their appearance. "Dinah, bring water to wash our friends' feet, and call Acsah."

Soon a lamb stew was simmering and bread baking for a company supper. Something about the extreme hunger on their faces as the food cooked made him urge Acsah to an early meal. Elimelech looked around as though in a daze. "How do you have this much food to share in the midst of all the suffering?"

"Eat first, my friend. Then you can tell me what's happening in the north."

Watching them eat as though starving reminded Othniel of their own early days in the Negev. Finally, when he thought his guests were satisfied, he sent the two boys off with Hathath and Meonothai. Acsah took Naomi into the house, and Othniel studied Elimelech, wondering what he planned. "Where are you going, my friend?"

"We're moving to Moab."

"Moab?" Othniel gasped, thinking of all the reasons Elimelech should turn back. "Aren't they still our enemies? You remember the trouble we had with them during our desert wanderings."

"Almost sixty years ago. Why should we allow an old enmity to distort our thinking now?"

"But what about their gods? You or your sons will be led to worship Chemosh. And how will you find suitable wives for Mahlon and Chilion?"

"Better to live there and have Moabite daughters-in-law than to die in Bethlehem. You don't know how severe the drought has become. Besides, with Cushan Rishathaim's invasion, we decided to get out while we could. He burns or takes whatever grain or animals anyone has. We have very little left ourselves, as you can see, but we have enough to get started in Moab."

Othniel looked out his door across the barren wadi below his house and thought it ironic Elimelech should speak of drought to him.

Elimelech continued. "You shouldn't think staying in Bethlehem would protect me from the temptation to worship other gods. Most Israelites in our area have Asherah poles near their fields, and some have even rebuilt the altars on the high places to Baal and Asteroth. It seems to me hypocritical to judge the Moabites for idol worship when the Israelites are no different."

Othniel's heart sank at Elimelech's words. "Surely not every Israelite worships idols."

"No, a few men, like my cousin Salmon, continue to worship Yahweh." Othniel gasped at Elimelech's irreverent use of the Lord's name, but Elimelech carried on with a shrug. "I can't see worshiping Yahweh has helped Salmon any. He's suffering the same as the rest of us."

"So you're determined to run away from the problem?"

"I wouldn't call it running away. It's practical. Moab has rain and crops. Israel doesn't. What alternative do I have if we want to live?"

"You could stay and encourage the Israelites to turn back to the Lord."

Elimelech shook his head. "It doesn't make any difference who we worship. We need to survive the best way we can. My parents insisted on absolute obedience to the law. I think they really believed in that, but I don't see it. Isn't it enough if we say we love God and believe in him and pray to him? Do we really have to obey every bit of the law?"

Othniel could not ignore Elimelech's question. "I understand your question. I've asked myself that many times. I think the answer lies in our history."

"In what way?"

"Simply this. When we as a nation obeyed the Lord without question, we had plenty to eat and victory in battle. When we stopped obeying, we had drought and defeat. God told us what would happen throughout the law, and it's happening again now. So I think we must obey to receive blessing."

"You just don't understand what it's like to be starving and see your family starving. When you reach that point, you get a little desperate. We've made up our minds."

Othniel didn't try to influence Elimelech anymore. Why would a sophisticated thinker like Elimelech listen to someone like him? His faith sounded so simplistic against arguments like Elimelech's, but he believed nevertheless. Instead he invited him to continue on with them. "Stay with us for a few days and build up your strength."

Elimelech shook his head. "We need to go on. I can't see delaying the journey any longer. Who knows when Cushan will come here?"

———

In the house, Acsah was getting reacquainted with the bubbly Naomi, who in spite of hardships maintained her good spirits. "Meonothai and Hathath are so good-looking. How wonderful that you have two sons. It's such a comfort to know we will have sons to care for us in our old age."

"Yes, it's wonderful to have sons. I've known a few women who had only daughters. They worried so much about the future." Acsah cuddled her two-year-old Rachel closer.

"Well, they must marry their daughters well. Then their husbands can help."

The mention of marrying daughters well gave Acsah an uncomfortable feeling, which grew worse when Naomi observed, "You surprised me when you married Othniel after having so many chances to marry into Judah. What was your father thinking?"

"Othniel's a wonderful man. I couldn't have married anyone better no matter what his lineage."

"I beg your pardon. I didn't mean to offend you."

A silence settled between them for a few minutes, giving Acsah time to reflect on the way her marriage appeared to other people. She knew now she had married the right person, but most of Israel couldn't understand putting godliness above lineage. Then she realized how she must have sounded. "I didn't mean to snap at you. Forgive me."

Naomi smiled. "It's all right. You should defend your husband."

"So where are you going?"

"To Moab. Elimelech says we'll have plenty to eat there. We've been hungry for so long. Your cooking tonight tasted marvelous. Do you remember our cooking classes with Rahab? Those were good days." For a moment her expression saddened, but she shook herself. "I'm sure when we get to Moab, we'll find wives for our sons. Elimelech says we should keep an open mind about other cultures and ways of worship, and I agree, but I intend to talk to our daughters-in-law about God's law. I wouldn't really want to live with people who worship other gods. Do you think they might become believers? Salmon's wife did."

Acsah thought she shouldn't point out that Rahab believed before Salmon married her. "Are you happy about moving to Moab?"

"I can't say I'm happy. But I go with my husband."

"I think you're right. It's very important to trust our husbands. They're the ones God will deal with directly." Acsah knew this from her experience. Her life had been so much better since she had learned to submit to Othniel, but a voice inside that she wanted to ignore reminded her that submitting is easier when everything is going well.

The next day, Elimelech and his family traveled on, carrying an extra sack of grain from their stores. "They need it even more than we do," Othniel said to Acsah.

She nodded, only a little concerned about the reduction in their grain supply. A good crop would fill their bins again.

Othniel continued, "I think we should change our plan to go north to Shiloh this year. From what Elimelech told me, Cushan has taken control of the tabernacle. We'd be better off taking our offering to Hebron."

"I could still see my brothers and their families."

"Yes. We should think about taking some extra food for them as well."

Acsah watched as Elimelech and Naomi passed out of sight at the eastern end of the wadi. "You're a wonderful man, Othniel. I appreciate your generosity. Perhaps helping our families is what you meant when you said the good harvest wasn't only for us." She hoped he would agree and save the rest of the grain.

"God takes care of us."

"Yes. He really does."

"Let's celebrate the Passover before we leave."

"I'll plan on that."

***

The wheat harvest and barley harvests passed with everyone helping. The yield impressed even Asa and Oren. A few days later, Asa stood by as Othniel carefully released the pent-up water into the ditch that carried it next to the tiny vegetable plants. "Master, can I ask you a question?"

"Certainly, Asa." Othniel looked sidewise at his servant, wondering what new attack he could expect about his farming methods or single-minded worship.

"I've been watching everything you do. You always take ten percent of your crops to the priests, no matter how little you have raised."

Othniel nodded, waiting for Asa to continue.

"And even in the worst of times, you never tried to worship any god but your own. You wouldn't even let us worship Baal or Asherah. I think you know I have resented your unwillingness to compromise."

"Yes, Asa. I knew that." Othniel still couldn't decide from Asa's face where this conversation tended.

"You're kind to us, never withholding food when your own family must have needed more. And now I see how your wife submits to you. My sister says it's because of your god. Is that true?"

Othniel looked at Asa, startled by the intensity of his gaze. "Acsah told me that, as well."

Asa looked away, picked up a shovel, and evened up some soil. Then he turned and said, "You're successful here in this desert land, even though the rest of Israel is suffering, but I know they have followed after our gods, not your God. I guess I never really believed that Baal or Asherah would help us; I just wanted to participate in the fertility rites. I know from what you have told me of your God's laws that I am not a good man, but..."

Othniel waited, his heart beating faster as he realised what Asa was confessing.

"I'm trying to say you're a good man; you really believe in your God, and He really blesses you. I want to know your God. I want to worship Him."

Othniel smiled at Asa and reached out his hand to grip his servant's shoulder. "I'm honoured to tell you all I know about the Lord. He's been good to me. He's a God worth worshiping."

"I'll have to be circumcised."

"Yes. But we can do that whenever you're ready."

Within the week, Othniel performed this operation on Asa, making him an official follower of God. Asa's brother Oren wasn't at all happy about his brother's decision, but he didn't openly defy Othniel.

Acsah called her servant girls to her. Dinah, heavy with her third child, waddled out to the courtyard where Acsah ground wheat flour. In a few minutes, Miriam joined them. "Tomorrow is the first day of Passover. We must clean out all the yeast from our houses."

They worked together to clean Acsah's house first. She handed each a broom. "Let's start by sweeping off the roof first." Acsah swept beside her girls, thinking about how God had blessed her with good servants. She never saw Miriam without thinking about Caleb's death. They had traveled north when they got word Caleb had fallen ill. They arrived in time to hear his halting blessing and to close his eyes. Her brother Iru inherited Caleb's land and possessions, but he generously gave them 100 sheep and Miriam as their servant. Acsah still felt grateful, but she had never stopped being sad about losing her father.

Shaking herself out of her reverie, she started down the outside stairs to begin working on the two rooms of the house. "You two can do the courtyard area." Inside the house she looked around at how much they had acquired, a table and chairs, more jars and pots. The Kenites kept her supplied with fine copper cookware and utensils. As her family grew, so did her need for blankets, mats, and clothing. Beginning in her kitchen area, she gathered up any bread or dough that might contain yeast, and took it outside to burn in the courtyard fire. Then the two women joined her in the house, where they scrubbed out all the cookware and swept the two rooms thoroughly. "Now we go to your house, Dinah."

"Mistress, you don't have to clean my house for me."

"Sharing work with others makes it lighter for everyone." She didn't add that she wanted to ensure they got all the yeast out. Everything had to be done right for this first Passover at home.

Their houses clean, they settled in her courtyard and ground grain for a week's worth of unleavened bread.

About noon, Othniel came bearing the lamb he had slaughtered for the Passover feast. With him walked Hathath carrying a hyssop branch and Meonothai carrying the bowl of lamb's blood. While Acsah watched, Othniel took the blood, and, dipping the branch in it, slapped some above and on either side of the door lintel. The words of the law came to her, "When I see the blood, I will pass over you." The blood saved the firstborn males from death in Egypt. Her dear Hathath, so mature now and serious, how could those Egyptian women stand what happened that night?

Now she and the other women had work to do to get the lamb roasting over the courtyard fire and the unleavened bread ready for baking. At twilight, everything sat ready on the table in the house: the bitter herbs, the bread, and the roasted lamb. Othniel, Hathath, Meonothai, Nathan, and Asa stood around the table, the women behind them. Acsah mourned because Oren could not join with them, but he had never chosen to be circumcised, and by law, could not join.

As the youngest male present, Meonothai asked, "Why do we eat bitter herbs and bread without yeast, Father?"

Othniel looked at Acsah with a smile in his eyes before he answered, "It is the Passover sacrifice to the Lord, because he passed over us in Egypt and did not kill our firstborn sons." The familiar words of the special ceremony filled Acsah with bittersweet feelings of nostalgia. She remembered her father saying those words so many Passovers in their tent in the wilderness, but now her father was dead. Tears filled her eyes. They were making those same kinds of memories for their children now.

Late that evening, Othniel asked her about her tears. "Were you thinking of Caleb?"

"Yes. How did you know?"

"Because I was thinking about him, too. We shared the same Passovers after my parents died."

"How did it make you feel, knowing they would die before the nation of Israel could enter the land of Canaan?"

"We all knew our parents had to die, but we didn't live like we knew it. I mean, maybe we just couldn't accept the truth; I don't know. But their deaths came as a shock to me."

Acsah put her arms around him in the darkness, speaking softly because the children slept nearby. "We all have to die eventually, don't we? I think I would live differently if I thought about that. Would you have done anything differently if you had accepted that your parents would not live to see the Promised Land?"

"I would have told them I loved them more often and expressed my appreciation, not only for what they did for me, but for who they were. I might have tried to marry sooner and have some grandchildren for them to enjoy, but..."

"You wouldn't have married me, then."

"No, I couldn't have. I think my parents would love knowing I finally married you. They loved you a lot."

"Did they know you loved me then?"

"No, I didn't know myself. But my mother might have suspected my feelings before I did. Mothers have insight into things like that."

"Since you believe that, I'm going to share a bit of insight I have."

"What's that?"

"I think Miriam likes Asa."

"Well, if he reciprocates, I'll give my permission, with your recommendation, of course."

Acsah chuckled. "Of course."

26

"Meonathai, keep that lamb from running away. Rachel, don't get in the donkey's dung." Ascah wiped her forehead with her head covering and checked to make sure they had everything for their trip—the first sheaves from the grain harvest and the tithe of all their grain on one donkey, separate from the load of grain for her brothers. "Asa, how many sheep are we taking?"

"Six for your brothers and three lambs for the priests." Asa's gaze wasn't on the sheep, but on Miriam, who packed the food for the journey along with the tent and skins of water.

Acsah smiled to herself. She'd have to watch those two.

Othniel brought up another donkey. "I want you and Rachel to ride on this one."

"Oh, Othniel, how thoughtful. Are you sure?"

"I'm sure." His smile at her pleasure warmed her through. Rachel could be a handful even at home, much less on a journey.

Soon they were waving goodbye to Oren, Nathan, Dinah, and their children. "We'll come back before you deliver," Acsah called back to Dinah.

They climbed out of their wadi and made the difficult trek over the rocky hills, heading for the gentler hillsides near Hebron.

That night, Othniel called a halt near what once was a spring, but no water ran there now. She congratulated Othniel for making them bring extra skins of water. This trip would be a dry one.

The next day, the roads were strangely quiet. They never got to the cultivated lands that marked the halfway point. Finally, Othniel realized all the land looked like the Negev now. Nothing grew except a few dying trees. Seeing the devastation shocked him.

They arrived in Hebron, and Othniel stopped at the gate. "Where are the priests receiving the first fruits offerings?"

One man scowled. "Who has any first fruits to offer this year? We're all starving. Try up the street at the fifth door."

Othniel knocked, and a man answered, wearing the priestly garb, though it hung on him several sizes too large. "What can I do for you?"

Othniel tried to explain. "I've brought the first fruits offering for the priests to bless. I understand..."

"Come in, my son. Yes. Come in." The man waved him into the courtyard, looking greedily at the donkey loads of grain. "Let's see, you'll need me to do a wave offering of your first sheaves." He did a cursory wave offering of the first sheaf of barley.

"Don't you need an altar to do that?"

"Well, yes, of course. I'll see it gets to the right people, and they'll handle it properly. And do you want to make additional offerings?" He eyed the other sacks of grain and the sheep.

Othniel pointed to a donkey load and a few sheep. "This is our tithe. These others we brought to share with our hungry family in this area."

"Who are you, and where are you from?"

"I am Othniel from the Negev, near Arad." Othniel wanted to laugh at his baffled face, but instead he said. "God blesses those who obey him." Then he took his family and went looking for Caleb's sons.

Elah's son Kenaz spotted them coming. A tall young man of nineteen, he called out to the household, "It's Uncle Othniel and Aunt Acsah."

Soon the whole family joined them outside. Like everyone Othniel had met that day, they eyed the grain and sheep with longing. He couldn't stand their suspense. "We've brought this for you."

To his surprise, Elah began to weep. "You're an answer to prayer. We have nothing at all left in the grain bins, and we have slaughtered all but a few of our sheep."

That evening, the whole family gathered at Iru's house. All the women helped cook the meal, small to Acsah, but Jerusha said, "What a feast." They slaughtered a sheep dying of starvation for a mutton stew and ground enough grain to make a piece of bread for every person.

Acsah couldn't help noticing how sparing the women were with water. No one offered to wash their feet when they arrived, and Jerusha saved the wash water from the dishes to use again.

Acsah asked, "Where do you get your water now?"

"One cistern for the city still has a little in it. They allow us one jar every other day. It isn't enough." Mahalath shook her head. "We never did without like this before in our lives, not even in the wilderness."

"The Lord met our needs in the wilderness," said Acsah.

"Didn't he promise to give us even more here in Canaan?"

Hearing the bitterness in her voice, Acsah kept quiet. She could tell Mahalath didn't want to hear God was punishing Israel. No one ever wanted to hear that message.

But later, they all gathered with the men in the courtyard. Iru pointed to a hill not far away. "Do you see that?" Acsah could see a faint gleam of a fire burning. "Someone's up there tonight, worshiping Baal. People have become so desperate they are sacrificing their own children, trying to get favor from some god."

Acsah tasted the bile rising from her stomach, but Othniel rose to his feet and started pacing. She knew him well enough to recognize his anger. His next words sent a thrill through her. "The Lord your God will cut off before you the nations you're about to invade and dispossess. But when you have driven them out and settled in their land, and after they have been destroyed before you, be careful not to be ensnared by inquiring about their gods, saying, 'How do these nations serve their gods? We will do the same.' You must not worship the Lord your God in their way, because in worshiping their gods, they do all kinds of detestable things the Lord hates. They even burn their sons and daughters in the fire as sacrifices to their gods. See that you do all I command you; do not add to it or take away from it."

Immediate quiet followed this speech. Her brothers would recognize the words of Moses spoken just before he died and repeated by Joshua at Shechem 14 years before.

Naam finally spoke. "What should we do now, Othniel?"

Othniel paused. Who was he to tell the sons of Caleb the law? But the sight of that fire on the hill moved him to speak. "We should return to the true worship of the Lord. We should tear down the high places and the Asherah poles, destroy manmade idols, and cease worshiping that way. We should return to Shiloh with sacrifices to the Lord through Phinehas instead of sacrificing all over the country. You know the law—give the Lord the first fruits, tell our children about the law. We've forgotten that our strength as a nation came totally from our dependence on the Lord, not from us."

Iru responded. "What you say is true. I had forgotten."

Elah shook his head. "Why do we have such short memories? Only seven years ago, we heard Joshua's farewell speech. I'll never forget that day."

Naam said. "That's when he called all of us to Shechem. He gave a powerful speech."

"Joshua looked feeble since the last time I had seen him," said Othniel.

"Yes, as if having done what God called him to do, his life began ebbing away." Others nodded agreement.

Elah continued. "Yet when Joshua started speaking, he spoke with power. He started as the leaders always do, reminding us of what the Lord had done in the past, from Abraham through their enslavement in Egypt and the grand exodus out into the wilderness. Then defeating the Amorites, entering land across the flooded Jordan, defeating Jericho, and defeating other tribes."

Othniel said, "I think the leaders rehearse our history to make us remember ourselves—the blood and sweat, the screaming women and children, the burning buildings. In every battle except one, the Lord was with us and defeated our enemies. We know he did it because he used earthquakes, hail, hornets, and other supernatural means. Even at Kiriath Sepher against the Anakites, I felt the presence and power of the Lord. Without his help, we could never have won that battle."

Acsah had not heard this from Othniel before. Sometimes, she thought, a man will say things in front of a group he never tells his wife in private.

Elah picked up the story again. "I have to admit I didn't understand when Joshua challenged us to get rid of all gods except the Lord. Even then, men had started worshiping Baal and Asherah."

"You wouldn't have known it from the crowd that day. They shouted, 'Of course we want to serve the Lord,' and 'We haven't forgotten what God has done for us.'" Naam shook his head.

"Did you get the impression Joshua didn't believe them?" asked Elah. "He must have known."

Othniel sat back down. "Of course he did; his next words prove that. The Lord must have given him a vision of this time."

"What did he say?" Acsah realized she had spoken aloud, something women rarely did with a group of men, but they didn't seem to mind.

Othniel answered her. "Joshua said, 'You are not able to serve the Lord. He is a holy God; he is a jealous God. He will not forgive your rebellion and your sins. If you forsake the Lord and serve foreign gods, he will turn and bring disaster on you and make an end of you, after he has been good to you.'"

"Of all those people who yelled back that day, 'No, no, we will serve the Lord,' how many do you think really meant it?" Elah asked.

Iru said, "I meant it when I said it, I really did; but I must admit, I've failed the Lord in many ways. I've comforted myself because I haven't done any really bad things like worshiping at Asherah poles or killing babies, but I've not always kept the Sabbath day holy."

Elah nodded. "I tried to plant crops during that first sabbatical year, but not one thing came up. That year began the drought."

Naam added. "You weren't the only one. In fact, I don't know anyone who didn't try to plant."

"Othniel didn't," Acsah spoke out again. The women around her stirred uncomfortably.

Othniel looked at her, bemused. "And Acsah supported me in that decision." Then he turned to the group. "The fact is, we made a covenant to do what Joshua said, 'As for me and my house, we will serve the Lord.'"

The group sat silent after that, each perhaps thinking of his or her failure to serve the Lord. Acsah knew she was.

The next day Acsah overheard Othniel proposing an idea to Iru. "Why don't all of you come back with us to the Negev? We have plenty of water and food. You can stay there until this drought passes."

Iru hesitated. "Somehow, I believe you're right. But we hate to burden you. Caleb told me how desperate things were for you."

Othniel smiled. "Come ahead and see. The Lord has blessed us."

Hearing this conversation worried Acsah more than she wanted to admit after the conversation the night before. Would they have enough grain to feed themselves and all her family? But, of course, they couldn't let them starve. She wasn't surprised that the idea seemed good to Naam and Elah as well when Othniel asked them.

As a result, a much larger group of people headed south than came to Hebron. Before they left, Othniel encouraged Iru to leave the uneaten grain with the neediest people he knew. "Perhaps this will keep a few more children alive in Israel."

On the way to the Negev, she saw Asa walking beside Othniel, speaking earnestly. Othniel told her in their tent that night that Asa had asked to marry Miriam. "We'll need to have a wedding feast soon."

"I'm so glad Asa believes in the Lord now, too. That means two of our Gibeonite servants have converted."

"Do you think Mehetabel believed before she died?"

"She never said anything to me. God alone knows what she really thought."

"Let's pray that Oren will want the Lord, too." Othniel took her hand and prayed in the darkness before they turned over to sleep.

After they got back, Othniel suggested her family settle in the area near the Brook Besor. "You'll have water there. Usually it quits, but this year the brook has run longer than ever before. After you get settled, come up to our house for a meal."

Acsah hurried up the hill to get food ready. Dinah, even in her advanced pregnancy, had anticipated her. "I've made the dough for bread and a large stew. We have plenty."

"How are you, Dinah? Any day now?"

"If it's like the last two times, I won't have to wait long."

That evening, a group of men sat on Othniel's roof, while their wives and children congregated in the courtyard below. Acsah laughed, remembering how Othniel had thought he wouldn't do much entertaining in the Negev.

27

Dinah's baby, a little girl, came a few days later. Acsah stayed very busy after that. The grain harvests were over, but now the vegetables on the highest terrace were producing. Every day, Othniel brought Acsah baskets of onions, leeks, lentils, peas, cucumbers, and melons. She preserved some by drying and others by pickling them in wine vinegar or salt brine. Their grapes ripened, and every evening, she could offer fresh grapes and melon to their guests. Jerusha accepted a piece of melon from her one evening. "After the misery of the drought, the peace and prosperity of this place are like another world."

"I'm so happy we could bring you here."

"Acsah, I need to say something. We..." She nodded toward the other sisters-in-law. "We should have stood up to Caleb all those years ago, made him give you more dowry or give you land in the area around Hebron. We just let him push you out."

"Hush, Jerusha. All that's past and forgiven. God meant for things to happen the way they have. If we had been in Hebron, we would have been starving now with you instead of here to save you from the drought." This conversation reminded Acsah of the story of Joseph and his brothers. Joseph realized if his brothers hadn't sold him into slavery, he wouldn't have been in Egypt to save them from starving.

One morning, Acsah had vegetables to process and needed to supervise her servant girls, but the courtyard looked untidy. "Meonothai?"

Her precocious five-year-old came running. "Yes, Mother?"

"Son, I want you to sweep up the courtyard."

"I don't want to." Meonothai kicked the ground, and Acsah knew he was waiting to see what she would do.

She tried reasoning with him. "A good soldier always obeys his commanding officer. To grow up like your father, you must learn obedience."

His lip poked out in defiance. "You aren't my commanding officer."

Suddenly a stern voice spoke from the doorway. "Meonothai!"

Acsah winced as Meonothai dragged his toes over to his father. She knew Othniel could be strict with the boys. Should she stand between Meonothai and the spanking he deserved? No, she needed to trust Othniel's love for them and remain quiet.

"What does the fifth commandment say, Son?"

"Honor your father and your mother."

"Yes. Does that mean you can disobey your mother?"

"But, Father, Oren says women aren't important. They are less than men."

"I didn't ask you what Oren says. I asked you what the law says."

"I have to obey you."

"And..."

"I have to obey Mother, too."

"That's right. I don't want to hear you insult your mother or refuse to obey her again. Do you understand me?"

"Yes, Father."

Acsah handed Meonothai the broom and saw him start sweeping before she followed Othniel into the house. She went over to where he stood and put her arms around him. "Thank you."

"You're welcome. If he acts up again, you can always remind him of what happens to a disobedient son."

"Stoning, you mean. Oh, Othniel, that seems so cruel."

"But it's the law, and he needs to know there are consequences for breaking the law."

"I don't want him to be afraid of us."

"A little healthy fear will make them respect you and love you more, if you enforce that respect now."

"You're right, Othniel. I'll try harder to be firm." She squeezed him tighter before releasing him to pick up his bag to go out. "Do you ever wonder if God feels this way about us?"

"What do you mean?"

"That God wants us to obey him from love and respect, not fear?"

"Yes, I think you're probably right. That deserves some consideration."

—◆—

That evening, a stranger came to their door, looking desperate.

Othniel went out to the courtyard with him. "What can I do for you?"

"Please, I heard you had food. My family is starving. Can you do anything for us?"

"Come and eat something now." Othniel called to Acsah. "Do you have any stew left from supper?"

She went immediately into the house and returned with some stew and bread and a bunch of grapes. "Why don't you take these up on the roof? You might get a breeze up there."

The man's voice cracked. "Thank you, so much. You don't know how wonderful this looks."

Othniel waited for him to eat most of his stew before he said, "Where are your people?"

"My wife has grown too weak to travel, and I don't know where my sons have gone. They left us when things got bad." He choked back another sob. "I'll repay you some day, if you will help me now."

Othniel asked him more questions about his situation. "You say your name is Josiah?"

He nodded.

"Do you follow the Lord, Josiah?"

"I did until things turned so against us. Then I began to doubt."

"And when did things turn bad?"

"About six years ago."

"During the sabbatical year, you mean?"

"Yes, not a single thing came up that I planted that year. Of course, we had plenty then, but not for long."

"Are you saying you planted a crop during the sabbatical year?"

"Of course—everyone did. Didn't you?"

"No, I didn't. I didn't even water my fields."

Josiah shook his head. "How did you live here in the Negev?"

"God provided enough from the year before to last us, just as he did for you," said Othniel.

"But I wanted more. I feared running out."

"So you didn't trust the Lord, and you did run out."

"I see what you mean. And you're right." Josiah rubbed his grizzled chin.

Othniel pushed the bowl of grapes over to him. "Israel has moved so far away from the Lord. Is it any wonder everything's going wrong? If we obeyed his law again the way we did when we crossed the Jordan, we wouldn't be having the drought and invasion."

"Do you think we must go back to our wilderness life? All day, every day worrying about how to carry water, what to eat or not to eat, how and when to have sex? I feared to breathe. And the way people acted if they thought us less than perfect! Most were breaking the rules themselves. I hated it."

Othniel pondered the truth of his words before answering. "I don't think that's what the Lord had in mind either. I think he wants us to know Him, not just his law. If each of us understands who he is and wants to please him, then the whole country will be good. Besides, we wouldn't judge each other, because meditating on God's goodness would keep us humble."

"You speak masterfully, Othniel. You almost convince me, but I don't think people will go back to restrictions. They don't want to be good unless they're afraid of punishment. The Israelites feel their freedom now."

Othniel looked down to the pool below him. Never had the water dried up in all the years of drought. How could he doubt God's goodness in light of all this? "You're right when you say people don't want to be good. But they do want to be loved. And God loves us. Why aren't people drawn to that?"

Josiah helped himself to more grapes. "Do you mean his love is conditional? We obey the law, and then he loves us? Was that part of the covenant between Moses and God?"

"I don't remember the law stating that his love was conditional, only his favor. Those aren't the same thing."

"What's the difference?"

"Think of it this way. When a father really loves his children, not for how they benefit him but with deep, selfless love that's willing to do what's hard, he punishes his children when they need it, so they will grow up as good men and women. He wants them to mature." The picture of Meonathai standing before him to be reprimanded came back to him.

"You're saying the drought and invasion demonstrate God's love for us?"

"Right, because he sees that as a nation we're disobedient and immature."

"So if we obey God, he'll give us favor again?"

"Yes, but I think he really wants more than obedience as a way of getting favor or avoiding punishment. Don't you want your sons to obey you because they love and trust you?"

In a bitter voice, Josiah said, "My sons don't obey me for any reason now. When they were younger, they obeyed sometimes because of fear. Now they do what they want. It breaks my heart."

"There, that's exactly what I'm saying about the Lord. We obeyed him in the desert because we were afraid of what he would do to us."

"Yes, the plagues." Josiah shuddered.

"But now Israel acts like your sons, doing what they want without regard for the Lord or his law. I'm sure he feels about Israel the way you feel about your sons."

"What about your sons?"

Othniel pointed to the two boys playing with sticks down by the pool. "My older son used to fear me. My younger son still does. I discovered I had to be firm. Whatever I told them I would do, I did, no matter how I hated to punish them."

"And God promised drought and famine if we disobeyed."

"Right, but I want to say this. My older son changed; I can't put my finger on when, but the more we worked together in the fields and shared stories around our family hearth, he learned to know me and finally to love me. Now I think he would do anything for me, even die, not because of fear, but because of love."

"But it took time." Josiah tossed his grape seeds over the edge of the roof.

"Yes, time together."

"So what does this have to do with Israel?"

"I'm not sure. We didn't obey him, so God is punishing us. We could go back to obeying from fear. But to know him better and love him more, we need to be with him, pray to him, think about who he is and what he's done."

"I wonder how all this could apply to my sons?"

"Do you want a word of advice?"

Josiah nodded. "Please."

"Don't protect them from the consequences of their bad choices."

"I know, I know. I nagged them on the one hand while giving them what they wanted with the other."

"It isn't easy to let them suffer or do without, but in time, you will see results, if you don't falter."

"Thank you for this talk. It's helped me a lot."

"It's helped me, too."

"In what way?"

"To clarify my thinking about things."

Josiah pointed a finger at Othniel's chest. "We need a leader like you to make all of us see things clearly again, like Joshua or Moses."

Othniel laughed to himself at this idea. Comparing him to Joshua or Moses was ridiculous. Maybe Israel did need another leader, but surely better men could be found.

The next morning, Othniel loaded Josiah's donkey with provisions to last for a while and sent him on his way. He knew Acsah worried when he shared their grain so freely, but he couldn't send Josiah away empty-handed.

28

Ever since Elimelech had told about Cushan's invasion spreading south, Othniel had been more deliberate about posting a watch around their valley. He knew they likely would have no warning. So one day as he worked in the vegetable patch far above the valley, he saw a sight that struck fear into his heart. He could see moving figures topping the pass on the opposite side, coming down into their secluded valley. "Please, Lord," he prayed, "Protect us."

Leaping down the terraces to the house, he grabbed the ram's horn he used for calling his sons and servants. The horn blast brought Acsah out of the house. "What's happening, Othniel?"

Othniel pointed to the dots descending the hills across the wadi. Acsah gasped, "You don't think the invaders would come this far south into the Negev, do you?"

"I don't know who it is, but I would rather meet them in battle over there than here at the house."

Acsah nodded and helped him gather his armor and weapons, which always hung ready. He could see her eyes tearing up. "The Lord will protect us, Little One." He held her close for an instant and hurried out.

By this time, Hathath and Meonothai had arrived along with the servants and Acsah's brothers. He had nine men capable of waging battle if needed. "Hathath and Meonothai, I want you to stay here with your mother. If the invaders prevail, I want you to take her and flee up into the hills." The two boys nodded with serious expressions on their faces.

In less time than it should have taken, the men collected their arms and headed out across the dry wadi toward the hills and the approaching figures, leaving the women they loved behind. But before they even cleared the wadi, Othniel could see that no army approached. Men in the garb of shepherds herded a small flock of sheep and goats, and he couldn't see any armor or weapons. Soon he could even see women on donkeys. He told his men, "I don't think these people mean us any harm. But stay alert, just the same."

Suddenly a figure broke away from the group and came toward him. Othniel strode forward on his long legs and soon recognized him. "Salmon," he cried in delight. "How wonderful to see you, my friend!"

Yet Othniel could not keep the shock from his face. Salmon appeared greatly altered, thin and worn, almost emaciated.

In a voice cracking with emotion, Salmon said, "Othniel! Oh, thank the Lord." Then he gave way to weeping as the remainder of his party caught up with them. Othniel could see Rahab, equally thin but smiling from the back of her donkey, and Boaz, a tall young man now. Othniel's eyes moistened as he turned to Asa and murmured. "Hurry back to the house, and tell the women we have guests. Then go find the fatted calf and slay it. We will have a feast for our friends tonight."

Then as they turned together to cross the wadi, Othniel said to Salmon, who had composed himself, "What news do you have?"

"Not good." Hearing the grief in Salmon's voice tore at Othniel's heart. "I'm sure you've heard about the drought?"

"Yes, Elimelech told us on their way to Moab."

Salmon grimaced at this mention of his cousin, then continued, "You also know about Cushan?"

"I assume he has taken Bethlehem now."

"Yes. Well, as you can see, we're in desperate need. Our crops failed for several years in a row, but we had some grain put by and might have made it on that by being very economical and by depleting the flocks and herds to what you see here." He gestured at the remainder of his once countless possessions. "But with the invasion we lost more because he burned some of our fields and took tribute to spare our lives. Then when Elimelech and Naomi left, I began to think about migrating, too, not to Moab, and not because of the drought."

"What happened?"

"Horrible things—fertility rites performed under the Asherah poles on every hillside, sacrifices to Baal, sexual perversion. Those of us who still try to worship the Lord are treated with contempt and derision."

"I heard some of that from Elimelech."

"Yes, he's quit trying to serve the God of Abraham, Isaac, and Jacob. But he wasn't alone. I never thought I would live to see such degradation." Salmon thrust his staff with unnecessary force into the sandy soil.

"So you decided to come here?"

"Yes, I knew that even if we died here in the desert, we would die surrounded by loved ones who share our faith in the one true God."

Othniel realized Salmon didn't know how God had prospered them. "You're not going to die, Salmon."

"You don't have to sacrifice what you have here for me, Othniel. I did not come to put your lives in danger, only to be near you."

Othniel's eyes stung again at the resignation and hopelessness in Salmon's voice, but he had good news to share. "The Lord has blessed us here, Salmon. We have enough and more. I consider it another blessing to have you here with me." Salmon looked unconvinced, so Othniel just laughed and said, "Come and see for yourself."

Acsah stood in the courtyard, uncertain of what to do as she watched their men march away resolutely across the wadi. Her heart stuck in her throat. After all their blessings here, would they lose everything now? She had heard enough from Othniel about battles to know what would happen to the women and children if the invaders got past those nine men. But she had faith in Othniel, still a mighty man, even in his fifties.

She could just make out a little of what occurred as the two groups met, and it didn't look to her like people fighting. She heaved a sigh of relief when she saw someone break away from the group and race back toward the house. How thoughtful of Othniel to let them know something as soon as possible.

Asa arrived, gasping for breath. "Master said to tell you we have guests and told me to kill the fatted calf."

Kill the fatted calf? Never before had Othniel done that for stray guests coming through. Then she reminded herself she trusted Othniel and rallied Dinah and Miriam to make preparations for a feast for a large group. She planned to make a large stew with the beef, and discovered she had plenty of ground wheat, all ready for baking. She soaked some dried figs for stewed fruit and sent Hathath to get fresh water from the spring to wash the travelers' feet. In her flurry, the crowd arrived before she realized it. She stepped to the doorway to see these guests who provoked her husband to give such a feast and found herself hugged by Rahab.

When they pulled apart, Acsah saw Rahab weeping, and her own tears flowed. "My dear friend, how I have missed you."

Rahab smiled. "I'm all right, now we're here." She drank the water with appreciation. "It's fresh and cool. How do you have this here in the desert?"

Acsah said simply, "God has been faithful in blessing us." Then realizing how that must have sounded, she added. "We couldn't have a drought here because we always are without rain."

"Don't apologize. I understand exactly what you mean. The abominations happened around us, and we did little to stop them, so we suffered along with everyone else."

Acsah turned to Dinah, who stood nearby waiting for orders. "Take some fresh melons up to the men on the roof and bring us some here as well. The meat won't be ready for hours."

She sat down then beside Rahab and said, "I want to hear everything."

"Things went well until two years after Joshua died. I know you remember."

"Yes, my father died that same year."

"During the sabbatical year, we didn't plant, but nearly all our neighbors did. They wasted grain they could have eaten. Nothing grew that year."

"So you were better off than they because you still had your grain."

"Yes, we had more for a while, and really our farm the next year did better than the surrounding farms. But now I realize the law breaking began before that sabbatical year. I noticed little things, like being cheated by a potter or treated with disrespect as a Canaanite."

Acsah nodded. "I can imagine what you mean. That sometimes happened even in the wilderness."

"Then I noticed when I talked about the Lord and his goodness, my neighbours would become impatient with me, more interested in what I could teach them about weaving or planting crops. Everyone still observed the Sabbath and took offerings to Shiloh, but some people complained aloud about how much they had to give up."

"I know. I remember feeling that way myself, especially those first years when we really didn't have enough. But Othniel insisted we give God his share without complaining."

"Othniel's a good man."

"Yes. He is. What happened after that?"

"Well, at first we heard rumors of the bad things—someone falsely accused another man of stealing his sheep and killed him in anger; some Benjamites not only allowed the Jebusites to set up Asherah poles, but put them up themselves."

"Yes. My father told me about some who did that."

"I think I know which one he told you about." She continued. "Later, some men denied some poor widows the right to glean in an already cleared field; I began noticing people out working in their fields on the Sabbath. It got worse and worse. After the drought came, the sexual orgies started under the Asherah poles, and some sacrificed babies. All the worst things about Jericho happened, families torn apart, children abandoned. Horrible."

"What did people say about the drought?"

"Instead of seeing that their problems resulted from their choices to sin, they said the Lord wasn't strong. I think they wanted an excuse to worship the Canaanite gods. Some even said that all the gods were superstitions and every man should do what seemed right to him."

"So everything started falling apart. How did you feel?"

"Sad. So much unnecessary suffering. Joshua told us exactly what would happen if we started following the gods of Canaan and ignoring the law, and it happened just as he predicted, first the drought and then the invasion by raiders. They took what little grain people had left. Finally, Cushan-Rishathaim came and made us pay such a heavy tribute that people began to starve."

"I'm so glad you came to us."

"It's ironic you have grain here in the Negev, while people are starving in the Hill Country."

"Yes. I'm not sure why." Before, Acsah would have said that they had plenty because they trusted the Lord; but if Salmon and Rahab went hungry, they could, too. She felt suddenly vulnerable.

The feast that evening tasted wonderful—the tender beef, fresh bread, leeks, onions, and fruit stew. Othniel took pleasure in watching his friend eat heartily.

Salmon spoke to Othniel by the fire afterwards. "I feel comfortably full for the first time in I don't know how long. Thank you for the excellent food."

"Thank the Lord. He provided all this."

"You don't know what a pleasure I feel hearing the Lord praised and revered again. It's been lonely in Bethlehem."

"Why do you say that?"

"Nearly everyone practices idol worship. Men don't talk about the Lord's provision."

"That's so clearly against the law—don't worship idols. I don't understand how they could miss that."

"At first they said they worshiped the Lord when they met on the high places, even if the shrines were originally designated to Baal."

"But the law forbids that, too."

"I know, and it's obvious why the Lord forbid that practice. It did not take long at all for many people to stop saying they worshiped the Lord there and admit they were worshiping the god of the high place."

"Why did any of this happen?"

"I think it started with the men who took Canaanite wives. Some married Gibeonites; others married Jebusites."

"But not believers in the Lord."

"Some of the women promised to convert for the sake of their husbands, but they must not have meant it. Those would say, 'Baal and Yahweh are the same. It doesn't matter what you call him as long as you're true to your own beliefs.'"

"And the husbands went along with that."

"I had a conversation with one man who married a Jebusite woman. You may remember him—Hamul?"

"Of course, one of the suitors for Acsah's hand."

"He told me he thought having peace justified compromises. He married a beautiful woman, and I think he's devoted to her, so he even put up an Asherah pole on his land."

Othniel shook his head in disgust. "I don't understand how we could have strayed so far from the law in so short a time."

"I've thought some about it."

Othniel looked at him. "What do you think?"

"Every culture I've ever encountered has this tremendous desire to put its faith in something tangible: the Egyptians worshiped bulls and the Pharaoh himself; the Canaanites worship figures of Ashteroth or sacred rocks or high places or poles."

"Yes, or bronze bulls." Othniel shuddered as he thought about the horrendous rites to Molech, the roasting of little children alive to appease the war god.

"Why should we believe we're any different? And if you look carefully at the reasons for this worship, it all comes back to one thing: the desire for possessions."

"I'm sorry. That's a leap for me. Could you explain?"

"Because they believe making some kind of sacrifice will give them better crops, more children to help with those crops, more power in battle to obtain more land to have more crops..."

"Okay, I see. So you're saying all idolatry stems from people's desire for gain."

"What do you think?" Salmon reached for another grape from the bunch close by him.

"It makes sense to me. Yet God promised us we would be blessed in this land."

"He did, but contingent on our obedience to the law. Perhaps the Israelites are looking for a shortcut to blessings that doesn't involve daily obedience and devotion."

"God does bless those who seek after him. I believe that with all my heart, but that doesn't mean all suffering starts from sin and disobedience."

Salmon looked surprised at this turn in the conversation. "Why do you say that?"

"You have suffered. Yet you remained faithful."

"Yes, that's because of the sin of others around me."

"That's been my experience, too. When Caleb, may he rest in peace, kept me from marrying Acsah at first, I suffered. And later after we first married, we suffered down here trying to start a farm. We hadn't really done anything to deserve that. But I can see now it was all part of God's bigger plan."

"So some suffering makes us into the people God wants us to be or prepares us for something he wants us to do, right?"

"Yes. And speaking of when we first married, we would have suffered even more had our good friends Salmon and Rahab not helped us. So I don't want to hear anything else about owing us for this hospitality. We are indebted to you."

"As if I'm not indebted to you for all the times you saved my life during our battles together, or how you stood by me during that time of waiting for Rahab to fall in love with me."

"I think as friends, we don't owe anything because love doesn't keep records of giving. Besides, in the sabbatical year all debts are canceled. I'll cancel yours now, if you have any."

All that summer, a steady stream of people came. Most were desperate, and Othniel couldn't turn any away. The field beside the Brook Besor contained more and more tents as people moved their families near the blessing of the springs.

29

Ǳ

One fall day, Acsah was serving Othniel his noon meal, when Oren asked permission to speak to him. "Master, we need to start preparing the soil for next year's crop. I've been collecting the animal dung to work into the soil, and ..."

"We aren't going to plant a crop this year, Oren."

"What do you mean we aren't planting a crop?" Oren's eyes stared in disbelief.

"It's the sabbatical year. We will trust the Lord to provide."

Acsah wanted to add to Oren's objections, but she kept quiet while he said, "Master, look out at all those tents. People are coming every day. All of them need food. I know we had an unbelievable crop last year, but can it sustain everyone who comes here? We'll all be starving before we can harvest a crop a year from now."

"I know how you feel, Oren. I've had my doubts about this at times, but what is trust if not exercised during impossible situations? We will not plant a crop this year."

Oren left shaking his head. Acsah came over to where Othniel sat and put her arms around him. "Have I ever told you how much I admire your godly faith?"

"If you have, I don't mind hearing it again."

"I do admire you, but I'm afraid Oren's right. We may run out if we have to keep feeding everyone who comes. Aren't you afraid?"

"Terrified. But, Acsah, you know that all through my life, whenever the situation seemed impossible, I've seen God deliver us, sometimes after a time of suffering. Always he's been true to his promises."

Acsah kissed the top of his head, which had become quite gray now, matching his beard. He reached back and pulled her around into his lap. His strong chest comforted her as she pressed her face into him. She wanted to trust Othniel and God, but she could see the store of grain going down every day.

———❦———

Acsah and Oren weren't the only ones with doubts. The men from the more than two hundred families who now resided in their wadi kept digging up the soil either around their tents or even up on Othniel's terraced fields. Othniel stopped them.

"Why won't you let us plant? We don't want to burden you. We can raise our own food while you observe the sabbatical."

Othniel insisted. "No one will plant during the sabbatical year. Put your trust in the Lord."

At last the people obeyed his command, but uneasiness stirred in the gathering of tents down in the wadi. He continued to provide them with food as they needed it.

One day, Othniel heard a shout from the lookout. He turned to see a line of what looked like armed men descending the hill on the north side. Instantly the alert sounded, and men came running with weapons in hand. The women gathered children and animals, herding both toward the valley of the springs, which could be defended as a fortress.

His men moved forward behind his leadership to meet the oncoming force, but suddenly a man ran ahead carrying an olive branch.

"What's this all about?" Othniel stopped.

Two more men broke away and came up to him, saluting him as though he were their commander. He recognized Josiah, the stranger who came months before needing help. Beside him, looking skeletal, stood Hamul.

"We come in peace, Othniel. We have come to ask you to lead us in driving Cushan out of Israel."

"You want me? Why?"

"We've never forgotten your military leadership at the battle of Kiriath Sepher, how you defeated the Anakites."

"Yes, but I'm only a farmer now."

"Look at what you've accomplished here in the Negev. Farms are failing all over the country, but you've managed to create a paradise here in this desert."

"The Lord gave this blessing."

"Are you saying the Lord blesses you while withholding his blessing from all of us?" This question from Nadab made Othniel hesitate. He really was saying that, but he didn't want to sound judgmental in front of all these men.

"I will have to think about this and pray."

The men nodded. Othniel could see they considered him their last hope. He recognized other men: Shemuel, Kemuel, Elidad, and many tribal leaders under Moses and Joshua. Their faces showed the effects of the famine.

"Come up to the house and be refreshed." Once again he was burdening Acsah and her servant girls with feeding famished men, but he needed time to get away and think. After settling the men with refreshments in the courtyard, he walked up to the area around the upper spring, which continued to cascade down to the pool below, a continuing reminder to him that God never stopped providing, that God had a plan. *Oh God, what is your plan now? Can we go up against these Arameans and win?*

The answer came to him as clearly as if he heard an audible voice— *Not while there is sin in the camp.*

He recognized the words God spoke to Joshua when Achan sinned, and he understood. *But God, I'm only an old Kenizzite, a stutterer, not dynamic like my Uncle Caleb. I've been farming for twelve years. Could I really lead an army now? Besides, they won't listen to me. They'll say I'm judging them or being intolerant of their choices if I tell them to turn away from their gods and turn back to you.* This time, Othniel heard no response, but the story of Moses and the burning bush came to his mind. God became angry at Moses for saying he couldn't speak to Pharaoh, and he understood why now. Moses didn't trust God to give him the words. He had to trust God. He had to convince those leaders to go back and follow God again before he would lead them.

He returned to the men where they sat in the fall chill by the fire of his courtyard. Josiah was telling how he returned to his home near Jerusalem and shared the miracle of this place down in the Negev and how inspiring Othniel had been to him personally. "After I told people about you, Othniel, they wanted to make you our leader."

Othniel let him finish before speaking. "I have prayed about your request, and the Lord says this to you. In his law God promised all the trouble that has fallen on Israel if our people intermarried with unbelieving Canaanites or followed their gods instead of following the Lord's decrees and commands. Do you remember the song we sang on Mt. Ebal and Mt. Gerizim? He told us what would happen—drought, wild animals, plague, famine, and invasion? How many of these has Israel experienced in the last few years?"

The men were nodding. Hamul spoke up. "All of those and in that order."

"You must do these before I will lead you—Chop down the Asherah poles; break down the altars to Baal; destroy the idols you have made

215

with your hands; give a tenth of your increase to the Lord; celebrate the Passover and other festivals before the Lord. And this year, do as I plan to do and leave your lands fallow for the sabbatical year."

Nadab shook his head. "This is a military matter, Othniel, not a religious matter. Don't confuse the two."

Othniel's courage rose. "I'm not confused. I know any success I've had as a military leader came because of the Lord. I cannot and will not lead unless he goes with me, and he will not unless Israel turns back to him."

Nadab turned away in disgust, but some of the other men were nodding. "We understand what you're saying, Othniel," said Shemuel. "We can stop serving the other gods, but we cannot leave the fields fallow. We're already starving as it is."

"Those are my conditions. God is faithful if we're obedient to all of his law, not just the convenient parts."

"Then we must return home to suffer and die," said Nadab.

"I'm not without compassion for your need. I will send a gift of food from the Lord's bounty to share with your loved ones." He ordered the servants to prepare sacks of barley to load on the leaders' donkeys.

As they turned to walk away from him, Othniel called out, "Return to me when you have returned to the Lord. Then he will help me lead you out from under the heel of your enemies." When they cleared the ridge, he went to find Acsah.

———

"You gave them sacks of grain?" Acsah couldn't believe he'd given so much away when their daily output to support the people in the wheat field already took so much.

"I couldn't let them starve, could I?"

"No, I guess not." Acsah wanted to say that they brought this on themselves and should face the consequences of their choices, but she understood Othniel's generosity. How many people could their grain supply support? "I'm glad the Lord didn't tell you to lead them against Cushan."

"The Lord didn't tell me not to lead. He told me to tell them we couldn't win unless they returned to the Lord." Othniel picked up a piece of melon left from what the men ate from the table beside them. "I told them, and they left. If they decide to take my advice, they'll be back."

"What did you tell them to do?"

"Tear down all the idols and leave their fields fallow."

Acsah nodded, thinking that if they did that, at least they wouldn't waste the grain they had sent by planting it during the drought. "Would you really go to war if they return?"

"That's up to the Lord."

She didn't like this answer. The idea of Othniel's going to war at his age against an opponent who had overrun Israel bothered her more than a little. For now, she could only wait and pray.

A few months later, the fields moved with activity. Othniel watched dozens of men harvesting grain in his terraced fields that no one had planted—a volunteer crop from the Lord. Gentle rains had fallen, so rare in the Negev. Since the Lord designated volunteer crops for the poor, and this year nearly everyone qualified except for his family, the fields would supply the needs of those living in the old wheat field. The Lord continued to provide. His heart filled again with praise, for the Lord's bounty exceeded his ability to doubt. And, he smiled to himself, he had enjoyed this year off from the constant backbreaking labor, another blessing from God.

As happened so many times, a lookout shouted someone was coming. His heart beat faster. He knew as a soldier any time could be the crucial time. Men scrambled out of the fields, throwing down farming tools and grabbing their always-ready weapons. Indeed, he could see arms flashing in the sun, but he quickly recognized the same leaders who had come before.

"We have come again, Othniel." Nadab spoke for the group this time. "You were right, and we were wrong. The grain we wanted to put into the ground would have been wasted. We did as you said. The Asherah poles provided us with heat this winter, and the hills have no altars on them anymore."

Hamul added, "We stopped anyone who tried to plant crops. We told them to live off their grain and trust God to supply. You know what happened? It rained. For the first time in seven years, the early rains came. We have volunteer crops, more than any crop we've had in all this time."

One leader, looking at the standing grain, accused Othniel. "But you planted crops here, didn't you?"

"No, this came up volunteer, too."

"But it's so much!"

"The Lord provides when we show him we trust him."

"So will you lead us against Cushan? We want to drive him out before he can burn up all our crops again."

"Yes. I believe the Lord will be with us, if all you say is true."

━━◆◆━━

"Acsah, I need to talk to you." Othniel's voice made her uneasy. The last time he had spoken that way, her father had been dying.

Putting aside the spinning wheel, she gave him her full attention. "What is it, dearest?"

"The leaders of Israel have returned, and they tell me they've obeyed what I told them to do."

"So you're going to lead in battle again."

"Yes. I've agreed to go. The people have proven to me they truly are willing to go back to serving and worshiping the Lord and only Him."

"Where will you get men to fight?"

"The leaders will return and spread the word among their tribes. Men can come down here in twos and threes, so as not to cause suspicion among Cushan's soldiers. They won't bring many supplies with them."

"Othniel, I know the volunteer crops came up, but how will we feed an army on what we have left from the sabbatical year and plant ourselves? And don't say, 'The Lord will provide.' I need more assurance than that." Her voice shook as the anxiety she had felt all this year spilled out. She didn't want to complain, but they had a family to support. Couldn't he see that?

Othniel looked surprised at her outburst. "All right, I won't say it." His silence then upset her more than arguing. Turning, she left the room calling over her shoulder, "You can tell the servant girls what you want them to fix for your guests."

Her mind in turmoil, she found herself standing by the splashing upper spring near the top terraces. From there she could see everything spread out before her—the hundreds of tents of the refugees, the men harvesting grain the Lord had watered, the melon and cucumber plants coming up volunteer beside her, soon to produce more food for those people. The Lord had provided.

She swallowed down a sob. Why couldn't she have faith like Othniel? All the fears she felt, like running out of food or losing Othniel in the wars, were not real, only imagination. At this moment, they had plenty for themselves and for others.

She knew Othniel waited in the house for her to come make things right between them, but first, she must make things right with God. *I know, Lord, that my fear is sin because I'm not trusting you. Help me remember that as I face challenges ahead, and help me do my part.*

Having surrendered her own wishes to the Lord's, she knew what she must do. Othniel was putting his own life in danger by taking on this leadership role. As the leader's wife, she couldn't shirk her duty. She must sacrifice the family's food for this cause. Not only that, these men must be fed by her hand.

❧

The leaders returned after spreading the word Othniel would lead Israel if they would come and fight. Over the next few weeks, men came to join them, some grizzled, clutching rusty swords not used in years. Others were young men carrying long knives or slingshots. Every day, more troops appeared on the ridge. Othniel posted a sentry on that side of the valley to cut down on the number of false alarms. As the men came, he checked their armour. Most of what they had wouldn't work. How could they win a battle without adequate weapons? *Dear Lord, this need is beyond me. I'm trusting you.*

Then one day, Jethro came striding up to his house. "Reporting for duty, Sir."

"You're welcome, Jethro. Would you lead a thousand? We probably won't have even ten thousand men."

"I wouldn't be too sure of that from what I've seen, but anyway, I've brought something for you. Come see." He led Othniel out to the path below the valley. There Othniel saw a train of donkeys, all loaded down. Jethro untied the bindings, revealing weapons, hundreds of them. "The Kenites have brought fresh supplies of armour from what we had to supply those men not ready for battle."

Othniel couldn't speak for a few minutes. "Jethro, I don't know how to thank you. This may be the saving of us."

Jethro didn't answer, just clasped Othniel's hand and began to unload the animals.

❧

Acsah dipped savory stew into the cups of the men who had not brought provisions. The line stretched far back and the look of hunger in their pinched faces hurt her. One man's lips trembled as he took the food. "Are you all right, Soldier?"

He shook his head and his throat moved in a convulsive swallow. "I wish I could give some of this food to my wife and children. Why should I eat while they are starving?"

Acsah handed him a piece of bread. "Because you need your strength to fight. The sooner we put Cushan out of our land, the sooner they can have food again." He moved on, but she couldn't help overhearing stories worse than his as men passed through the food lines— fields burned and sheep stolen, women raped and carried off, children dying in their mother's arms. How much suffering did it take to get people's attention?

"Mother, can I talk to you?"

"What is it, Hathath?" Acsah saw that most of the men had been served, so she set down her copper ladle and gave her attention to this twelve-year-old with the earnest expression.

"I think I should go with Father."

She could see he was serious, so she proceeded carefully. "Why do you want to go to war?"

"I overheard Father say they needed more troops. I've been practicing with my sword, and I'm almost as tall as a man."

She didn't laugh, but she didn't think he would be hard to dissuade. "Your father would be proud of you for wanting to help, but I need you here to protect me and the other children."

"You'll have Oren and Asa and Nathan. I should fight for my people, shouldn't I?"

Acsah took him into her arms and said with a sigh, "Not yet, my son. Wait until you're older."

He didn't answer her, so she thought he agreed.

30

Othniel underestimated the number of men who would come to fight. Salmon came to him one day after the new men coming slowed to very few. "We've counted. You have over 30,000 men."

"That's more than I expected. We need to get organized. I want you to be my next in command. What do you think about Jethro, Elah, and Shemuel as leaders of ten thousand?"

"That's good. You have a balance of Kenite, Kenizzite, and Israelite among your leaders. And they're the best, I think."

"We'll let them choose their own leaders of thousands and hundreds. I've been doing training exercises with the men, but we really need to organize that by units. We need more bows and arrows."

"Do we have wood for making them?"

"We can organize a search party. I'll ask Acsah if the women can make string for the bows."

Acsah saw Othniel coming up to the house in the middle of the day. Lately, she didn't see him unless around a cooking pot with other men or very late at night. Was something the matter? She almost spilled the barley meal in her hurry to go to him. "Othniel, what's happening?"

"Nothing to alarm." His abrupt manner and preoccupation reminded her of how shut out she felt when he got into his military mode, more concerned with weapons and strategies than with his family.

"What can I do for you?" Acsah dusted her hands on her shift and waited, tense with overwork and nerves.

"We need about a thousand strings of medium weight, as strong and tight as you can make them for bows. Two cubits in length."

Acsah stared at him. He couldn't be serious, could he? She and her servant girls had been cooking food for so many men for days—and now *this*. She answered slowly. "I'll see what I can do."

After he left, she turned to Dinah. "Did you hear what he said?"

Dinah nodded. "I'll get my spindle. We have plenty of wool floss in storage."

Acsah sighed. "If you can make the strings, maybe Miriam and I can handle the food."

One day as she and Miriam ground grain for the huge pots of porridge she prepared each day to feed the men, Rahab came to see her. "What are you doing?" Rahab's gaze went from the large mound of ground barley to the pots of boiling water.

Acsah pushed her hair aside with the back of her hand. "I'm grinding grain."

"I can see that, but why so much? Are you expecting guests?"

"We already have guests." Acsah waved her floury hand in the direction of the tents in the old grain field.

Rahab's face reflected her dawning comprehension. "Why didn't you let me know? I could have been helping you. Does Azubah know what you're doing?"

"I hadn't really thought about asking for help. God wants me to feed these men."

"And I believe he wants me to help you. This is too much work for you and Miriam alone." She took the grinding stone out of Acsah's hand. "Here, let me."

Acsah watched as Rahab began to grind the grain with her skilled fingers. Then she turned, and after wiping her hands, picked up a knife to skin the carcass of a sheep for the evening stew. She looked up and saw Rahab looking at her again. "What?"

"You can't keep this up. Let's ask all the available women."

The next day, Rahab arrived with Azubah and thirty other women with her. Azubah ran forward and shook her finger at Acsah. "We all want to help. Tell us what you've been doing."

Acsah beamed at her friends. "Miriam and I make several large pots of barley porridge for the morning meal and bread with meat stew for the evening meal. And Dinah is spinning strings for bows."

"Where are you getting the food and wool to do this?" Another woman spoke up then.

"From her own stores and flock." Azubah answered before Acsah could stop her.

"That isn't right. You shouldn't have to bear the entire burden. If each of us donates a sheep, we can keep this going for a month and deplete no one's herds." Other women nodded their heads at this idea.

"I can provide a sheep for this evening." A young woman whom Acsah knew had come with her husband and very little else dashed off before Acsah could object.

Rahab laid her hand on Acsah's arm. "Let them share, Acsah. God is honored when anyone gives for his service."

After that, things got better for Acsah. She organized the women to prepare food in shifts, so no one had too much to do. They made pot after pot of porridge and stew, and mountains of bread. The grain supplies never ran low. To remind Othniel that he had a family, she took little Rachel to carry water to her father out in the fields where the men practiced archery with the bows newly strung with Dinah's good string. Othniel looked up when he saw them coming, and his expression turned from stern to doting. Acsah liked to watch this change from the leader of men to the tender father of a small daughter. She could remember her own father treating her so. She had forgotten how things could be for the military family. *God, help me remember to support him and not become a burden on him by my selfish demands.*

One day, Othniel appeared at the house again. "Acsah, come walk with me."

She looked up from the grain she was grinding, surprised to see him at this time. She hesitated, looking at the bag of grain still waiting to be ground. What new project might he have for them to do? But seeing a look of yearning in his eyes, she set the grinding stone aside. Covering it with a cloth and dusting off her hands, she joined Othniel as he led the way up the hill behind the house. They reached the top of the hill, and he led her out above the terracing, where she could see all the activity in the fields below them.

"Do you see that group over there?" Othniel pointed to some men practicing their archery. "They've been working on their own, and I think their aim has gotten pretty good." He turned to her. "Thank you for supplying us with string for the bows."

Acsah blushed, remembering her earlier reluctance. "You're welcome. So do you think you'll need to use archers against Cushan?"

"I honestly don't know. But I wouldn't say that to anyone but you."

"I won't tell." She looked out at the area they still called the wheat field after all these years, though no crop had grown there in ages. The number of tents in the wadi now reminded her of the camp of Israel in the wilderness. "What do you think your chances are?"

Othniel rubbed his graying beard in a characteristic movement she loved. "So many things could hamper us. If reinforcements come from Aram, or Cushan manages to set up in a walled city, we don't have the resources to do a siege. We'd starve before they would."

Acsah turned and put her hands on either side of his face, forcing him to look at her. The uncertainty of his expression reminded her of the way he used to look at the mention of her father. "You believe the Lord is on your side, don't you?"

"Yes."

"Well, then." She stopped talking and watched as his brow unfurrowed and a smile came into his eyes.

"Thank you, Acsah. I needed to remember that."

As she continued looking at the troops, Acsah saw that given this group of men, the Lord would need to be with them.

"Have I told you lately that I love you?" Othniel spoke softly, but she heard every word.

"I don't mind hearing it again." She knew he would understand the depth of her emotion, though she kept her tone light. Then there in full view of anyone who might be looking, the leader of the Israelite army pulled her into his embrace and kissed her deeply. No, Othniel hadn't forgotten he had a wife.

—◆—

Othniel met with his leaders to plan. Salmon spoke first. "Cushan is relying on starvation to keep the population under control. He has very small units of men at all the small towns and cities, spread very thin over all of Israel. But Cushan himself has a larger force, which he has billeted at Gilgal."

Jethro laughed. "Maybe because he didn't want to stray far from water himself."

Othniel drew a map on the ground. "We need to strike directly at Gilgal, then. We don't want to give away our approach by going up through here." He pointed to the hill country. "We'd be fighting small skirmishes the whole way and delaying. By the time we could get to Gilgal, their larger force would be ready for us."

He remembered the trek he made south from Gilgal when Caleb banished him. He had seen no one the whole day. People didn't frequent the path along the Salt Sea as much, and the army could avoid En Gedi. He drew a line from Arad to Gilgal through the Negev. "By going this way, with disciplined marching we can get within striking distance in less than 24 hours."

"We'll need to take plenty of water with us." Shemuel made a good point. "But we can do it." The others nodded.

The next day, Othniel announced that the army was ready. They made preparations to leave the next morning. Acsah could feel fear rising in her, but she tamped it down. The men she loved made war all through her childhood. But this time, if Othniel didn't come back, she had three children still not raised and the responsibility of the farm and all these women whose men were also going away. But she summoned her courage, cooked a marvelous dinner, and then met him in their room after everyone else went to sleep.

She pulled off her shift and settled down on the mat, pulling her blanket close and watching him as he rubbed oil into his leather shield. "You're going to be a brilliant leader."

"I'm unworthy."

"No one but you thinks so. Don't you believe God prepared you for this time?"

"I want to believe that. With so many things against us—untried youths, aged soldiers, a shortage of good weapons and supplies—we should fail. But the Lord promised to be with us. The people have chosen to trust and follow him again."

"Your speeches have inspired them."

"Ironic, isn't it? I, who could hardly talk without stuttering." He set the shield aside and picked up his sword to sharpen it.

Acsah remembered with regret the time she once made him stutter.

"I haven't stuttered in years, and I only did when I talked to your father."

"Or me," Acsah muttered.

Othniel's look was tender. He stopped sharpening his sword and set it back in its sheath. Then blowing out the lamp, he came to lie beside her, pulling her into his arms. "We went through some hard times before we married and during those early years, but you've been a wonderful wife to me, Acsah. I could never have asked for a better one." The familiar comfort of being nestled against his chest filled her with bittersweet feelings. How had they come to this point of loving understanding?

She lifted her lips to his for a long tender kiss. "You know, when we were younger, I thought you were blessed to have me for a wife, but now I know I should be grateful to the Lord. I'm blessed to have you."

Othniel lay so quiet that Acsah stirred in his arms. "Are you all right?"

Othniel replied, "I was remembering a dream I had on perhaps the worst night of my life."

"Tell me about it. Was it a nightmare?"

"No, my life felt like a nightmare at that time, but the dream wasn't like a story. I thought…"

She waited in the dark, her breath against his chest warming her nose in the chill air.

"You might think I'm crazy. I believe the Lord spoke to me through my dream."

"What did he say to you?"

"He said what was happening at that time—my being sent away from you, believing you would be married to someone else, even my stumbling through the Negev to find these springs—would somehow work out not only for my good and yours, but for the whole nation of Israel. I couldn't see it then, but the words gave me comfort. Now I can see how all the parts fit together."

"You're right. These springs have provided for us and the army of Israel during this time of crisis."

"Yes, and God knew my marrying you would involve conquering Kiriath Sepher. People remembered that, so they called on me to deliver the people now."

"And to call them back to the Lord."

"What the Lord said came true. I had trouble believing it then. My future seemed in ruins." He pulled her closer to him and kissed her nose. "I wonder how much heartache we would avoid by trusting that the Lord has a plan. He makes the bad things of life turn out better than we can imagine."

"I think I'll trust God to take care of you in the battle to free Israel from the king of Aram. But I will miss you."

Othniel hugged her again. "I'll miss you, too, my love."

Acsah held his embrace and words close to her heart in the days that followed.

31

The next morning, Othniel stood on the threshing floor, overlooking the troops before him. Among those below stood men he'd known for years, men he'd fought beside in battles from the east of the Jordan through the whole of Canaan. His friend Salmon looked up at him with an encouraging smile.

Behind those ranged younger men, many too young to fight when Joshua died. And behind those stood Canaanites, Gibeonites, Kenites, and others who had joined with Israel. What could he say to make them understand?

"Men, we would not be standing here at all if not for one thing— the greatness of our God. Many of you were with us and saw the miracles he performed to bring us to this land. If not, I hope your parents or neighbours have told you of how God delivered us out of slavery in Egypt, provided us with all we needed to live for forty years in the desert, gave us good laws for our benefit as a people, and brought us into this land, driving out our enemies before us as we trusted him to do so.

"Yet our people have sinned against this wonderful God, not counting on his consistency. He blesses those who trust in him; he promises to punish those who do not. Has he broken covenant with us? No, we have broken covenant with him."

The men were looking up at him now with rapt attention. "We promised Joshua we would worship the Lord only eleven years ago. Yet we have had orgies around poles, sacrificed our children, and committed abominations far worse than just forbidden adultery. So why are we surprised that there has been a drought, that our prosperity has failed, and that foreign invaders have come and stolen away our property, our wives, and our children? Didn't the Lord say this would happen?"

Some men were nodding now. Others, even some younger ones, shifted uncomfortably. But Othniel continued, "Those of you who have gathered here have told me you have burned your poles and broken down the altars on high places. That's a start, but if we want the Lord on our side, we must do more than just temporarily remove temptation from around us. We need to change the way we think. The Lord loves us. He has chosen us. He wants to bless us, but he is holy and jealous. He will not tolerate our infidelities to him and to his law. We must worship him and him alone. We must obey his laws. But most of all, we must love him with all our hearts, and souls, and strength! Do you agree?"

"Yes! We will!" The roar of 30,000 male voices echoed from the walls of the wadi's hills.

Othniel waited until the sound died down. "Then I believe we can go into battle with faith the Lord will be on our side. If the Lord fights for us, we cannot fail."

Another roar greeted this pronouncement. Some held up their swords and spears and shook them. Their reaction to his speech dazzled Othniel. Would Uncle Caleb have believed his stuttering nephew could ever speak and get this kind of reaction?

Taking his own sword in hand, he made his way down off the rock and led north from the wadi toward Cushan-Rishathaim, king of Aram Naharaim.

———————

Acsah waited until the men had cleared the ridge. She had kept her composure for Othniel's sake while he said goodbye and made his stirring speech, but now she gave vent to her feelings in the inner room of the house, away from the children and servants. "Oh, God, protect him," she moaned with tears choking her and an ache growing inside her. The silence of the house after all the activity of the last few weeks oppressed her. She had little to do except fix meals for the children, so she gave herself up to the luxury of self-pity.

Finally, in late afternoon, she rose from her mat and began grinding the barley for the evening meal. She finished putting the hot bread and fruit on the table, calling to the children. "Hathath, Meonathai, Rachel. Come to supper."

Meonathai and Rachel came running from play down by the pool, but she saw no sign of Hathath. "Did Hathath go with Boaz to his tent for supper?"

"I don't know, Mother, maybe." Meonathai reached for a piece of bread.

Acsah debated with herself. Should she go looking for Hathath now or wait until after they had eaten? It wasn't like him to be late for a meal or not to tell where he was going. She chided herself. He was twelve now and needed more independence.

Bedtime came, but he still hadn't appeared. Acsah began to wonder. This behavior was so unlike her compliant son. She walked down to Rahab's tent. "Have you seen Hathath today?"

Rahab looked surprised and turned to Boaz. "I haven't. Have you, Boaz?"

Boaz shook his head. "Not today."

Rahab threw on her head covering. "Let's check with the other mothers who have children his age. I'll go with you."

They went from tent to tent, but no one had seen Hathath. Acsah couldn't imagine where he might have gone. Finally, one young boy spoke up. "He told me he was going to battle with his father. I saw him with the soldiers today carrying his sword."

The realization hit Acsah like a stone, and she lost consciousness.

Her next awareness was waking up on the floor of Rahab's tent with several concerned people looking at her. She groaned, "What happened?"

Rahab wrung out a cloth and put it on her head. "You fainted, so we brought you here."

Then Acsah remembered. "Hathath has gone to the battle. We must do something." She scrambled to get up, but Rahab gently pushed her back down.

"There isn't anything we can do now. We don't even know for sure where they went, and by now they may be engaged in battle. He's with his father, Acsah."

Rahab's calm voice helped some, but Acsah couldn't push her panic down. "He told me he wanted to go, but I didn't take him seriously. I should have told Othniel. This is dreadful." The image of her son, her baby, in harm's way made her frantic, especially knowing he was beyond her help. She had to trust him to Othniel's and God's protection.

———————

As they marched, Othniel wondered about the men with him. How many broken hearts were making this Salt Sea journey, men who lost wives or sweethearts to the drought or had them snatched away by rapacious enemy soldiers? How many children died of starvation or were sacrificed in the fires? So much pain they could have avoided if they had not stopped following the true God.

Now he needed to concentrate on winning this battle, to end the devastation from the outside force and bring faith in God back to the people. He called the two men he had chosen as spies. "Run ahead of us to Gilgal. Find out the strength of the city's defenses, number of troops, the expectations. Come back to me as soon as possible."

"Yes, Sir." They set off at a swift pace that he knew would get them back in time.

His hope lay in surprise. If Cushan weren't concerned about an armed force coming against him, he might not have built a wall. Gilgal didn't have a wall before.

All day the troops marched. The sun became hotter. Two hours before sunset, the spies came back to them from Gilgal. Othniel called a halt and a rest while he consulted with them. "What's the news?"

"Cushan's there in the city. He has 40,000 troops." The breathless spy bent over, wheezing from running in the heat.

"And a wall?"

The other spy answered. "They have built a wall around the city, but they haven't finished it yet on the east side. That side has a heavy guard on it. Their gates are wooden logs. They have no moat, but the city sits on a hill, so they will see us coming."

"What about expectation?"

"They do not fear an attack at all. They're confident of no resistance."

"Give these men some water and food." Othniel thought hard. They had the advantage of surprise and the weakened wall. The disadvantages included the large force there and the city's high ground.

He called his leaders over. "I think we need to make best use of our archers. If they can get off several good volleys at the force on that weakened east side without retaliation, we could charge without danger from their archers. I want all the archers on the east side, regardless of unit. Then I want one unit to feign an attack on the northwest side as near the gate as you can without being hit. You must draw attention away from the east side.

"Meanwhile the rest of us will rain arrows on the guards on the east side, then charge in before they can recover themselves."

Salmon approved. "Sounds brilliant to me."

The others promised to do their parts. Othniel would lead the charge, flanked by Salmon and Shemuel. Jethro would bring up the second unit behind the first on the east side, and Elah would lead the diversion force.

With their plans firmly in mind, they marched on past dark, getting as close as possible to Gilgal without being visible from its elevated position surrounded by the Jordan River plain. They rested for a few hours, but Othniel had them up before dawn. He then spoke once more to the troops. "Remember to trust God, obey orders, and fight for your lives and homes."

Then in the gray light of early dawn, he watched as Elah led troops over to the northwest side. The unit looked tiny in comparison to the city and the walls that towered above them. Then Elah's troops yelled and began their feigned attack. Arrows rained down, falling short of them.

Meanwhile, Othniel led his troops on the double quick from their position to the east side. The darkness gave them some cover. By the time they were in place, they could see the city. He gave the command for the archers to move in and begin shooting inside range. Their accuracy impressed him as a hail of arrows fell among the guards standing by the eastern side. The guards fell or pulled back from their positions. As he hoped, the enemy archers were distracted by the attack to the west, so no arrows came in return.

"Now!" Othniel shouted and ran forward with Salmon by his side and Shemuel just behind on his right. They reached the wall before the Arameans could recover and began battling one-on-one with the men pouring out. Man after man came toward him. Othniel lost count of how many heads he severed from bodies or legs he slashed from underneath. Around him he glimpsed Israelites fighting manfully. But he noticed another phenomenon as they made their way deeper into the city. The Benjamite residents of Gilgal were fighting as well. He spotted one woman on a roof, pouring boiling water on an Aramean soldier as he hurried down a street. Old men were using their hoes and shovels as weapons. Cushan had enemies on the inside and the outside.

Suddenly Israelite soldiers before him gave way. He didn't know, but he guessed the muscular Aramean coming toward him to be Cushan-Rishathaim, King of Aram, bellowing with rage. Just as Othniel planted his feet and prepared to engage him, a small Israelite dashed between them and challenged Cushan. "Don't you hurt my father."

Hathath! Here? But he had no time to think or question. Cushan raised his sword to decapitate the small soldier in front of him. Before he could bring it down, Othniel's shield came between them, taking the stroke, which jammed his shield arm into his shoulder. He winced in pain, but his drive to save his son made him come forward with his sword to block the next few strokes, matching Cushan's power and speed. The whole battle seemed to hinge on what happened between them. In the midst of dodging strokes and dealing them, Othniel remembered that the Lord was his strength. He felt the Spirit of the Lord giving him the power he needed. With a sudden upper cut he drove his sword into Cushan's side. Cushan's eyes lost focus, and he fell over at Othniel's feet—dead.

The Aramean soldiers who saw Cushan fall panicked and ran toward the city gates. Othniel turned to see where Hathath had gone. Was he safe? He found his son at last, crouching in a doorway with sobs shaking his small body. The would-be soldier had become a small boy again as Othniel put his arms around him.

"Oh, Father. He tried to kill me."

"I know." As Othniel hugged him, he became aware of his injured shoulder throbbing with pain. "But it's all over now."

They heard a cry of victory. Othniel and Hathath walked to the western gate, where they saw the last of the Arameans who had run out that way battling with Elah's men. Soon those Arameans also were dead. Elah told Othniel later how they opened the gates and poured out, trying to escape. "But we were waiting for them, ready to have our share in the fighting. No one got past us."

Othniel took Hathath with him to stand on the ramparts looking down on the city and field of battle. Victory gave exhilaration, but he felt humbled, knowing the victory came from the Lord. *Thank you, Lord for blessing your unworthy servant and freeing Israel from her oppressor. And thank you for protecting this son of mine.*

Later, Salmon noticed how he favored his left shoulder. "Okay, commander. What have you done to yourself?"

Othniel told him about the battle with Cushan. "I couldn't believe it when I looked up and saw Hathath. Acsah must be frantic."

"Do you have any men who didn't handle the bodies?"

"I'll find out. Why?"

"If I were you, I'd send a message back to Brook Besor that we've won the battle and attach a message that your son is safe. You don't have to supply the details." Salmon grinned at him.

"I'll do that." He turned his body too quickly and gasped.

"But first, I'm going to bind up that sprained shoulder so you don't make it worse." Salmon pulled some strips of cloth from his pack that could be used for binding.

Hathath shared his blanket that night, but the next day, Othniel sent him to stay under the watchful eye of his uncle Elah and cousin Kenaz. He had plenty to do as commander. He called everyone to attention. "Phinehas has come himself from Shiloh to help perform the cleansing ceremonies. The priests will come around to sprinkle you with the cleansing liquid."

A young man standing near him looked surprised. "What are we doing, Sir?"

"The cleansing ceremony for those who have handled dead bodies. And your name, Soldier?"

"Abiathar from the tribe of Benjamin."

"What do you know about God's laws, Abiathar?"

"My parents told me a little, but they didn't seem to think they mattered too much. My father worried more about crops than religion."

"What laws do you know about?"

Abiathar shifted his feet. "Didn't God forbid having sex?"

Othniel cringed at this misunderstanding of God's law. "No. He only forbid adultery, sex outside of marriage."

"That would do away with Asherah pole parties and Baal prostitutes, wouldn't it?"

"Precisely. Those things are specifically forbidden in the law, as is any worship of gods other than the Lord. Abiathar, if we organized some studies of the law this week, would you and your friends like to understand why this matters?"

"I suppose we should. You really believe it made the difference in this battle, don't you?"

"I do."

Later that evening, Othniel found Phinehas in his tent. "Do you happen to have a copy of the law Moses read before he died?"

Phinehas rose and brought out a scroll. "I brought this, hoping it would be of some use."

"Tomorrow, I want you to read this aloud to our troops. Some younger men in particular haven't heard it." Othniel peered at his face in the gloom. "Do you think it's a good idea?"

"Wonderful. It's so good to have a leader again who motivates the people to repent and worship the Lord."

"I'm only a military leader. I agreed to defeat Cushan, not lead all Israel."

"From what I've heard, the whole country has turned back to worship the Lord as a result of your influence. We need another Joshua."

"Another Joshua? I'm not fluent when I speak. Joshua gave marvelous speeches."

"Now you sound like another national leader we both knew and loved. I don't think you can escape the expectations, Othniel."

Othniel couldn't respond. For the first time in years, he feared a stuttering episode.

"Pray about it. The Lord will show you. By the way, one of my cousins in Hebron told me you saved their lives last year when you brought your first fruits offering to them. He sends his gratitude."

Dazed by Phinehas's assumption that he would lead Israel, Othniel went out to the Jordan River to think and pray. *Lord God. Is this part of your plan for Acsah and me?* He heard the sound of the river flowing nearby, a call of a bird not quite settled for the night, crickets chirping. *I am willing to do whatever you show me.*

The next day, Phinehas stood and read the law aloud to the soldiers. Some townspeople came out and stood listening as well. The reading caused a lot of comment among the soldiers. Many came up to him afterward to ask questions. "That part about the blessings and curses, you believe the drought and invasion happened to us because we followed after idols, don't you?"

"I do believe that."

"Couldn't it have been coincidence?"

Othniel shook his head. "Not in my experience. All my life, I've found obedience brings blessing and disobedience brings suffering. I've observed it, and I believe it. You won't know for yourselves unless you put the law into your own lives. But everyone must do it before Israel can be blessed."

"I'm going to follow the law," said Abiathar. Several others nodded.

As the time drew to an end, the word came from all over Israel that Aramean soldiers were abandoning their posts when they heard about Cushan's death, or, in some places, the local men overcame them. Othniel realized they had won the war by killing Cushan. They could all go home now. Would Acsah be all right? He hoped she had received the message. She would be so upset. The thought of her reminded him how much he missed her.

The last sprinkling and bath ended. Othniel made a speech to the men gathered below him as he stood on the walls of Gilgal. "Now that you have turned back to the Lord and learned more about him, don't go back to worshiping the gods of Canaan. They could not save you from Cushan as the Lord has done. They do not control the rains as the Lord does. He is a good and loving God. Worship him and him alone. I expect to see all of you at Shiloh at the First Fruits Festival."

His own band of men whose wives and children waited back in the wadi by the valley of the springs fell in behind him as he started south with Hathath safely by his side. As they walked, Othniel looked at his son, so tall for his age, but still just a boy. "Hathath?"

"Yes, Father?"

"I want you to know that I'm proud of you for wanting to fight in the battle and for coming against Cushan in my defense."

Hathath nodded with a solemn expression. His look of childlike innocence would never fully return after what he had seen.

Othniel gripped his shoulder. "Son, I need to tell you this. A man doesn't become a soldier from practicing a little with his sword or from wanting to defeat the enemy. A soldier has to endure training and become mature and strong before he can fight in the battle."

"I know now, Father. At least I wasn't killed."

"No, praise the Lord. Why do think that's true?"

"Because you took the blow intended for me."

"That's right. You couldn't survive the battle without my help, just as I couldn't win the victory without God's help. Never forget that, Son. God loves you even more than I do."

"Mother's going to be upset with me, isn't she?"

"I imagine so. Let's not tell her too many of the details, okay?"

"Okay, Father."

32

━━━━━ ❦ ━━━━━

Acsah sat with Rahab in the courtyard listening to the water splash down from the upper spring into the lower spring. She wasn't as distressed as she had been earlier in the week. A messenger had come from Othniel, assuring them that they had won the battle and Hathath was all right. Still she wouldn't feel comfortable until she saw them herself.

Rahab spun wool while Acsah made baskets. "Rahab, why do I prefer making baskets to spinning and weaving? You don't seem to mind, but dealing with cloth makes me irritable."

Rahab laughed as she threaded her yarn into the loom. "Perhaps God did that on purpose, making each of us good at different things. Instead of feeling inadequate or jealous, we can work together as we are today. You supply me with baskets, and I make blankets for both households."

"The best part is doing it together this way. I'm almost glad for the drought. It's been wonderful having you here." She picked up another wheat straw and worked it into the pattern she was making.

"At least we're finished with the ceaseless cooking for now except for ourselves and the children."

Acsah sighed. "Yes, you're right, but I'd love to be cooking again if it meant the men were back and safe."

"They have to fight, don't they?" The wistful quality of Rahab's voice made Acsah smile in sympathy.

"I believe so. I would like to think all the fighting Othniel and Salmon have ever done, they did because they sincerely believed God was telling them to do it."

"Yes. Even the conquering." Rahab stopped to tie off some threads.

237

"That's harder to understand in some ways. To the Canaanites, we're invaders come to take their lands and drive them out. And I suppose that's true."

"But God ordered it because Canaanite culture is so wicked he used the Israelites to clean that out, just as he used the Arameans to punish the Israelites when they fell into the sinful Canaanite practices."

"Do you think God would have spared the Canaanites if they had turned to him in repentance?"

"He spared me."

"I'm so glad he did." They sat working in companionable silence. Acsah looked over at Rahab as she wove the cloth. Rahab understood the nature of God better than most Israelites, even though she had grown up in Canaanite culture. "Well, now at least, Israel has repented and the Lord is blessing again. I wonder if a time will ever come when Israel will refuse to repent, even when they have the chance. What would happen then?"

"According to the law, the enemies will overrun the country and take the people into exile. I shudder to think of the misery that will produce."

"Why can't we learn from studying the law, Rahab? Why do we have to have terror and hunger before we are ready to listen?"

"I don't know, Acsah. Maybe because of our sin nature, the sin of Adam inside all of us. We want to do what we want without interference from anyone, even God."

"Yes. That makes sense."

As she and Rahab continued their work in the courtyard, she thanked God again for the wonderful friend he had given her in Rahab. The thought of all Rahab meant in her life, strengthening her faith and showing her how to be a good wife and mother, made her teary.

"Are you all right, Acsah?"

"I'm thinking of what a dear friend you are. I suppose when the men come back you'll have to return to Bethlehem."

Rahab set her spindle down and hugged her. "Your friendship rescued me when I didn't know anything about life in Israel. You taught me to speak Hebrew and how to follow the law. When no one else would be my friend, you were."

"Your faith has steadied me through the years. You taught me how to really love God, not just obey him from fear."

Rahab smiled at Acsah, then took up her spinning again.

"Mistress?"

Acsah looked up in surprise to see Oren and Asa standing at the entrance to the courtyard. "Yes, Oren?"

He came forward in uncharacteristic shyness. "Asa and I have been talking a lot lately about your god. But this week when we got the word that Othniel had won the battle against Cushan, I finally understood something."

Looking at Asa's smile, Acsah nodded her head. "What do you realize?"

"Othniel is the only truly godly man I know, and God blesses him every time. Only a true and powerful God could have taken the troops that I saw here and used them to defeat seasoned warriors. I believe in him now myself."

"Oh, Oren. That's wonderful. We've been praying for you for a long time."

"Really, Mistress. You cared enough to pray for me?"

Rahab entered the conversation. "The law of the Lord commands us to care about our neighbors, to love them as ourselves. Oren, you knew I became a believer as a Canaanite, didn't you?"

Oren nodded. "I thought you did it to marry Salmon."

"No, I believed because of God's love for me, long before I met Salmon. His love is his best attribute, better even than his power."

Asa commented, "You know you'll have to be circumcised, don't you?"

"Yes, I'm ready, as soon as Master Othniel returns."

Acsah felt such joy at Oren's declaration that it took her several minutes to sense a change in the activity around the tent encampment. She stood and looked out into the wadi. Why were people milling around like that? Then her children and Boaz came running up. "They're coming."

"Can we go meet them, please?"

"Some older boys spotted them."

"Rachel go, too?"

Acsah laughed with delight at their exuberance. Turning to Rahab, she said, "Let's go greet the men when they come into camp."

"That's a good idea. I like that."

Acsah picked up little Rachel and carried her on her hip while she and Rahab started down the path to the wadi.

They didn't have to go far before Acsah could see the men marching over the ridge to the northeast, with Othniel and Salmon leading. Othniel looked so tall and commanding that for a moment she became the young girl with a crush she once had been. Her hero had returned. Then she saw the sling holding up his left arm and hurried faster. Behind him she caught a glimpse of Hathath walking double-quickly to keep up with the long legs of the leaders.

Before the army came very far, a crowd of women and children surged into the middle of them, and order collapsed as men and women embraced and children clung to their father's legs.

Othniel grabbed Acsah and Rachel together in a big one-armed hug. Acsah clung to him, so relieved to feel him alive and victorious. "Welcome home, my husband. What have you done to your arm?"

His bronzed, muscular arm tightened around her. "I'll tell you about it later. I missed you." His voice was soft, but she cherished his words. "Now, let's see this little girl who came all the way out to see me." He picked up little Rachel with his right arm and swung her into the air as he had Acsah so many years before. Acsah found Hathath being questioned by his adoring younger brother. "How was the battle?"

She took Hathath into her arms, her tears freely falling on his shoulder.

"Mother, I'm so sorry. I know now I shouldn't have gone." He pleaded with his eyes for forgiveness.

"I forgive you, Son. You wanted to help. I need to remember that you are becoming a man and to take your words seriously next time." Acsah clung to him a while longer, so happy to feel the life in his young body.

Soon the whole crowd moved back to the wadi. Acsah clung to Hathath's hand on one side and Othniel's good arm on the other. When they reached the house, she hurried in to fix a good welcome home dinner for her men.

— ◆ —

After they finally settled the children that evening, Othniel took Acsah by the hand. "Let's go for a walk by the cascade from the upper spring."

She turned to him. "Oren has decided to believe in God. He wants to be circumcised."

"Wonderful. What made the difference?"

Acsah told him what Oren had said. "I believe he's really sincere, though he has a lot to learn yet."

"I'll have a talk with him. God has answered so many of my prayers. That one has taken over thirteen years." They stood in the peaceful glen below the waterfall, feeling a mist rise from it and enjoying the evening coolness. "I missed you, Acsah."

"I know. I missed you, too. But to be honest, my terror about Hathath overwhelmed all other emotions." She looked at him with a question in her eyes. "You haven't really given me a straight answer about your shoulder sprain. How did it happen?"

Othniel knew he had promised Hathath not to tell much, but he couldn't withhold information from Acsah. "I was defending a soldier from being killed by Cushan and held my shield too far extended."

"Which soldier?"

Othniel sighed. How did she know to ask that? "Hathath."

Acsah turned pale. "He was in the actual battle?"

"I didn't know until that moment that he had come with us." He could tell the news brought horrible images into her mind. "The Lord protected both of us."

"Yes, I know. I've never prayed so much in my life before."

He squeezed her hand. "I can understand that. I learned something from this incident."

"What's that?"

"I always believed I loved Hathath, but not until I saw that sword about to take off his head…" Her gasp interrupted him. "I'm sorry, bad choice of words."

"Go on. I can stand it."

"I was going to say I never realized how much I loved him until that moment. I couldn't let him die, even if it cost me my life." He turned from her to stare into the darkness, listening to the peace. "I've been thinking that God loves me so much. I wonder if he would be willing to die for me to save me from an enemy's blow, if it were possible for God to die."

Acsah shook her head. "That's deep for me, Othniel."

"I suppose so, but it just came to me."

She kissed him lightly on the lips. "It sounds beautiful anyway." She glanced around again. "This place is wonderful, isn't it?"

"It's wonderful to be home."

"Do you remember what you said to me once about home?"

"Remind me." He was bending low now to kiss her earlobe.

"You said walls and a roof do not make a home. Home is the presence of those we love."

"Like I said, it's wonderful to be home." Then standing next to the springs that represented God's care for them, he held her close to his heart.

Epilogue

———— ✦ ————

"Grandfather's home." The children's voices rang out as they tumbled down the path towards the wadi.

Acsah dusted the flour off her hands and stood to follow them. Ahead she could see Othniel picking up their little granddaughter, Meonathai's youngest, and swinging her in the air. Surrounded by the chattering children, he came up to her and gave her a warm embrace. She could feel the heat of his body through her shift. "Come, let me get you a drink."

She made him sit in the courtyard and went to the jug to pour out some cool water. She grabbed a bowl of grapes on her way back to him. "How was the trip?"

"Not too bad. Most cases could be solved easily. Law-breaking has declined markedly over the last twenty years." He absently mussed the curls of his granddaughter who knelt by him.

Acsah sat down nearby. "That's because of your leadership. You've been a wonderful leader and judge for Israel."

"With the Lord's help." He smiled at her. "But I'm not sure how deep the transformation goes, if they obey because they follow me or obey because they love the Lord themselves."

"Why does that matter?"

"Because if it's only about me, their obedience will end when I'm gone."

She didn't like hearing him talk about dying. "You can do God's will yourself in your lifetime, no more. Each one is responsible to Him."

"You're right, as always."

"Now, I'd better see about getting you a good dinner. I imagine we'll have a houseful tonight."

That evening, after the children and grandchildren went to their rock homes nearby, Acsah took Othniel by the hand and led him to their bedchamber. There they lay in each other's arms on their sleeping mats. Acsah still drew such comfort from his embrace. She knew he needed sleep after his long journey from Shiloh, but she had a question for him. "Why do you love me? I'm trying to figure that out, and I can't."

"What do you mean?"

"Oh, I don't know. All the reasons you married me have diminished with time—beauty, figure, wittiness. Yet you continue to love me."

Othniel nuzzled her neck. "I didn't love you then because of your beauty or your wit. I loved you because of who you are—the essential Acsah."

"The essential Acsah—I like that."

"Now your turn. Why do you continue to love me?"

"I would say exactly what you've said but add because..." She stopped as she tried to put the idea into words.

"What?"

"Because you're mine. Does that sound strange?"

"No. I understand. We belong together."

"Yes. That's what I think. We've shared so many experiences together..."

"Good and bad." Othniel tickled her ear with his beard.

"We've built a life and home together."

"We share our children..."

"... and grandchildren."

"And we finish each other's sentences."

Laughing, they ended their day with a warm kiss.

Proof